# Notice

If you have not read *BST Book Zero* yet, please make sure to do so. It includes the first two chapters of Darcy's journey and context behind the series as a whole. Life Timeline, Death Timeline, and Revival Timeline all begin the same way, with the timelines splitting apart upon the end of Book Zero.

# Revival Timeline

**Banana Split Timeline, Volume 1**

Sol Quasar

Published by Pen Reilly, 2024.

This is a work of fiction. Similarities to real people, places, or events are entirely coincidental.

REVIVAL TIMELINE

**First edition. November 11, 2024.**



ISBN: 979-8227154828

Written by Sol Quasar.

# Table of Contents

# Warnings

This series has a bit of nightmare fuel, as many of these scenes are fueled by my nightmares. I have many subconscious fears and concerns, and placing these nightmares into fiction seems to be a successful outlet. My nightmares are quite vivid, however, so please take care of yourself if you are uncomfortable with disturbing imagery, including body horror. This has been toned down compared to earlier drafts, but care should still be taken when reading.

As mentioned before, this series has an emphasis on spiders, including descriptions of spider body parts. Those with arachnophobia will likely want to avoid this series.

One of the main characters suffered from depression in the past. This includes brief stints of suicide ideation. While these moments are quickly argued against in preference towards being alive, these moments can still be triggering for those who struggle with these same thoughts. If you yourself wrestle against thoughts of death, please, *please* choose to keep on living. It is always worth it.

Another one of the main characters is a victim of emotional abuse, which is heavily explored. I even struggled writing certain scenes because they reminded me so much of the abuse that I myself had suffered from. The use of electricity was also involved in the abuse and discussed.

There are recurring characters who are parents who lost their children and children who lost their parents.

The Salavites are trying to resist a genocide, which is shown by not being free to live in their cultural home, their resources being restricted, and suffer acts of intimidation by their oppressors.

If you continue on, please keep these factors in mind.

# Revival: Extra Note

The Salavites are a species of sapient reptiles. Like spiders, reptiles are often villainized in stories, which is quite saddening. Every time I see a fantasy story where the Lizardfolk are always evil, I'm disappointed. Reptiles are so incredibly cool, but are merely written as literal cold-blooded monsters. Did you know that the *Aspidoscelis uniparens* reproduce asexually? Not only that, but thanks to chromosome tripling, the resulting offspring are genetically diverse from their parents instead of being direct clones. This is so unique! How has a story not been written about this yet?

Reptiles should have a chance to be the heroes of a story and I wanted to explore what a society based on *Aspidoscelis uniparens* would be like. And since I needed to explain where magic comes from in this universe, I got an idea: a society of magic asexual lizards.

The Macbeths, in the meantime, represent old money. They are a long line of privileged people who keep all the best resources (in this case, magic) to themselves. They stepped on the Salavites just because they could. We as people like to think that these villains of history are artistic, wise, or well-spoken, but they are just bullies. There is nothing special about them, nothing to admire. They're cowards who hide under a veneer of jewels.

# Chapter 1

"...Revi."

Revi squeaked in excitement. "Thank you so much! I promise you won't regret this. We're gonna have so many good times together!"

Life nodded to Revi. "Congratulations." They disappeared.

Death patted Revi on the head. "Good luck, lil sib! Let us know if you need help with anything." They disappeared as well.

Darcy asked, "So you guys are pretty close, huh?"

"Yup! And once you're officially installed, I can tell you all about them!"

Darcy tilted their head to the side. "Installed?"

"Sorry, that's the best word I can think of for it. Initiated? Employed? Accepted? Part of the system?" They tapped their claws against their head. "There's a very specific vibe that English doesn't have a word for."

"Fair enough. How does the initiation go?"

"Well, first, I turn the contract into pizzazz. Poof!" They tapped on the contract and it transmuted into a cloud of blue sparkles. "Then I put it into an object so it can safely be absorbed into your body."

"Wait, why does your pizzazz have to go into something? Why not just...?"

Darcy reached for the pizzazz. Revi pushed them away.

"DON'T TOUCH THAT!"

They left the pizzazz floating in the air. They checked Darcy's hand.

"Did it get you? Are you disintegrating?"

"What? No. I couldn't even get close."

"Phew!" Revi wiped away nonexistent sweat. "That was close!"

"What's going on?"

"Well, the thing about pizzazz is that it absorbs anything that touches it. So when it's freestanding like this, it's really dangerous. It's gotta go into something so its power can be directed. I need a non-living object to use as a conduit."

"Well, I've seen you turn pizzazz into objects before. Can't you do the same now? Just make it into apple juice again."

"Are you okay with apple juice?"

"Yeah, I'm up for it."

"Okie dokie, then!"

Revi conjured another cup and turned the freestanding pizzazz into apple juice. Before they gave it to Darcy, they said,

"Remember: once you accept this pizzazz into your body, there's no goin' back. You'll be a warlock. If you quit or get fired, you'll lose your pizzazz and all the memories associated with it. If you change your mind years later, you'll lose a lot of time."

"I understand."

Darcy drank the apple juice. It tasted just as good as before, but now had a powerful, energetic zip to it. It was like drinking the juice of a freshly-squeezed granny smith apple.

"Wow, this is some good stuff."

"Thank you! And check it out!"

Revi pointed at Darcy's torso. It had changed from its gray coloration to that of a nice blue tone, the same blue that Revi had.

"Congrats!" Said Revi. "You have pizzazz now!"

"Sweet!"

"And now that you're officially a warlock, you get one of these!"

Revi conjured the blue box from before. Darcy immediately placed it on the table.

"Oh my god, thank you so much! I'm gonna make all kinds of food with this!"

"Like what?"

"Like... like..." They paused. "I don't know. I've never had this much freedom with food before."

"What if you made something that you never got to eat? Like a fancy meal?"

"Hm..." Darcy shrugged. "Well, I always did wanna try pizza bagels."

"Ooo, yeah! Pizza bagels!"

Darcy wrote "12 pizza bagels" down onto the whiteboard and opened the box. Lo and behold, twelve pizza bagels sat inside. They were hot and perfectly toasted, as if they had been pulled fresh from the oven.

"Yum!" Said Revi.

Darcy sat down and took slow bites. As much as they wanted to shovel them into their mouth, they also wanted to savor the sensation of actually eating something.

"Want some?" They offered.

Revi shook their head. "Oh, Patrons don't need to eat."

"Why not?"

"We don't have bodies like you do. No organs or anything."

"Huh. Wild." They ate another pizza bagel. "Hey, can I ask you something?"

"Sure!"

"How old are you guys? I don't mean kid or adult, but like... how long have you existed?"

"Oh, a very, very long time! I'm as old as human civilization and I'm the *baby* of the family!"

Darcy's eyes widened. "Oh. Oh, wow. Holy shit. How have you guys stayed hidden this whole time?"

"By working really, really hard. We gotta be super careful on who we associate with."

"Yeah, why *is* that? If you're all about helping people, then why not work out in the open? Like, I know that not everyone likes spiders, but with good enough marketing and PR..."

"There's a bunch of reasons. Some people would see us as a threat. Others would find ways to control us or drain our pizzazz. I personally like taking care of my warlocks. If we got exposed, they would be vulnerable, too. And even if there wasn't a danger, being public knowledge would make it harder for us to hire more people."

"Why's that?"

"Well, remember the test we use to determine if someone would make a good warlock? Let's say that someone knows about the test beforehand. They'll know to help the spider and get the result they want. And if they do that, then that person's character isn't actually being tested."

Darcy nodded. "I see. If a cruel person knows that they have to do an act of kindness to get power, then they're just gonna pretend to be kind until they have what they want."

"Exactly. And then there's... the reason why you can't tell your friends or family. Why you can't recommend people that you know."

"Why's that?"

Revi held their hands behind their back. They rocked back and forth on their feet as they explained.

"In 1900, Life hired a warlock. The warlock really wanted to tell their family about the Patrons so they could become warlocks, too. Life agreed to an introduction, but it was actually a trap! All the family wanted was to take Life's power for themselves."

"Holy shit. What happened next?"

"The warlock helped Life escape, but they stopped talking to each other. Thankfully, that family only learned that powerful beings existed, nothing about pizzazz. But still... Life was never the same after that."

"I see." *That must be why Oliver never told me about the Patrons before today—he didn't want to betray Life's trust.*

After they finished eating, Darcy stood up and stretched. Revi asked,

"So what do you wanna do now?"

"Well, I should think about the immediate future. I can't work at my job anymore, and if I stay at this apartment for too long, people will connect the dots between me and Julia."

"Oh! Then why don't you stay in my pocket dimension? I'll need some time to make your home, but a lot of my warlocks live there, so you wouldn't be alone."

"I'd be grateful, Revi! Should I get my stuff right now?"

"Sure!"

Darcy packed away their phone and their family photo. In complete honesty, those were the only things of value that they had.

Revi said, "Okay, you'll need to hold my hand. Or just any physical contact will do."

"Gotcha."

Darcy held Revi's hand. In a flash of blue light, the two vanished from Darcy's apartment.

To Darcy's surprise, they arrived at a grassy field. Hordes of blue flowers of every species populated the field. Four giant blueberry bushes grew in this field as well, one in each cardinal direction. They were as huge and thick as redwood trees and had openings big enough to step inside. Bright blue signs hung above the openings. Darcy approached one and read it aloud.

"Break chambers."

"For when you just wanna chill out," Said Revi. "The other three bushes go to the work sites, the living quarters, and the Wraith Lodge."

"Can I check out all of them?"

"Sure thing!"

The break chambers were made up of circular rooms carved out of the wooden interior. Chairs and sofas of various materials lay scattered about in each room, many accompanied by coffee tables. The rooms were connected by carved-out hallways and spiral ramps. Humans and Venutians rested in these rooms, with some carrying quiet conversation. Every room had a hologram projector, and some people used it to watch movies or show off slide shows.

"Well this place is quaint," Said Darcy, "But I don't know if I'll personally be using it. Is everyone in this pocket dimension a warlock?"

"Yup. Well, 'xcept for the Wraiths. I'll show you those last."

Revi then led Darcy to the living quarters. Like the break chambers, the rooms were carved out of the wooden interior. They were sorted like an apartment complex, with each door leading to a unique living space. One person had their music playing at full volume, yet when they shut their door, the sound muted entirely. Revi said,

"Every place is soundproof so everyone is comfortable. Then I carve out each apartment to fit the preferences of its warlock. I can even make them bigger on the inside! As big as you want."

"That's incredible!"

"But, um, the more personalized and specific your request is, the longer it'll take for me to finish it."

"Totally understandable."

A human warlock passed by the duo. Upon seeing Darcy, he stopped in place and looked up and down at them.

"What are you supposed to be?"

"Hey, be nice," Said Revi. "Darcy is an arachnomorph, and they're a warlock just like everybody else."

He shrugged and went on his way.

"Sorry," Said Revi. "Most of my warlocks are more polite than that."

"You're good," Darcy replied. "That reaction's pretty mild, all things considered."

"So, have an idea on what you want your apartment to look like?"

"I, uh... don't really know what kind of place I would want at the moment. Can you do something generic?"

"Sure! Which number do you want for your address?" Revi conjured a list of numbers. "These are all the available ones."

Of course, the obvious numbers were already taken: 666, 420, 69, and so on. Darcy hummed with thought.

"Today is August fifteenth, so... do 815."

"8-1-5?"

"Yeah. I want to remember this day."

"Okie dokie! Would you want to continue the tour or have me start working now?"

"I think I can continue the tour on my own."

"Alright! I'll let you know when your place is done. If you want to go back to Earth, go to the tree that says 'work sites'. There is a hole in the side that will teleport you back to wherever you were last."

"Sounds good!"

Darcy left the living quarters. Sure enough, they found the tree with the exit, but their attention trailed over to the one that said "Wraith Lodge".

*What is a Wraith?*

Darcy entered the lodge.

It opened to an expansive forest meadow surrounded by trees. Blue fruits and veggies grew from the trees and earth. A dark shadow emerged from the trees and grabbed one of the fruits.

Darcy gasped, which grabbed the shadow's attention. Eight white eyes formed and the shadow solidified into something monstrous. The monster stepped over to Darcy, easily dwarfing them in size. It looked down at them with its glowing eyes.

Darcy gripped their drawstring bag. They hurried for something to say, but not words had formed; all they could do was stare.

The monster still carried the fruit in one of its massive claws. It lifted the fruit forward so it could be easily seen. The fruit looked soft and perfectly round. The monster leaned forward so that their face was only inches away from Darcy's own.

<...Want some?>

Darcy exhaled. "What?"

<Want some fruit?>

What in the world? Not only was this creature speaking with telepathy, of all things, but they were willing to share their food. The monster seemed to sense Darcy's confusion, as a white jagged smile appeared on their face.

<I was just messing with you. I'm not going to attack you.>

If Darcy was certain about one thing, it was that they didn't want to make this person mad. They accepted the fruit and took a bite. It was juicier than a peach and carried an apple-like aroma. It reminded Darcy of Starburst candies.

"It's good," They said. "Thank you."

<Isn't it?>

The monster formed shadowy chelicerae and protracted fangs. The fangs pierced the fruit like needles through wet paper. Deep blue energy appeared within the creature. The fruit changed to an indigo color and became stiffer. The monster removed its fangs, and to Darcy's surprise, no holes were left within the fruit; only the bite Darcy had taken had remained. Darcy took another bite, this time met with a burst of sour flavoring.

"It's like you... unripened it."

<That's the power of a Decay Wraith.> The Wraith extended a clawed hand. <Nice to meet you.>

Darcy shook their hand. "Nice to meet you, too."

The Wraith introduced herself as Sky. She explained that Wraiths were what happened when a warlock's pizzazz got corrupted.

<Think of it like data corruption,> She said. <The pizzazz no longer has the right data to work with, which in turn affects the mind and body. It begins a feedback loop that distorts all three until they're unrecognizable.>

"So you're not human anymore?"

Sky shook her head. <My body was destroyed by the corruption. Now I'm just a shell with pizzazz inside. But on the bright side, I can eat rot now.>

"Eat... rot?"

<What I did to that fruit. You see, aging is technically just another form of rotting. The cells in your body are dying faster than they're being replaced. But I can use my power to reverse those effects.>

"Reverse aging? That's... that's incredible!"

<Yes, and it tastes good, too. And Revi designed this lodge to be the perfect home for us. Go into any direction and you'll find something to keep us Wraiths busy. Punching bags, hot tubs, gymnastics courses, bowling...>

Darcy chuckled at the image of shadow monsters trying to get a strike.

"Would you say that it makes the corruption worth it?"

<By Time, no. If I could go back to my old life, I'd do it in a heartbeat. There's a certain peace that comes from growing older, especially when you have loved ones to do it with. And I wouldn't mind being able to use my vocal chords again.> Sky turned to Darcy. <And now, I must ask: why do you look like that? Is it magic?>

"No, I'm a warlock. An arachnomorph."

<Ah. Was it Revi?>

"Yeah."

<Yup.> Sky patted Darcy on the back. <Well, if you ever want to visit, you're free to.>

"I'll keep that in mind, thank you. Nice to meet you, Sky."

<Same as well!>

Darcy then wandered to the work site. Like the other areas, it was carved out of wood, but the interior was not what Darcy expected.

A movie theater with plush velvet carpetting. A Venutian warlock resembling an emerald beetle sat at the front desk in theater getup. Posters lined the walls, each labeled with a different type of training. Darcy approached the warlock.

"Um, excuse me. Is this the... work sites?"

"It is. If you've entered this room, that means that you haven't finished your training yet."

"I didn't know there was training."

"Oh, yeah. You're required to complete Revi's Safety Seminar before you're permitted into any work sites. Got to make sure anything you create is OSHA-compliant, you know?"

"OSHA?"

"The Official Spider Health Association. Apparently the name used to be different, but then Revi saw humans make OSHA and was inspired by the acronym."

"Huh. Is there a particular place I should go first?"

"The first course of the seminar is the first door on the left. It'll begin in ten minutes. Note-taking materials are on the counter by the wall."

"Okay, thank you."

*I guess I'm taking classes, then.*

Rows upon rows of plush seats faced a massive screen. This theater had only a couple other warlocks within it, giving Darcy free choice of where to sit. They picked a central seat and readied themself.

A trailer appeared on screen, complete with subtitles. Revi's voice said,

"Are you tired of this happening to you?"

A human warlock appeared on screen. They said in an exaggerated tone,

"I don't know how to spend my time!"

Revi said, "Then you need a change of pace! If you're in a rut, try a different role? As the Revival theme, we don't just experiment with powers, we also help people in our community!"

A Decay Wraith appeared on screen. They held a sheet of paper and a text-to-speech synthesizer. They said,

"Thanks to the support I was given, I don't..." They glanced at the paper, "...Have to worry about slipping into madness."

Revi appeared. "That's right! Helping the Wraiths counts as doing your job as a warlock. The same goes for lounge cleanup, theater work, and other odd jobs. Because I'm Revi and I care."

Text appeared on the screen saying, "Thank you for becoming a Revival warlock!"

The room then went dark, indicating that the actual movie was going to begin. Darcy looked around to see if anyone else had joined the theater, but it still only had them and the two other warlocks.

The screen showed Revi speaking in front of a white void. Revi said to the camera,

"Welcome, new warlocks, to Revi's Safety Seminar. We're so glad to have you with us! And when I say 'we', I just mean 'me'. I don't know why people say 'we' in these videos." They cleared their throat. "Um, but, in this first lesson, we shall be going over the basics. Because the process of resurrection doesn't technically exist, I do my best to fulfill my role in other ways. This includes testing out powers so that we can help other Patrons and their warlocks. This includes making sure that regular stuff like super strength still works as intended, as well as updating those powers so they can be even more efficient and helpful. And if you create or discover a new power, you can even apply it to the active power list! But first thing's first, we must ensure that it'll be safe. Now, it's important to..."

Darcy tried to pay attention, they honestly did, but Revi's voice droned on and on. Darcy's mind wandered to nothing in particular as they stared into space. If a person looked into their thoughts, they would find radio static. Before Darcy knew it, the entire lesson had passed them by.

"...And that is the end of course number one. We look forward to seeing you in course number two!"

Darcy blinked and sat up. *Oh, god dammit.*

They rubbed their eyes as they returned to the entrance. The theater worker asked,

"Did you have a good time?"

"I, uh... zoned out. I think I'll have to take it again."

"Ah. That happens, don't feel too bad about it. The course will be running again in a few minutes if you want to try a second time."

"Okay, thank you."

This time, Darcy leaned forward in their seat as they watched the course. They glared at the screen with absolute concentration.

*Focus. Focus on the lesson. Focus real hard! I'll be focusing so well that everyone will be surprised by how focused I am! Focus on... wait, is the lesson going right now?!*

Indeed, the course had begun and Darcy hadn't even noticed. It was halfway done and Darcy had no context on what was going on.

*I was focusing so hard on focusing that I forgot to actually focus! Dammit!*

Darcy exited to the lobby, then entered again when the course restarted, but once again, something happened that simply made it impossible to follow along. Darcy would get distracted, or their thoughts would drift away, or a combination of the two would occur. No matter how hard they tried, they just couldn't get their brain to follow along. It was like trying to go rock-climbing with hands and feet made of jelly.

After the latest failure, Darcy leaned their forehead against a wall and stared at the floor. The theater worker asked,

"Are you alright?"

Darcy sighed. "Why am I stupid?"

"You're not stupid."

"Yes I am, the same thing happened in school. In some lessons, I could focus just fine, but in most of them, I was just..."

Darcy made a vague gesture with their hands.

They asked the warlock, "How many courses are there in total?"

"In total, Revi's Safety Seminar is two hundred hours long."

Darcy swiftly turned to look at them. "Two *hundred*?!"

"Revi really cares about warlock safety."

"No kidding."

"Oh, and there's a test at the end of it to make sure you were paying attention. It's a thousand questions long."

Darcy choked. "A thousand?! Jesus!"

"They really, *really* care about warlock safety."

Darcy considered whether or not they had the mental fortitude to do this. They eventually made a defeated sigh.

"I don't think this particular role is for me."

"I'm sorry. You can always help with the Wraiths."

Darcy stepped out the door. "Have a nice day."

"You, too. Have a nice day!"

Outside, Darcy sat down in the grass. They pulled out a small handful and played with it mindlessly.

Revi appeared next to them. "It's done!"

Darcy screamed in surprise.

"Sorry!" Said Revi. "How're you doing?"

"Just, uh... checkin' everything out." Darcy scratched their fuzzy head. "To be honest, I thought the training would be more... engaging."

Revi giggled. "Darcy, safety is what's important here."

"Yeah, I got that. I guess I didn't know what else I expected. I *am* glad that you prioritize it, though. Just don't know if I have the, uh, fortitude."

"That's okay! It's not for everyone. But if you *do* come up with a cool idea for a power, I won't be able to approve it until you finish the training."

"I understand." Darcy stood up. "Okay, let's check out my place."

Darcy's new apartment was noticeably larger and more spacious than their previous one. Each room was big enough for Darcy to lie down in with all their limbs outstretched. It had a bedroom, bathroom, kitchen, dining room, living room, and a personal study. Every room (save for the kitchen) had a plush floor that regained its shape upon stepping off of it, and the sanded-wood furniture had plush coverings that could slide off with ease. Darcy's favorite part was the bed, as it had multiple different blankets, each of varying thickness.

"Your bed is fully customizable," Said Revi. "And if you need any more blankets or pillows, the chest in the corner can make more. Ooo, and let me show you the fridge!"

The fridge was big enough for a person to step inside, and that wasn't even including the freezer it was attached to. Revi opened the top section of the fridge.

"Place your food box in there."

"Uh, okay."

Upon Darcy doing so, the fridge briefly shined with a blue light. Revi explained,

"Now you can conjure an entire fridge's worth of food! It only works when the food box is *in* the fridge, though. Oh, and if any food rots, you can ask one of the Wraiths to help you!"

"Actually, I already met one of them. They can reverse aging!"

"Hehe, yup. But they also forgot who they were before. Any friends or family are gone to them. And since they lost their organic bodies, they can't eat or drink anymore, not like you can. It's really sad, actually."

"Yeah, but what causes corruption? Will I ever become a Wraith?"

"No, don't worry." Revi shut the fridge door. "Y'see, there's a special mental lock in place to keep pizzazz from affecting your mind. You can use your thoughts to control your powers, but you never have to worry about your powers changing your thoughts. And so, the feedback loop can't start and corruption can't happen."

"But could something break that mental lock?"

Revi put a claw against their chin and looked upwards.

"Hm... brainwashing would do it. Also getting zapped in the brain. Specific stuff like that. It probably won't come up in regular warlock adventures, but if you ever *do* see something that could cause corruption, please let me know."

Darcy nodded. They placed their family photo on the drawer next to their bed. With their drawstring bag still in tow, they turned to Revi.

"Well, I think I'm ready to head back."

"Really?"

"Yeah. I want to update a friend of mine. Remind me, where will the exit drop me off?"

"You'll be dropped off exactly where you entered. In this case... your bedroom! Well, your old one."

"Gotcha. And what will I do if I want to come back here?"

Revi handed Darcy a blue crystal in the shape of a heart. Not a heart symbol, but a human heart. It was small enough to fit in Darcy's palm.

"Use your pizzazz to activate the crystal, then it'll send you back to my pocket dimension." They then added, "I made it into a heart to make it cuter!"

"That's... nice." They placed the heart into the bag. "Thank you for everything, Revi."

"Yeah! Always happy to help my warlocks."

With Revi's voice and behavior, Darcy couldn't help but be reminded that they were speaking to a child. They said to Revi,

"And listen... I know that you're thousands of years old, but if anyone is creepy towards you or makes you feel unsafe, let me know okay? I'll beat 'em up for you."

Revi looked at them in confusion. "You know, every one of my warlocks has told me that."

# Chapter 2

Once they arrived at their old apartment, Darcy wrote down a note explaining that they were leaving and left it on the door. They hoped that this would be enough to suffice, but if it didn't, there wasn't much they could do without revealing themselves. They wrote a similar note for the tech store and made their way there.

*I told Oliver that I wouldn't be at work today. Man, how am I gonna find him? We never shared phone numbers. I guess I could always try the headquarters.*

They dropped off the note at the store without wasting time for conversation, then ran to the Almond Industries headquarters.

The headquarters was a building tall enough to look like it clawed at the sky. Its shiny chrome exterior matched its interior to a T.

Darcy's foot-claws clicked against the metallic floor of the building, and suddenly they felt very underdressed.

*Maybe I should've gotten some clothes first. Well, too late to turn back now! Guess we die like men.*

They approached the secretary. "Uh, excuse me. Can you tell me where Red Arachnid is?"

"Are you an employee of Almond Industries?"

*Shit!* "Uh, no. A... friend of mine is, but she can't come with."

"I'm sorry, but unless you have express permission from the company, we cannot connect you to our ambassador."

"What if I told you that I'm a superhero? I want, uh... I want a crossover."

"Once again, I am sorry, but that is still not the precedent for a meeting. Unless you are also sponsored by the company, we simply cannot allow our ambassador to team up with other superheroes."

*No superheroes whatsoever?*

Darcy decided to cut their losses before they drew too much suspicion. They sighed.

"Alright. Thanks, anyway. Have a nice day."

They strode back out the doors, too lost in their thoughts to notice anyone around them or where they were going.

*God, how am I gonna do this? Should I just meet him at the store tomorrow? I really wanted to tell him as soon as possible, but I might just have to wait. Man, I was hoping we could finally hang out as friends. Now what am I gonna do for the rest of the day?*

"Hey, look! A Venutian!"

The voice came from behind Darcy and belonged to a young man in ripped-up clothing. Two other men in similar getups approached Darcy from the front. The trio had closed off the alleyway Darcy was in, and each carried a metal baseball bat.

"Not often we see Venutians," One of them said.

*Shit.*

Darcy tried to play along. "Maybe you're just not looking in the right places."

"Yeah. Sure."

One of the men in front of them pointed at Darcy's bag with his bat. He asked,

"What you got in there?"

"Not money. Sorry to disappoint you, but I'm broke."

This didn't convince the men, as they stepped closer to Darcy. Each was only a few feet away from them now. Darcy's mind ran for a solution.

*Maybe I can slip between two of them? Or maybe turn around and try to get past the first guy? Or... wait. Wait! I have powers now! I'm a spider, for crying out loud!*

"Sorry to disappoint you," They said. "I won't be easy prey."

Darcy leapt and clung to a wall. Just as the Patrons and Oliver had said, Darcy's powers activated in response to their thoughts.

Darcy desired to stick to the wall, so they did, and with super strength, it took no effort at all to carry themself. Darcy scurried up the side of the wall as a spider would. The astonishment from the men below was like music to their ears.

"Did you see that?!"

"Dammit, I forgot that Venutians are bugs."

"How could you forget something like that? Look at them!"

"Man... this robbery was poorly planned."

Once at the top of the building, Darcy shuffled very, very quickly away from the edge. Sure, sticky powers meant that they wouldn't have to worry about falling off of things, but their fear of heights was still as strong as ever. Once at the center of the rooftop, Darcy lay on their back and watched the blue sky above.

*If I was still human... god, that would've been bad. But wow, talk about a test drive for my powers. Nothing like life-threatening pressure to get you going, I guess. But if they were supervillains, I would've been fucked...*

A voice came from a few buildings over. "Darcy?"

Darcy sat up and looked. Red Arachnid excitedly waved to them.

"Darcy!" He said. "Hi! It's me!"

He leapt from building to building with such ease that it put Olympic athletes to shame. He practically trembled with excitement.

"Omigosh, hi! How are you? Are you good? It's me, Red Arachnid!"

"Yeah, I know it's you, bud. Uh, there were a few guys who tried to rob me. I think they're down there..." Darcy glanced over the roof's edge, only to find an empty alleyway. "Huh. They must've scattered."

"Really? Are you okay?"

"Yeah. A little spooked, but unharmed. Let's talk."

The two sat cross-legged on the rooftop. Oliver deactivated his mask.

"So, um... which Patron did you choose?"

"Revi. I thought I could, um... be more productive there. But, uh... not exactly."

Darcy explained their attempts at Revi's Safety Seminar and consequent failure.

"I thought I could force myself through it, I really did. But in the end, everything turned into radio static."

"Really?"

"Yeah, but it's just my brain being stupid."

"Darcy, your brain isn't stupid."

"Yes it is, it's always been like this."

"That still doesn't mean that you're stupid. Darcy, you're an intelligent person with a lot of good ideas."

"Really? How so?"

"Oh, uh..." He scratched his head. "Well, um... well, you just need a good outlet to apply yourself, you know?"

"Like what?"

"Are there any learning environments that engage you?"

"Well... I want to learn more about pizzazz stuff, but if it's going to be like the training seminar..."

"No, I mean, what kind of learning do you react to best? Do you learn best by doing things in person? Or having a visual aid?"

"Oh. I guess I learn best by doing stuff? But seeing how it works also helps, I suppose."

"Then the next time you learn something, we can try doing it together."

Darcy smiled. "I guess we could try it."

Something shuffled nearby. Both Darcy and Oliver stood up.

"What was that?" Darcy asked.

"Don't know." Oliver tapped a foot against the ground. "Hm..."

He looked over the side of the building. He turned to Darcy and shrugged.

"Nothing here."

"But it sounded heavy."

Oliver knocked a hand against the rooftop. "Vibrations say that there's something clinging to the side of the building. I don't *see* anything, though."

"Maybe it's invisible?"

"No, that would take magic." He shook his head. "I'm probably just... interpreting things wrong. I should head back to the headquarters."

Oliver turned his mask back on, but he stopped before leaving. His body trembled. He fell to his knees and yelped in pain.

Darcy ran to his side. "Another panic attack?"

Oliver's arms wrapped around his midsection. His breaths came out short and labored. He shivered and whimpered.

Darcy wished that there was something they could do, but unlike anxiety attacks, panic attacks were often random and did not have a "source". Sometimes, they simply came and went without explanation, leaving the victim with nothing but pain and exhaustion.

"I'm okay," Oliver finally said. "I think it's over now."

"Want me to walk you home?"

"Thanks, but no. I appreciate the offer, though."

Oliver stood up, took a deep breath, and leapt away as if nothing happened. Darcy considered going to the headquarters anyways and finding a way to sneak inside.

*No. I need to respect his wishes. I'm sure that he'll be fine.*

Darcy took out the crystal heart that Revi had given them. They focused on their pizzazz to activate it. In a flash of blue light, Darcy teleported back to Revi's pocket dimension.

— — —

That evening, Oliver journeyed back to his home at Almond Industries. But just as the headquarters was in sight, he became overcome by the sensation that someone was watching him. But, no matter where he looked, nobody was there. Sure, civilians watched him go by, but they didn't activate his anxiety. Well, they *did*, but whatever watched him this time gave him even more anxiety.

This was *advanced anxiety*.

But after a half an hour of searching for nothing, Oliver rationalized the feeling as simply being a small panic attack. They had varying levels of intensity, after all. Perhaps this was simply one of those mild times.

Oliver climbed up the side of the Almond Industries headquarters. Unfortunately for him, his fears were correct: someone of note *was* watching him—they were simply unable to be seen. This invisible force crept closer and closer to him until he was within arm's reach.

*Maybe Darcy was right. Maybe something is-*

Five invisible claws grabbed the back of Oliver's costume. It yanked him away from the building and flung him into the air. Oliver had tried to stick to the building, but he had been grabbed with such force that bits of metal had broken off and stuck to his hands. Now he flew through the air with only seconds to think.

*Who did this what did this what's happening what do I do how do I-*

He crashed to a rooftop and tumbled a few feet. He unstuck the metal bits from his hands and rubbed his head. He jumped to his feet and glanced around for the attacker.

*Okay. Invisible. Invisible. I need to-!*

He tapped a hand against the rooftop. All sources of vibrations came from inside the building. Whatever had attacked him, it hadn't reached him yet. Oliver leapt down to ground level and ran as fast as he could. Whatever this thing was, he didn't want to fight it around people. He opened the first manhole he saw and climbed inside.

Newstone City had a large sewer system underneath it. This was because it was a city built on top of a city: Old Newstone. The top level of the city had been built over with sewage lines and old mining facilities, but the rest of the ancient city lay untouched and abandoned. If Oliver was going to fight something, this would be the safest place to do it.

Something heavy landed behind him. It was still invisible, so Oliver tapped a nearby wall. The vibrations helped him figure out the shape of the creature: something large and reptilian with a pair of wings attached.

"A dragon warrior!" He gasped.

The dragon made a sound of surprise, then a sigh.

"So, you figured me out."

The invisibility dissipated, revealing a violet dragon with yellow eyes. Its wings resembled violet flower petals and folded against the creature's back so as to not bump against anything. Its cone-shaped ears pointed backwards in irritation.

Oliver squeaked. He was tall for a human, but his head only barely reached the dragon's chest. If the dragon wanted to, it could tear his head off with a single bite. Oliver's voice cracked when he spoke, but he didn't care about sounding cool right now.

"I'm sorry, sir or ma'am or nongendered friend. Um, if we can avoid a fight, that would be really nice. If that's okay with you?"

"Personally, yes," The dragon answered. "Come along with me and I won't have to use force."

Oliver tapped his fingers together. "Come along... where, exactly?"

"I need to get you out of the city, out of **his** reach."

"His?"

"The CEO of Almond Industries. You *must* get away from him."

"What are you talking about? Why would I ever want to leave him?"

"You're in danger."

"*How*?"

The dragon's crystalline eyes focused on Oliver's mask.

"Turn off your recording software."

"What? No."

"I can't say more until you do!"

Oliver stepped back. "I don't trust you enough for that."

"Then I'll destroy it myself and take you by force!"

The dragon lunged at Oliver. He only barely jumped out of the range of its claws. He kept dodging as he hurried for a plan.

*I don't have experience fighting dragons! I'll just have to calculate where their pressure points are. Let's see, a lot of muscles meet at the base of the neck...*

One advantage of the dragon being so much bigger than him was that it was easy to treat its body like a jungle gym. All Oliver had to do was wait for a swipe of its claws and use the creature's arm to vault himself closer. He jumped over the shoulder and spun himself around to stick to the dragon's back. He placed a hand on the base of the neck and applied pressure.

Thanks to his speed and agility, all of these actions happened in the course of two seconds, and the results were immediate.

The dragon's body stiffened. "W-what?!"

"I'm really sorry."

Oliver increased pressure. The dragon became so stiff that it lost balance. It fell onto its belly. Although it couldn't move, that didn't stop the dragon from growling.

"Let me go."

"Only if you promise not to attack me."

"You can't go back to that man."

"Why?"

"He's hurt you, just like he hurt the others."

"The... others?"

"The previous ambassadors."

Oliver considered this information. It was true that the previous ambassadors had vanished or quit for one reason or another. But that would imply that Mike Harrell did something to them, and Oliver couldn't accept that thought.

"That's... just what happens to superheroes. Sometimes we disappear. Sometimes we die. It's natural."

"Haven't you felt it? Your mind losing control, your pain intensifying... it had to come from somewhere."

Oliver paused. "How did you know about that?"

"Wikham told me."

The name sounded vaguely familiar, but Oliver didn't know enough to put a face to it.

"Well... whoever they are, it's probably just a coincidence. These things just happen."

"So there's no getting through to you?"

"I'm sorry."

Now the dragon was the one who paused. "If you let go of me, I will leave this city and never bother you again. I have just one request, though."

"What is it?"

"The white spider. Talk to the white spider."

"Darcy?" He blurted. He covered his mouth with his free hand.

"Yes. The white spider with the blue center. Find them."

"I-I will. But please don't attack me."

"I will not."

Oliver finally let go of the dragon. He stepped off of it and helped it back up. It placed a clawed hand on Oliver's shoulder.

"Thank you," It said. "I'm sorry."

"Me, too. I wish the world was simpler so we wouldn't have to fight."

"Yes. I apologize for that... and for this."

The dragon placed its other hand against Oliver's forehead. It felt as if something entered his mind. An immense pressure filled his head, as if every thought and feeling was being rearranged.

The dragon let go. Oliver fell to his side.

"You'll thank me later," Said the dragon.

"Hey!" Someone called.

Oliver's consciousness dimmed, but in the corner of his eye, he spotted an armored figure down the hall. He recognized the voice, but his mind was too frazzled to acknowledge anything.

The dragon hissed and became invisible. Its heavy steps ran in the opposite direction. The armored man knelt down next to Oliver.

"It's alright," He said. "I've got you."

# Chapter 3

Mike Harrell was the one who had rescued him. Because Oliver had never turned off his mask, Harrell knew exactly where he had gone and how to find him. Harrell carried Oliver back to his room in the headquarters. He remained in the armor in case something happened. He sat in a chair and watched Oliver until the latter awoke. It didn't take long.

"Where...?"

"Back home," Harrell answered. "How do you feel?"

"Tired..."

Oliver took a deep breath. His head pounded with the worst migraine he had ever known. It was too much to even think, and his body had become incredibly sore.

"Everything... hurts..."

"We'll have to check you over tomorrow. For now, just rest."

"Yes... yes, sir..."

Harrell placed an ice pack on Oliver's forehead and a glass of water next to his bed.

"Recover soon. You're too important to lose."

"I... will..."

Harrell double-checked the locks in the room before he left.

— — —

Oliver awoke at midnight in a cold sweat. His whole body trembled and he breathed heavily. He had just suffered a nightmare, and although he couldn't remember its contents, it was terrifying enough that it had caused him to wake up with an anxiety attack. He tried to ignore these sensations and return to sleep, but his own mind turned against him. He couldn't focus, couldn't settle down. Even worse, his stomach felt like it was caving in on itself from hunger. In fact, his entire body felt like something was off.

Oliver sat up. He still trembled and couldn't stop hyperventilating. It took every bit of his willpower to think of what to do.

*Food. I'm just hungry. Get food.*

His fridge was only a few feet away, but every step clouded his mind further. His cold body had been dampened with sweat. He shivered so intensely that he couldn't grip the handle of the fridge door. He fell to his hands and knees.

Something inside him woke up. *Hungry.*

It was the last coherent moment.

— — —

Darcy slept great! Their new bed was so soft that they had fallen asleep the moment their head hit the pillow. Although Darcy wasn't typically a morning person, the excitement of seeing Oliver again made them bright-eyed and bushy-tailed. They checked the news on their phone as they ate breakfast. How wonderful it was to eat breakfast! It was just a simple sugary cereal in a bowl of milk, but for Darcy, it felt like a feast. Unfortunately, the news they saw wasn't so pleasant.

"Multiple people have reported seeing a 'night creature' late last night. It apparently had broken into multiple stores and places of residents. Thankfully, nobody had been harmed in this incident, but doors have been torn off of their hinges, walls have been left with claw marks, and large amounts of food had been eaten. The prime suspect of the Night Creature is someone within Almond Industries, as a gaping hole was found in its headquarters. Some witnesses claim that it is a spider monster, leading authorities to believe that it may have something to do with the current company ambassador Red Arachnid."

Darcy hurried to finish their meal. The moment they could speak, they called, "Revival Patron!"

Revi appeared in front of them. "Yello?"

Darcy showed them the news. "I think this is Oliver!"

Revi grimaced. "Oh, yikes! Let's get you there right away!"

The two left the pocket dimension and arrived on the same rooftop as before. Revi said,

"Oh, wait. What if people mistake *us* for the Night Creature?" Without waiting for a response, Revi conjured trench coats, shades, and fedoras for the two of them. The outfits were all in blue, of course.

"Ta-dah! Nobody will ever suspect us now!"

Darcy gave a nervous thumbs-up. "Uh... sure."

"And check this out: there are slits in the sides! So you can hide your extra arms in the coat but also put them through the slits so you can still use them."

"Oh, that's actually pretty cool." Darcy put on the outfit. "Alright, let's go."

And so, the duo took to the streets. Their destination was the headquarters, but they stopped by every location hit by the night creature on the way there.

"Good morning," Revi would greet. "I am Agent Blue-One and this is my partner, Agent Blue-Two. We would like to ask you some questions about the Night Creature."

This ruse was enough to get most people to talk, and every story was the same: an arachnid monster had broken into the home, but never attacked anyone directly. In fact, one person had attempted to strike the beast, but instead of retaliating, it merely screamed and ran off.

Darcy asked Revi, "What would've caused this? Oliver was never like this before."

Revi replied, "I'm scared to think of it, but it might be corruption. Maybe he became a Wraith."

The thought made Darcy's mouth go dry. They gingerly asked,

"If he did, can you reverse it?"

"It depends. If his body is still intact, then I can try, but if his organic form has shed away... there's not much I can do."

Darcy tapped a claw against their skull. "Okay, so where would he be right now? Not the headquarters, everyone would know to look there first. He hasn't mentioned being connected to any other heroes..."

"You two are friends, right? Do you think he'd be at your place?"

"I guess it'd be worth a shot."

Darcy climbed up the fire escape and into their apartment.

"Oliver!" They called. "It's me, Darcy."

"Darcy?"

Oliver stepped out of the bathroom. He wore clothes that looked like they were pulled from the garbage, and stunk like it too, but that didn't stop Darcy from running over and giving him a hug.

"Oh, thank god!" They quickly backed away. "Shit, sorry. Are you okay with hugs?"

"I am." Oliver giggled. "I'm happy to see you, too. Um, sorry about breaking into your place. I couldn't think of anywhere else to go."

"Yeah, I saw the news-"

"But it's not me!" He blurted. "Please don't listen to what the news is saying. The Night Creature isn't me!"

"Huh?" Darcy pulled back. "What do you mean? Who else could it be?"

"I-I..." He rubbed his arm. "It's... not."

"If it's not you, then why isn't Red Arachnid investigating this?"

"The whole thing is just a hoax. Nothing to look into."

"Then why are you hiding?"

Oliver backed away. "I-I'm not a monster. I'm still human, see? It's... it's just a nightmare." He smiled. "Yeah. Just a nightmare. I'm going to wake up any second now and everything will be A-okay."

Darcy shook their head. "Never mind, we'll talk about it later. Let's go, Revi's just outside."

"Why is Revi here?"

"We were worried that you got corrupted. C'mon."

The two met back up with Revi in the alleyway below. Revi clapped.

"You found him!"

Oliver gave a nervous wave. "Um, hi, Revi. Don't worry, I'm fine."

"Oh, great! Problem solved! Okie dokie, let's hold hands!"

The threesome held hands and Darcy pulled out their crystal heart. They then vanished to Revi's pocket dimension.

Oliver fell in the grass. "Woah!"

Revi stood in front of him and Darcy. "What do you think of this place? Do you like it?"

Oliver glanced around. "It's... uh... a lot."

"Hm, how 'bout you two chill out in your apartment. I gotta check on my other warlocks, but let me know if anything happens."

Darcy replied, "We will."

In Darcy's new apartment, Darcy explained their side of things. Oliver paced back and forth. He rubbed his wrist.

"But I can't be the Night Creature. I don't remember doing any of that. Honest!"

Darcy scratched their head. "So this is like a werewolf situation?"

"But werecreatures don't exist."

"Still, turning into a monster and not remembering what happened is pretty peak werewolf stuff."

He turned to face them. "Do I look like a monster to you? Do I look like I would break into people's houses and eat all that food?

I don't even have a good relationship with food! Besides, the Night Creature could be anything! Maybe it's a mutant Venutian?"

"A mutant Venutian just so happened to tear a hole out of the Almond Industries headquarters? I saw the articles, Oliver."

Oliver clenched his teeth and looked away.

Darcy's voice softened. "Listen, I want to believe you, but if you're right, then what were you doing? Why were you hiding?"

"I-I was just lost. My costume got damaged. I knew that people would blame me, so I ran off. But it *wasn't me*."

Darcy showed him their phone. "Here. People have already uploaded videos of the Night Creature. Look at this one."

The video had been taken from behind a couch. The hallway light gave the video just enough brightness to show details on the creature. It looked like Darcy, but red, twice as large, and wore the shredded costume of Red Arachnid. The creature dug through the fridge, shoving anything it could into its mouth. It then crawled to the nearest window and burst through.

Another video had been taken from just outside of a kitchen, from around a corner. The Night Creature gnawed at a plastic container, struggling to get it open. The lighting revealed that its eyes had a different formation than Darcy's—instead of two large primary ones and six secondary ones, the Night Creature's eyes were all the same size and had four distributed in the front and two on the left and right sides of the face, respectively. In the video, the Night Creature had failed to open the plastic container and promptly climbed to the ceiling, where it scurried out of view.

Darcy said, "There's at least a dozen more of these."

Oliver backed away and shook his head. "No... no..."

"If it helps, you didn't seem to hurt anyone."

"But that won't matter. It won't matter because... because Harrell..." He closed his eyes before he could form tears. "He doesn't like monsters."

"Denying it won't make anything better."

"But if I just pretend it was all a bad dream... if enough time passes... maybe everything will return to normal. Can't I have that?"

Darcy sighed. They said slowly,

"Oliver, if we *do* wait, and everything *isn't* back to the way it was, then what will you do?"

"It doesn't matter," He said, "Because it *will* be."

# Chapter 4

Oliver refused any tests or analyses on his situation.

"Just give it a day," He said. "After a day, everything will calm down and go back to normal. You'll see."

Revi still had Patron work to catch up on, so they were kept busy. Thus, it was up to Darcy to try to pull Oliver out of his bubble of denial.

"I mean, look at it this way," They said. "You looked pretty cool."

"It was just a nightmare," He replied. "Just a one-night thing! Everything is fine now."

Oliver himself struggled to believe his lie, but he felt that he had to. Mike Harrell was a ruthless man when it came to the company—anything that could threaten its image was a stain to be eliminated.

*But that would never happen to me*, Oliver thought. *I'm different. He's good to me.*

And in his denial, Oliver convinced himself that his encounter with the violet dragon was also part of the nightmare. He couldn't acknowledge that was real because that would mean everything that occurred afterwards was also real. And so, he didn't mention it.

But the stress of pretending wore him down faster than any marathon. By the time afternoon rolled around, he had stopped talking entirely. He would simply sit somewhere and stare into space. At the current moment, he sat in Darcy's living room. Darcy sat down next to him.

"Hey, bud."

No answer.

"It's okay if you're scared."

He turned his head away from them.

"I'm going to make some late lunch. Are you up for anything? We could have chicken nuggets together."

Oliver's stomach growled at the thought. He was always taught that asking for food was greedy, and enjoying the food was gluttonous, lessons that were only hammered deeper when he became a superhero.

*"You must look like the ideal human."*

But his body had gotten weak from hunger, and Oliver didn't wish to die. He whimpered out,

"Okay."

He followed Darcy to the kitchen. They conjured the nuggets with their food box and set a plate for each person.

"Do you want ketchup for yours?"

"I dunno."

"That's alright. They taste good plain anyways."

Oliver nibbled on a nugget. His instincts craved the meal. He wanted more than anything to just enjoy himself and have a good moment with his friend, but years of learned hatred stayed embedded in his mind.

*Look at you, eating like a pig. What kind of a person does that? There are thousands of people in the world who are starving. You don't deserve this. You don't deserve anything.*

He tried to ignore it.

*Heroes don't need to eat, especially not garbage. You should be ashamed of yourself.*

He covered his ears as if it would help. Instead, the guilt became stronger.

*Trying to hide it? Really? You can't even block out intrusive thoughts correctly. How much of a loser* **are** *you?*

*No wonder Darcy pities you.*

A pressure welled up in Oliver's soul. He gritted his teeth and tightened his grip on his head.

"Stop it... stop it..."

Something in his hands crunched. Darcy gasped.

"Oliver!"

"What?"

"Your arms..."

He moved his hands in front of his face. His fingers had become claws and his arms were covered in a red, chitinous substance.

"No..."

"Are you hurt? That looked painful."

He wasn't sure if "pain" was the right word for it. It was the same sensation he felt every time his anxiety got bad or his stress reached a boiling point.

Oliver squeezed his eyes shut. "It's not real."

Darcy put their arms around him. The hug helped him steady his breathing and slow his heartbeat. He hugged back. He watched his hands as he did it, and to his surprise, they morphed back into human ones. Oliver separated from the hug and looked at himself.

"Huh?"

Darcy said, "Oliver, I know that it's hard, but what is happening to you *is* real."

Oliver didn't reply. He opened and closed his hands in curiosity.

*I wonder if...*

"Darcy," He said. "I think I can still pretend to be human."

"That's, um... great. But what do you mean?"

"I... in my nightmare, I was attacked by a dragon. It did something to my head. Now it's like my powers are connected to my emotions."

"So as long as you stay calm, you won't transform?"

"I think so." He smiled. "Darcy, this is great! If we explain this to Harrell, he'll understand. I can still live with him and everything will go back to normal. Maybe he'll even find a way to fix me."

Darcy didn't appear convinced. "Woah. Hang on. While I'm glad to see you hopeful, what if he still just sees you as a monster? What will happen if you have a panic attack? Or transform at night again? Are you sure you can fully control this?"

"He'll understand."

But Oliver knew that Darcy raised some good points. If he didn't have a handle on this situation, then history would just repeat itself.

He asked, "But, um... can you help me?"

"Of course."

Oliver forced himself to eat the rest of his meal. At this point, the chicken nuggets had cooled down, and that ironically lessened the guilt that came from eating them. The sensation of having food in his belly made him shiver.

"I'm proud of you," Said Darcy. "You should reward yourself."

"With what?"

"I... uh... hm. Want another hug?"

Oliver smiled. "I'm always up for those."

They duo spent the rest of the day understanding Oliver's new situation. He could still activate his powers like a regular warlock could—the spidery transformation seemed to exist alongside them, like an addition rather than a replacement. As for the transformation itself, any form of anxiety seemed to cause it; even something as simple as a jumpscare caused his limbs to morph. The more frightened Oliver felt, the more he changed.

"I'm willing to bet that's why I... *may have* become the Night Creature," He said. "I had a nightmare, and it triggered my anxiety so bad that my entire body transformed."

"Do you think you could learn to control your full-spider form?"

"I don't know. I don't want to know. And if everything goes according to plan, I won't have to. Which means I can't fall asleep."

"Woah, are you sure about this?"

"I can't risk having another nightmare. Darcy, I know that this is a lot to ask, but can you please watch over me tonight?"

Darcy's face was cast with doubt, yet they nodded along.

"I'll watch over you. But if this doesn't work out-"

"It will. It *will.*"

"Can we at least tell Revi about what we've learned?"

"We'll... talk to them tomorrow."

But tomorrow seemed to come slowly. No matter how many times Oliver checked the clock, time moved at the same rate it always did. Darcy offered for the two of them to watch a movie or play a game together, but Oliver worried that they would make him tire out faster. So instead, he laid on the living room floor and stared at the ceiling. Unfortunately, the floor was so plush and soft that it made him want to sleep anyway.

His stomach gurgled.

*Maybe the kitchen will be better.*

Oliver stood in front of the fridge, but stopped himself from opening it.

"It's okay," Said Darcy. "We can snack on something if you want. After all, the Night Creature seemed pretty hungry. Maybe stocking up on food will help things."

"Maybe."

The duo had a simple snack of cheese and crackers at the kitchen table. Darcy ate the cheese with vigor.

"Man, I'm so glad that arachnomorphs are omnivorous. If I became lactose-intolerant, I would lose my goddamn mind."

Oliver made a weak laugh. "Yeah."

He had to admit, the cheese tasted *really* good. The cheddar had enough flavor to be exciting, but not so much that it was overwhelming. Oliver found himself grabbing multiple slices of it.

"Sorry," He said.

"Don't apologize. I can always conjure more." Darcy then said, "If I may ask, why are you uncomfortable around food? Let me know if this is intrusive."

Oliver retreated into his chair. "Well... the foster system I grew up in didn't have much funding. Whenever I was between families, food security was... lacking. And when I *was* with a family, I always felt like I was burdening them, so I tried not to eat much. I didn't want to take up space. Then when I aged out of the system, I became a warlock and suddenly had access to infinite food. I got so excited that I conjured myself an entire feast, but I ate so much food at once that I got sick."

"Refeeding syndrome."

"Yeah. I got sponsored some time after that." He sighed. "The thing about superheroes is that we're supposed to represent the best of mankind, not just in ideals, but in body as well. If you don't look perfect all the time, then you're not... good enough."

"So it's like a hellish combo of being a celebrity and a bodybuilder."

"Pretty much. But it's not all bad. Being sponsored gave me access to top-of-the-line training. I was able to master my powers much more efficiently. And I *belong* somewhere."

"But is it worth it?"

Oliver couldn't look them in the eyes. "Of course. It's... always worth it."

But the wheels in his head kept turning.

*Eating is good for me, but the company says it isn't. Mister Harrell is a good man, yet he'll reject me if things don't go well. I belong somewhere, but if I'm not perfect...*

*If a home doesn't allow imperfection, then is it a home at all?*

He shook his head in an attempt to get rid of these thoughts, but the funny thing about anxiety is that it causes a person to second-guess **everything**, even if that person saw something as an unshakable truth.

*What if Mister Harrell was just waiting for something like this to happen? What if I already failed somehow and he just needed an excuse to get rid of me? What if I was never good enough? What if everyone is just pretending to be nice to me?*

He got out of his chair. "I'm sorry. I need to be alone."

*It's only a matter of time before they realize I'm not the person they want. Then they'll just leave me. I'll never be good enough.*

Oliver hurried into the bathroom and locked the door. The downward spiral of fear had already caught him and set his heart racing. He gripped the edges of the sink and tried to force himself to calm down. But without any emotional tools to ground himself with, the anxieties ate into each other like an ouroboros.

*Everyone hates me. Everyone's sick of me. They were just putting up with me. Even Darcy's sick of me. They're just pretending to like me so I won't feel bad. Everyone's just* ***pretending****!*

This event triggered the transformation, the *full* transformation. Extra arms tore through his clothes, already armed with claws and chitin. The chitin spread over his body as he grew larger and developed extra eyes. He looked into the mirror and saw a monstrous red spider staring back.

Despite this monstrous appearance, his actions were still driven by fear. He didn't recognize his reflection and screamed in fright, backing into the wall. His animal instincts only understood two things: that he was in a locked-off place and there was another spider in the room with him.

Oliver clawed at the bathroom walls until he found the door. He scratched and pushed against it until he forced it open.

A small white spider squeaked in surprise. Trying to fight for its territory, no doubt. Oliver ran past it and into the kitchen.

*Hungry.*

He didn't know why he was starving—it was just a hole he had to fill. Then he would find a literal hole to hide away in. He climbed onto the kitchen table and shoved the cheese and crackers into his mouth.

The white spider ran up to the table. They said something in a vaguely familiar voice, but Oliver couldn't quite understand it. It stepped between him and the fridge. It put its hands out and said something again.

Oliver stepped back. The spider only reached his waist, but the thought of getting into a fight still terrified him. If it didn't want him in its fridge, then he had to oblige. He'd have to find more food somewhere else.

He crawled along the walls in hope of an exit. He reached a door, but a webline stuck to one of his limbs. It trailed back to the white spider, still connected to the spider's abdomen. Oliver bit the webline in two. He only made a couple more steps before the white spider put their claws on him.

*Afraid.*

Couldn't the white spider see that he was trying to leave? He didn't want to cause trouble, he just wanted to feel safe. Yet the white spider pulled him to the floor. Oliver closed his eyes and readied himself for pain.

And yet... the pain never came. Instead, the white spider stroked Oliver's fuzzy head and spoke softly to him. Oliver's heartbeat slowed, and without panic screaming in his head, it was easier to understand the sounds around him.

"It's okay," Said the white spider. "You're okay. You're safe. You're safe."

*Safe.*

His mind cleared. He understood what those words meant as well as who spoke them. He managed a word as well.

"Darcy."

"Yeah." They placed their head against his own. "It's going to be okay."

Oliver let out a breath. His shape shrunk back into human form, but an exhausted one.

"Darcy," He said. "Oh, god. Darcy, I'm so sorry."

"You're okay. Sorry for getting rough with you."

"It's fine." He gulped "I... I need to tell Harrell. I need to tell him the truth. I can't keep ignoring it."

"But what if he...?"

"Then that will be the truth," He admitted to himself. "I *am* the Night Creature."

# Chapter 5

Oliver was scared out of his mind. Rejection was imminent, he was certain. Darcy even offered for the two of them to stay home, but Oliver turned it down. He had reasoned that Revi would need time to fix the damage he had caused to the walls and bathroom door (which he had apologized for immensely). He had a second reason as well: that he needed to have this conversation. He worried that if he didn't, then he would be eaten away by temptation. He would doubt himself and think, "Well, maybe things won't be so bad." But, by going as soon as possible and mentally preparing himself for the outcome, he would be able to rip off the bandaid. Only then would he be able to start moving forward.

Darcy dressed themself in their hat-trench coat combo while Oliver still wore the clothes he found in the garbage. The duo left Revi's pocket dimension and arrived back in Newstone City.

They found Mike Harrell patrolling around Almond Industries headquarters. Darcy and Oliver hid in a nearby alleyway to steel the nerves.

"He's right there," Said Oliver. "He's right there..."

"Okay, here's what we're gonna do," Said Darcy. "I'm gonna go up to him first and try to explain things. Hopefully it'll keep him from assuming the worst. If things are chill, I'll give you the signal."

"Please be careful."

Darcy approached Harrell as Oliver went over the script in his mind.

*"I'm sorry, Mister Harrell, but my condition is unstable right now. I understand that you're disappointed, but I can't represent the company for the immediate future. I hope we can still retain our relationship, as you've told me that I'm like a son to you. I hope those words ring true."*

Things seemed to have gone well on Darcy's end, as they gave a thumbs-up in Oliver's direction. Oliver gingerly stepped into view like a deer leaving a forest.

"H-hello, sir."

"Ollie! Welcome back."

The armor around the head retracted to show a man wearing beige-rimmed sunglasses. Darcy pointed at the sunglasses.

"Uh, do you always wear those?"

"Of course. Don't want the sun getting into my eyes." Harrell put his hands on Oliver's shoulders. "Oh, Ollie, it's good to see you!"

"Really?"

"Yes! I was so worried about you! How have you been? *Where* have you been? You smell like a dumpster."

"I, uh... well, sir-"

"Never mind, you can tell me all about it later." He placed a hand against Oliver's back and led him to the headquarters. "I missed you so much, kiddo."

"I-I did, too. But sir, there's something I need to tell you."

"If it's important, we'll get to it. Let's get us some **privacy** first."

Harrell looked to Darcy and snapped his fingers. Upon nothing happening, he snapped his fingers again.

He said in an annoyed tone, "Come on. You can go now."

"No. I'm not leaving my friend."

"He doesn't need you anymore."

"Wait," Said Oliver. "Sir, I..."

*Tear off the bandaid, tear off the bandaid.*

Oliver took a breath. He said, "Sir, my powers are unstable."

"I'm aware."

"I know that we- I'm- that I can't represent the company in my current state-"

"Yes, I figured that out when you trashed every other place in the neighborhood."

"But sir, I hope that maybe we can still be... well, it's just... you said that I'm like a son to you."

Harrell stopped. He slowly turned to face Oliver. With his sunglasses on, it was difficult to read his expression, This caused Oliver to assume every worst thing imaginable. He felt the now-familiar sensation of transformation in his hands. Oliver swiftly hid them behind his back.

Harrell watched him in silence. After a long moment, he said,

"You know, Ollie, you remind me of my sister. Have I ever told you about her? She and I used to be *so close*."

Harrell grabbed one of Oliver's arms and pulled it into view. He stared at the spider hand. His grip tightened enough to break circulation in Oliver's wrist. Harrell spoke with venom on his tongue.

"...Until she **changed**."

Harrell pulled Oliver closer so his face was only inches away. He spoke with a monotone intensity.

"Change back."

"I'm trying."

"Do it!"

"I'm trying!"

Harrell grimaced. He pulled Oliver towards the headquarters.

"I know how to deal with this."

"Sir, please! I can do better! I'm not a monster!"

"Then change back."

"I can't!"

Oliver's arm had entirely morphed now. Harrell let go in disgust. He glanced at the building doors, then back at Oliver. He pressed a button on his suit. His helmet went back over his face and his arms glowed. He placed a hand on Oliver's shoulder.

"Goodbye, Oliver."

Electricity shot through Oliver's body. He screamed from the pain before falling down. He only barely hung on to consciousness as he saw Darcy jump into view. Darcy lunged at Harrell and punched him in the face. His helmet made a cracking sound and he collapsed.

"Count yourself lucky, fuckweed," Darcy roared. "That hit was *mercy*!"

Darcy carried Oliver away from the area. Once they were out of view, they pulled out their crystal heart and teleported the two of them back to Revi's pocket dimension. Darcy set Oliver down and checked him for any injuries. Oliver rubbed his wrist as the past few minutes caught up to him. He fell to his knees and cried.

"It's over," He whimpered. "It's over..."

— — —

Darcy had grabbed a blanket from their apartment and wrapped it around Oliver's shoulders. They sat in the grass for a good while. How long, Oliver couldn't tell. Revi's pocket dimension had its own sky and sun, but he didn't keep track of its movement. He merely let himself cry into Darcy's shoulder.

It was strangely nice to let himself feel emotions like this. He no longer had a reason to bottle them up, so they flowed out of him like a dam. He had no job, no home, no role to speak of... but at least he didn't have to lie to himself anymore.

"I'm sorry," He said to Darcy. "Sorry that I dragged you into this."

"No apologies," They replied. "You're my friend. Friends are there for each other."

"But I haven't done anything for you in return."

"Just existing is enough." Darcy nuzzled their head against Oliver's. "Love isn't transactional."

Oliver collapsed into more tears.

"Thank you," He managed to say. "Thank you..."

Revi met with the duo to tell them that the apartment repairs were finished. The three met up in the living room so Revi could finally run an analysis on Oliver. They placed a hand on top of Oliver's head and their eyes shined bright.

"Sorry for the physical touch. The details become more clear this way."

"It's okay."

"Would you want me to project it, or just tell you what I see?"

"Only tell me."

"Okie dokie. So looking into your past, your pizzazz had it rough. Really rough! Looks like you suffered from repeated brainwashing!"

Darcy yelped. "Brainwashing?! When?!"

Oliver answered, "Mister... well, Harrell... had a way of, um... weeding out certain behaviors. Every time I did something that wasn't appropriate for the company, he sort of... put me into an special chair. It was for my own good, really."

Revi squinted at him. "Buddy. Dude."

"I'm sorry."

"It's not your fault, it's just..."

"It *was*. I agreed to it."

"Coerced consent still isn't consent. Brainwashing is bad, no matter how you slice it." Revi sighed and continued. "Aw, man... that explains the next part, too. You see, Oliver, the brainwashing didn't just mess with your head—it messed with your pizzazz, too. It started corrupting. If your pizzazz was left alone, you would've become a Wraith by now."

"Holy shit," Said Darcy. "What saved him?"

"A... dragon? A Salavite! Yeah, a dragon Salavite."

"Like a dragon warrior? I thought they were extinct."

"Oh, no. Plenty of Salavites still exist. They've just been forced into hiding. A few of my warlocks are Salavites, actually."

Oliver asked, "So what did the dragon do to me?"

"Well, it seems like you tangled with a violet dragon. Salavites from the Violet Clan specialize in purification spells. Hm, purification removes toxins from plants, water, soil... and dragon warriors are powerful enough to remove toxins from the mind."

Oliver said, "They *did* say something about Harrell being dangerous."

"That must be it," Said Darcy. "Some sort of attempt to cure him of brainwashing!"

Revi said, "Well, if that was the plan, then they succeeded. From that point on, your pizzazz was restored to factory settings. No more risk of corruption! The mental lock was even put back in place, too."

Darcy asked, "So what caused the whole transformation situation?"

"Ironically, the purification spell. You see, any spells that affect the mind require consent to work properly. Because Oliver didn't consent, the purification did its job, but also intensified his connection to his powers. Hence the morphing caused by fear."

Oliver was nearly too afraid to ask.

"Can... can it be fixed?"

"I... um... I'm not certain. There are certain factors here that still don't line up. Like how you specifically transform into an arachnomorph, and a big one at that. That's so *strange*. Why isn't it the design from Form Change?"

"What is the difference?"

"The Form Change design only has two arms and doesn't have chelicerae or an abdomen. They're meant to look more human-like."

Darcy said, "Is it possible for a non-Patron to turn someone into an arachnomorph?"

"No. But then again..." Revi tapped a claw against their chin. "Back in dinosaur times, my siblings apparently created warlocks by taking regular spiders and turning them into arachnomorphs.

Could it be that the arachnomorph design exists within the pizzazz itself, just lying dormant? Did this situation accidentally re-activate ancient spider powers?"

Darcy said, "That sounds cool as hell!"

Oliver said, "I'm really sorry, but I don't want to find out."

"But if we figure out how this stuff works, we can use it to change you back, right?"

"I don't want to have special powers, I just want to be me again."

Revi said, "Well, good news: your pizzazz is fine. I double-checked the mental lock just in case, and you won't be corrupted in the future unless you get brainwashed again. Bad news: your morphing is a magic problem, so our best shot is a magical solution. And, um... Patrons can't do magic."

Darcy tilted their head to the side. "Really? Aren't you guys super powerful?"

"Having power doesn't mean we can do everything. And when it comes right down to it, pizzazz can't make magic and magic can't make pizzazz. You're gonna have to find magic users, and good ones at that."

"Any direction you can point us in?"

"Good news again! Yes! I'll take you to Akio. They're a Salavite warlock and they used to be in training to be a dragon warrior. They could never complete the training, but they come from an entire *place* and it's full of *people*! If they know anyone who can help you, Akio will tell you."

This gave Oliver some relief. "Thank you, Revi."

"Uh-huh! Glad to help! And take care of yourself, too. Emotional balance will help you big-time."

# Chapter 6

Revi led Darcy and Oliver to Akio's apartment, numbered 008. There was a delay before Akio answered the door, and when they did, they only opened the door a hair's width.

"A little busy at the moment."

"Hi, Akio," Said Revi. "We were wondering if you could help us with a magic problem."

"Magic?" Akio opened the door wide. "Come in!"

Akio had blue hair tied into a ponytail and bangs that faced forward. The ponytail was long, thin, and reminded Darcy of lizard tails. Akio wore a red-and-white letter jacket over a black t-shirt and complemented by matching red pants. The pants tucked into black-and-white all-terrain boots. Akio sized up the visitors with dark red eyes, their focus especially on Darcy.

"Woah. What happened to you?"

"Revi turned me into an arachnomorph."

Revi shrugged with a smile. "Whoops?"

"I'm fine with it, but I'm not the one who needs help."

Akio replied, "Alright, come in."

Akio's apartment had walls and flooring in soft, earthy tones. Akio had the visitors sit down in their circle-shaped living room. Its sofas all had a curve to them to fit the room's shape.

"Sit down and I'll get us some tea."

"Want any help?" Revi asked.

"No, just stay in that room."

Darcy leaned forward to catch a glimpse of the connecting rooms. Sheets of paper and small stone sculptures littered the floor and furniture.

As the trio waited, Oliver said to Darcy,

"Did you see how much red they were wearing? They're so cool!"

"Yeah. I wonder how they got their eyes and hair like that."

Revi explained, "Salavites keep their eye color no matter what. And Akio's hair is just dyed. It's usually black."

"So do Salavites start out as humans?" Darcy asked.

Revi giggled. "Find out for yourself."

Oliver rubbed his arm. "How am I going to explain my situation? What if Akio says no? What if we're forced back to square one? What if we go through all this effort only for nothing to happen?"

Revi chirped, "Well, we won't know until we find out!"

Akio returned to the room. "Hope you like green tea."

"I'm not picky," Darcy replied. "Though I've always wanted to try dandelion tea. I heard that you can use the leaves."

"You use the flower, actually, but I think every part of the dandelion is usable for something."

Akio sat on the arm of a chair as they conversed.

"So how much did Revi tell you about me?"

Darcy replied, "That you're a Salavite, you used to be in training to become a dragon warrior, and you know a 'place full of people'."

Akio's face became somber upon hearing the term "dragon warrior".

"I see," They said. "Well, what can I help you with?"

"Well, we have a problem caused by magic and we're hoping that magic will also be the solution."

"And have either of you seen a Salavite before?"

"Not in person," Said Darcy.

"Ditto," Said Oliver. "Unless you count the one who attacked me."

Akio's eyebrows raised. "Someone attacked you?"

Oliver nodded. "A violet dragon with yellow eyes. They also had wings, but didn't use them."

"A dragon warrior from the Violet Clan. Did they tell you why?"

"They kept trying to warn me about 'him'. I think they were talking about Mister... Mike Harrell. They wouldn't explain why I was in danger, but we think it was because Harrell was... hurting me. They also told me to look for Darcy, but I don't know why."

Darcy said, "Hey, do you think that dragon was watching us talk the other day? Was that why they knew about me?"

"Probably. I *did* sense something back then."

Akio asked, "What did the dragon warrior do to you?"

"Well..." Oliver explained his corruption and the violet Salavite's role in haphazardly curing it. Akio listened closely.

"I see," They said. "And you haven't seen them again since then?"

"No. If they are invisible, I haven't sensed them nearby."

"Hm. Well, I don't know much about Mike Harrell, but I doubt the Violet Clan member would want to be on his radar for long. I'm willing to bet that they returned home."

"Would you know where that is?"

"Unfortunately, no. The different Salavite clans have been separated since before I was born. It's always been my dream to reunite them, but I only know where some of the clans might have gone. Even then, my clan doesn't have any leverage to form alliances."

Oliver's face fell. "So you don't know anyone who can help me?"

"Hey, now. I never said that! Just because we won't be able to find the person who changed you doesn't mean we can't reverse it. My clan has someone who studies magic's effects on the body; if anyone can help you, it's them. But before we continue, I think you guys need to know what a regular Salavite looks like."

Akio pulled a small sphere from their pocket. It was the size of a marble and glowed with olive-green light. Akio placed the sphere onto the couch cushion next to them. Once the sphere left their hand, an olive-green veil surrounded Akio's body like an egg. After a second, the "egg" broke and dissipated, revealing a Salavite.

They were a lizard-like creature, especially with the shape of their head and tube-like body. Like lizards, they had five claws at the end of each limb. Their dexterous tail whipped back and forth. Two cone-shaped ears rested at the back of the head and moved independently of each other. Akio's eyes caught Darcy's attention in particular: they were crystalline with lightened pupils. Both light and shadows were captured in their blood-red hue. Darcy realized that they had been staring at the eyes for too long and shifted their attention towards the rest of the body.

Akio had red scales, but the scales were so dense and smooth that Darcy would have to get up real close to see them. White lines with black dots ran down Akio's sides and tail. The black and white met together at the head, with white on the top half and black on the bottom half. Black markings decorated their eyes like eyeliner.

To Darcy's surprise, Akio's clothes had transformed with them and changed proportions accordingly. Their pants even gained a third pant leg to fit over the tail. Akio got off the couch's arm and stood tall, showing that they had gained an entire foot in their transformation, now being six-foot-seven. They gave a bow.

"This is my true self: Akio Ashlath."

"Wow," Said Darcy. "You look amazing."

"Thank you!"

Oliver said, "So that stone turns you human?"

"Yup! Like so."

Akio put the sphere back into their pocket. An olive-green egg appeared around them once more, and once it dissipated, Akio stood in human form once again.

They said, "The process is a bit showy, but transformation spells go all the way back to the start of our species. The very first Salavites used to be regular mundane lizards, after all."

Darcy said, "Nice. A transformation spell might be just what we need."

"Sure, but it wouldn't be a permanent solution. Oliver here would have to wear the stone constantly. But if I can take you back to my clan and introduce you to Varia, then I know for certain that they'll find a way to help you." Akio raised a finger. "But I'll need something from you guys in return."

Oliver replied, "What is it? I'll do anything."

"Well, how much do you two know about the Macbeths?"

Darcy said, "Aren't they a family that lives off old money?"

Oliver explained, "They own all the newstone in the world, letting them control all the magic by proxy."

"Yes," Said Akio. "And Salavites evolved because of magic. It literally runs through our bloodstream. So, of course, the Macbeths want to control us as well."

"I see," Said Darcy. "So that's why the clans are separated. You're not as much of a threat if you're not united."

"Exactly."

Oliver asked, "But why not use your own magic against them? If Salavites are naturally magical, wouldn't that give you the advantage?"

"Because the Macbeths also have dispels: spells that neutralize all magic within a certain radius. You can imagine what that does to a species with magic in their bodies."

Darcy sucked in the air through their teeth. "So they can just dispel you guys and make you helpless." Their eyes widened. "Oh! That's what you want help with, isn't it? Oliver and I don't run on magic, so dispels wouldn't affect us."

"Yes, exactly! And being warlocks gives you more of an edge than a regular person."

Oliver asked, "What about other superheroes?"

"Trust me, if they were willing to help, this would hardly be a problem. But I can't contact any registered heroes because they answer to the government, and the government wouldn't ever want to do something to anger the Macbeths." Akio hissed. "Because god forbid they do something that could inconvenience the rich and powerful. I can't contact any sponsored heroes for the same reason: the Macbeths are stockholders."

"But what about heroes who aren't registered or sponsored?"

"Not trustworthy. They could become turncoats the moment the Macbeths flash them a better deal. The only people I can trust with this are other warlocks."

Revi raised their hand. They had been silent in the conversation up until this point.

"It sounds like you want Darcy and Oliver to help you fight the Macbeths," They said. "Um, I thought you would just help them with their own problem."

"Revi, I told you, a warlock would be the best person to defend us from the Macbeths."

"But what if a warlock gets captured? The Macbeths could torture them or use a telepathy spell to breach their mind or do both at the same time! What if they find a way to wield pizzazz? We'd be giving the family even more power."

"But we can't go on like this," Akio argued. "With every passing year, we're growing weaker and weaker. We need help!"

"And I'm fine with getting help! But I can't approve of open rebellion against the Macbeths." Revi clasped their claws together. "I'm really sorry, Akio, but it's just too risky."

Akio's brows lowered and they glared at the floor.

Darcy said, "What if it was only defense?"

Revi tilted their head to the side. "Hm? What do you mean?"

"What if Oliver and I- or even just me- helped Akio's clan as just guards or something? That way, the focus will be on helping the Salavites instead of fighting the Macbeths, so there will be less chance of getting captured."

Revi put their claws next to their mouth. "Hmmmmmmmm. Would you guys promise not to chase them down, even if the

Macbeths run away? Would you promise to stay away from their mansion, no matter what?"

Darcy nodded. "I promise."

They said with uncertainty, "Okie dokie. You two have my permission to help Akio. Just... *please* be careful."

"We will!"

Revi stood up. "Okay. I'm gonna go check on the rest of my warlocks. Stay safe, love you! Ciao!"

Akio breathed a sigh of relief. "Thanks, Darcy."

"No problem."

"Um, I have a question," Said Oliver. "Revi mentioned other Salavites being warlocks. What about them?"

Akio sighed and lay backwards. "I already asked all of them. Everybody wants to focus on providing for their own clans, not somebody else's. While they *have* told me where their clans are, my clan doesn't have anything we could trade in return, so we won't be getting their help."

Darcy leaned forward. "I want to check out their museum."

"Huh? Why?"

"Well, the magic museum doesn't just talk about newstone, but the Macbeths, too. If I go there, I could learn more about the enemy. Plus, I promised to never go near the *mansion*, but I didn't say anything about the *museum*. So technically not breaking my promise to Revi."

"Fair enough."

"Please be careful," Said Oliver.

"Good luck," Added Akio. "Hope you have the money for it."

"Wellllllll, I don't have some right *now*, but I *do* have an idea." Darcy checked the time on their phone. "I can try that idea today, but I'll have to wait until tomorrow to visit the museum proper."

"Alright. Let me know when you guys are ready, then."

"We will!" Darcy took a step. "Oh, but before we go, you mentioned Salavites being magical. Does that mean you can do spells without newstone?"

"Yup." Akio changed to Salavite form and put out their hand. A red, sulfur-like substance covered their claws.

"That's incredible," Darcy replied. "Which spell?"

"Poison augmentation. My clan's specialty." Akio deactivated the spell and put their hands in their pockets. "But even poison magic is useless against a dispel."

"Damn. Well, I'll come back tomorrow, okay?"

"Yeah. Stay safe out there."

Back in Darcy's apartment, Oliver requested Darcy to call Revi. Once the Patron appeared, Oliver asked,

"Um, is it okay if I get some new clothes? Preferably something that stretches, if that's okay."

"Yeah, I can do that!" Revi conjured a blue, sleeveless bodysuit. "Will this do?"

"Um... does it come in red?"

"I only make blue clothes."

"Oh..."

"Sorry."

"No, it's okay."

Oliver went into the bathroom to change. Revi asked Darcy,

"So any leads yet?"

"We'll be seeing Akio's clan tomorrow. That's all at the moment."

"Tomorrow? Why not tonight?"

"Oh, uh, you know... wanna keep things low-stress for Oliver."

"Ah, that makes sense! Okie dokie, then!" Revi disappeared.

Oliver exited the bathroom with the old clothes in hand. He said,

"Did Revi leave already?"

"Yeah. It was just a quick check-in."

"Alright, then. So, um, what should we do with this hoodie and pants? They're so... ripped up."

"I'll take them. I have an idea."

"Oh?"

"Yeah, wanna visit the Wraith Lodge with me?"

"Wraiths? Gosh, I don't know." He rubbed the back of his neck. "They sound terrifying to be around, and with my anxiety..."

"Ah. Yeah, you should probably stay here. Be back soon."

"Okay. Be safe."

— — —

Because they were grabbed from the garbage, Oliver's old clothes had rips and tears and stunk of something awful. His transformation into the Night Creature had not helped things either, as it stretched out his clothes and formed even more holes. Darcy carried the articles of clothing to the Wraith Lodge.

"Sky? Hello?"

No answer. Sky must have been busy doing something else. Darcy decided that it would be a good idea to travel deeper into the lodge. They took a right turn and found a log cabin among the trees. Darcy knocked on the front door before entering.

Whatever Darcy expected, they were not ready for a bar. A counter stretched from one wall to the next with stools sitting along it. No other furniture existed—it was as if this was a child's vague idea of a bar rather than being based on something real. A human warlock in a barkeep's outfit stood on the other side of the counter. Their dark hair had been tied into a neat bun.

A Decay Wraith sat on one of the stools. They were solid enough to have a coherent shape- that of a spider monster- but their eyes lacked definition. In fact, the eyes blurred together into two white masses on their face. The Wraith gave Darcy a halfhearted nod.

<Welcome to the party.>

"Uh... thanks."

Darcy sat next to the Wraith. The barkeep said to them,

"Just so you know, Wraiths are weak to light, so try not to use your phone or photography in here."

"Okay, thanks for letting me know."

The barkeep pointed a thumb at the shelves behind them. One of them held a food box.

"Want anything?"

"Thanks, but I have my own food box. Nice to meet the two of you."

"Same. I'm Perci."

<If you translated my name into Modern English, it would be Dusk. Dusk Nocturne.>

Darcy said, "Woah. That name's cool as hell."

<Thank you.>

Darcy decided to cut right to the chase. "So Dusk, I understand that Decay Wraiths can reverse aging."

<Yes, we eat the rot.>

"Yeah! And I was wondering if you could eat the rot from these clothes. Can you restore them to be new again?"

<I can try.>

Dusk held the clothes in their claws. They protracted sharp fangs and injected them into the clothing. The clothes regained their color and original texture, yet the rips and tears remained.

"I don't understand," Darcy said.

<We can only reverse aging, not injury.>

"But don't clothes tear more easily when they get old?"

<Yes, but that is a symptom, not a causation.>

Darcy recalled when they had taken a bite of the fruit with Sky. It still retained its bite marks even when made younger.

Dusk said, <It was still a decent enough meal. I've had worse.>

"What did it taste like?"

<White bread with slices of ham.>

"So like a sandwich?"

Dusk made a *tsk* sound. <Is that what the children call it these days?>

"Uh... yes? If you take bread and add meat to it, you get a sandwich."

<Why? Just call it bread-with-meat!>

"Dusk is really old," Perci explained. "I think they're older than the human race. They still struggle with certain concepts."

"Woah, really?" Darcy leaned closer to Dusk. "How old *are* you?"

<Old enough to remember the old days. You see, back in *my* day, people didn't prepare their food. We ate it as it was and it was great.> They formed shadowy claws specifically to do air quotes with. <Then the humans started the trends of "cooking" and "agriculture".>

"Yeah, those... those are pretty important things. I don't think I would call them trends."

<*Psh*. They'll die out, just you wait. Then everyone will go back to living in caves and eating raw meat.>

Darcy and Perci shared a glance. Darcy said,

"Well, I should get going. I gotta take these clothes back."

Dusk returned the clothing, then said, <Before you leave, I would like to ask something.>

"What is it?"

<Did Revi transform you?>

"Hm? Oh, yeah. I got sick and apparently was bound to get even more sick. Maybe even dying? I don't know for certain. But I'm an arachnomorph now! It's actually been really nice."

<Hm. Good to hear.>

Darcy then remembered what the Patrons had said about arachnomorphs existing in the past. They asked Dusk,

"Did you know any arachnomorphs back in your time?"

Dusk hesitated for a good while before answering, <Yes.>

"Have you ever heard of magic causing strange transformations for arachnomorphs?"

<I didn't study magic.>

"Do you know anyone who did?"

<I try not to converse with the other Wraiths.>

"Do you know of any ways to change a person's pizzazz?"

Dusk blinked. They averted their gaze. <...I do.>

"Really? That's great news! Can you tell me how? Is it true that you can use pizzazz to activate dormant powers?"

<Yes. Even when they are removed from the active list of abilities, old powers still remain in the history of the pizzazz. When I was alive, I played with the concept quite a lot.>

Perci said, "Uh, I wouldn't recommend trying it yourself, though. If you mess with your pizzazz, you'll break the mental lock and risk corruption."

<Yes. Consider me a cautionary tail.> Dusk raised a single claw. <However... I have had a lot of time to analyze my mistakes. It **is** theoretically possible to test with pizzazz safely... if you can find a way to get a sample.>

"Like a blood sample?"

<A sample of your pizzazz. If you can remove a small piece of your pizzazz and store it within a container... yes, I believe you could safely test with it then.>

"Hm, okay. Thanks for the tip."

Perci asked, "Are you trying to become human again?"

"No, but my friend is... in a way. Well, thanks for the help!"

"Yes, have a nice day."

"Have a nice day!"

Dusk turned to Darcy as if to say something, but turned again to face the counter.

<...Good luck.>

"Thanks, you too."

Revi met Darcy outside of the Wraith Lodge. They greeted,

"Hello! I got the ping that you fed a Wraith! Thank you."

"Yeah, I was hoping for a different outcome, though." Darcy showed Revi the tattered clothes.

"Ah. Here, lemme fix 'em up for you." Revi conjured a blue string and sewing needle. "Give me an hour and these will be good as new!"

"Thanks. In the meantime, the reward for the job..."

"Right! Which do you want, money or a new power?"

"Money." Darcy gave them a note. "I wrote down how much I want and how I want it to be stored."

"Okie dokie, I'll get right on it. The money will appear in your apartment soon."

"Thanks."

Darcy returned to the apartment to find the money in containers just as they requested. Each container was labeled with how much money it had, with one dedicated to singles, another dedicated to fives, and so on. Oliver commented,

"They just appeared in a cloud of blue sparkles."

"They're for me, don't worry. Although you can take some if you want."

Darcy placed some of the money into their drawstring bag so they would be ready tomorrow. Oliver asked,

"So... why not go tonight?"

"The museum is going to close in a couple hours. By the time I get into the building, I'll barely have time to observe anything. I wanna take this safe and slow."

"Well, what if we did something tonight? We could stay up again."

"I'd love to, but I want to be well-rested." Darcy paused. "...Oh."

Oliver rubbed his arm. "I'm just worried."

Darcy thought for a moment. "Well, what if we shared a bed?"

"What?"

"Whenever we didn't feel safe, my family and I would all get into the same bed. That way, if anything dangerous happened, we could easily protect each other. We were like cats. Maybe doing the same can help you feel safe, too."

"Maybe... hopefully..."

In bed, Darcy held Oliver close. Unfortunately, with them being so small and him being so tall, there wasn't a way for them to fully protect him. This affected Darcy's thoughts as they drifted into sleep.

*I wish there was a way to make myself as big and strong as the Night Creature. With that much power, I could protect people for certain...*

# Chapter 7

Darcy awoke alone in their bed. At first, this seemed like a normal, rational thing... until they remembered that they weren't supposed to be alone this morning.

*Oliver! Did he change again? Did I sleep through it? Oh god, please don't let him be far!*

Darcy rushed through the rooms of the apartment, but skid to a halt in the kitchen. Oliver, in human form, stood in front of the stove with a pan.

"Morning, Darcy," He chirped.

Darcy let out a heavy exhale. "Oliver. Oh, thank god."

"Sorry for worrying you. I wanted to surprise you with breakfast."

"So you didn't have nightmares? No transformation?"

"No," He said with relief. "I can't remember the last time I slept so well. I felt so safe! So I, um, wanted to thank you with some eggs."

Darcy looked at the pan. The egg yolk had cooked enough to be semi-solid, so Oliver flipped it over to cook the other side. Darcy asked,

"Which kind of egg are you making?"

"I... don't know. It's been a few years since I last prepared my own food. But I *do* know how to make pancakes, so I thought that eggs worked the same way."

"If you know how to make pancakes, then why didn't you just make pancakes?"

Oliver paused. "I... did not consider that."

Darcy giggled. "You silly billy."

"Haha, sorry."

"No, no. I'm excited to eat your eggs. Are they seasoned?"

"I used butter on the pan as the non-stick solution. There isn't any salt or pepper, but I can conjure some if you like."

"Thanks, but I can do it."

Darcy grabbed a plate of flat eggs, then slathered them with butter with just a pinch of salt and pepper. The eggs were well-cooked, not being too gooey nor too crunchy. The butter, salt, and pepper added to the flavor to create perfection. Darcy gobbled up the rest of their serving.

"Oh my god, this is amazing!"

Oliver beamed. "Really?"

"Dude, you gotta try this! Have you eaten yet?"

He looked away. "I... I actually did already."

Darcy watched with suspicion. "Did you actually eat, or...?"

"I... well... let's just say that it took a lot of tries to get these eggs right. First, I made them too hot, then I made the heat too low, and I kept making mistakes like that. But I couldn't just throw the eggs away! It would be wasting food, you know? So I used that logic to convince myself to eat them." He gave a nervous laugh. "Now I'm so full that I can't try the attempts that actually succeeded."

Darcy checked the nearby trash to make sure. About a dozen broken egg shells littered the trash can, and no sign of anything else. Although Darcy was still uncertain, they decided to take his word.

"Nice work! I'm proud of you."

"Thank you. Maybe next breakfast I can make us some pancakes."

"I'll make 'em with you. I've always wanted to try making peanut butter pancakes."

"Ooo. That actually sounds delicious."

As they ate another serving of eggs, Darcy conjured a glass of apple juice. They studied while they thought.

*Revi had placed the pizzazz into apple juice to give me my warlock powers. And before that, the apple juice turned me into an arachnomorph. Theoretically, I can do the same thing. Take a piece of my pizzazz... and place it into the juice.*

They placed a hand against their chest and shut their eyes. They exhaled and focused on the pizzazz in their body. They placed another hand onto the glass of apple juice. They concentrated on moving a bit- just a tiny bit- through their arm and into the glass.

It was like an electric jolt ran down their arm. Darcy shivered from the sensation. They let go of the glass and studied it.

The apple juice retained its golden coloration, no different than before. Darcy touched the glass again. They focused on activating the pizzazz. Their torso glowed blue, and to their surprise and delight, the apple juice glowed blue as well.

"Yes!" They stood up. "I did it!"

Oliver jumped and yelped. He shut off the stove.

"What? What happened? What's going on?"

"Sorry, didn't mean to scare you. But check it out!" Darcy showed him the apple juice. "I got a sample of my pizzazz."

"Wow. Darcy, that's... that's incredible. How did you even do that?"

"Well, if Revi can remove bits of their pizzazz, then why can't I?"

"I suppose I always assumed it would be a Patron thing. So what are you going to do with it?"

Darcy paused. "...Actually, I don't know. I didn't think that far." They looked at the glass. "I guess I could try messing with it, but I wouldn't know what that would do until I drink it and it rejoins my body. Not really the safest way to go about this, huh?"

"I'm sure you'll think of something. You're smart."

Darcy rolled their eyes with a smile. "I'm not smart."

"Yes you are. You're the one who thought of this."

"Yeah, well, let's hope I'm smart during the mission." They downed the apple juice.

After breakfast, Darcy got dressed and hurled their drawstring bag over their shoulder.

"I'm heading to the museum now. Wanna come with?"

"Thanks, but that place is always so crowded. I'm worried that I would get overstimulated and scared."

"Ah, yeah. Well, I'll be back in a few hours. Wish me luck!"

"Good luck! Please be careful!"

"I will! I won't cause trouble, I promise."

— — —

The Macbeth Museum of Magic was, without a doubt, the second-biggest collection of magical items in the world, beaten only by the Macbeths' mansion. People traveled from all over the world just to get a glimpse of the objects stored within this museum. This tourism inspired hotels, restaurants, and other tourist sites. As a result of this economy, the northwest part of Newstone was high-class and well-funded, which also meant that it was unbearably expensive. Admission prices were sixty dollars for each person and charged extra for those with children (on account of them being chaotic little monsters).

But there were people in this world that viewed expense as value, and so assumed that being able to pay such a fee meant that they were superior to everybody else. Some people merely wanted to see magic and saw the admission price as a worthy expense. For Darcy, it would be a way to understand the Macbeths better. Considering that they were the ones who created this museum, it would undoubtedly skew the facts in their favor, but this would give Darcy an opportunity to see just *how* they spoke of themselves. Just how much would they steer away from the truth?

Darcy waited in the crowded line of people to pay their fee. They gazed at the white marble exterior of the museum and its posters.

A warning sign read, "All exhibits are replicas, but any attempts at theft will result in a lifelong ban."

Darcy thought, *So they don't actually put real magic here. Guess that makes sense—anyone getting a hold of this stuff could threaten the Macbeths' power. Not to mention all the movies and shows where someone robs a museum...*

*But if that's true, then wouldn't that mean that the mansion is the biggest and* ***only*** *place holding magical objects? The Macbeths are either overconfident or their security is just that good.*

It came for Darcy's turn to pay admission. While the kiosk accepted their money, the security guard glared at Darcy in suspicion. Darcy spoke in the heaviest, most ridiculous midwestern accent they could muster.

"Venutian from out east. Y'know, I ollways wanted t'see this place."

The guard spoke with a gruff voice. "Don't cause trouble."

"*Oh yeh*. I get'ya, do'n worray."

Apparently their accent became too thick, as the guard gave up trying to understand them. He simply moved Darcy along and said,

"Just... don't cause trouble."

Darcy shuffled along in relief.

The inside of the museum was also made of white marble. Sunlight poured through the high-arched glass ceilings and illuminated most of the building. Each exhibit was protected by a wall of thick glass and a rope fence. Thick crowds stood at every exhibit, so much that Darcy would have to climb on top of someone just to catch a glance. As tempting as doing that was, Darcy elected to move along with a random group and simply catch whatever information they could see.

Darcy's group passed by an audio recording. It spoke with a faux-friendly voice.

"The Macbeths began as English nobility. Naming themselves after the historic Shakespearian play, they moved to America for new opportunities, which they found in the California Gold Rush. In the year 1850, they moved to the west coast, but it was not gold that they found, but newstone. They took advantage of this discovery and founded the newstone mines. They stimulated the careers of many men and women in those days, and thanks to their work, the city of

Newstone was built. Fun Fact: Newstone City is the only place in the world where newstone deposits can be found."

*I see. So they didn't just buy the newstone from people—they've had a chokehold on the source since the very start. The Macbeths having all the magic is simply seen as the status quo.*

Darcy's group next stopped at an exhibit that Darcy could just barely see. Through the gaps of people, they just barely caught sight of a colorless, glassy sphere. The audio voice explained,

"In ore veins, newstone appears as a thick, colorless mineral. It does not erode in water, so it is mined with the surrounding rocks, then washed and filtered. The newstone is then carved into a spherical shape. It is important that the newstone does not have edges, as cuts can poison a person's bloodstream. Once the newstone is carved and ready, it is activated and exposed to an element to create a spell. For example, activating newstone while dipping it in water will give it a water spell. It is then that it gains color and becomes a spell stone."

While learning about newstone was interesting enough, Darcy was particularly invested in the possible blood poisoning. They had heard that newstone was toxic if ingested- even just licking it could cause illness- but if newstone could cut a person and kill them, then perhaps Darcy could take advantage of that somehow.

And while Darcy did not want to think about it, it also laid out the possibility of magic being in Oliver's body. What if he was poisoned as well?

*Have to find out more.*

Darcy found another audio recording. It said,

"Magic is wonderful, but also dangerous. If any amount of newstone enters the body, it will cause necrosis to living tissue and eventual organ failure. Human bodies are not designed to handle such a mineral. This is why the Macbeths must keep magic close—to keep people from hurting themselves with newstone or others with spell stones. The Macbeths have everyone's best interests at heart."

*But what about spells?* Darcy wondered. *What about magical effects that remain in the body?*

Unfortunately, Darcy could not find any further information on the subject, but they did notice that there had been no mention of Salavites. No meetings, no conflicts, no relationship with the Macbeths of any sort. It was as if the species never existed.

*In school, they were only called dragon warriors and apparently went extinct long ago. I thought the Macbeths would mention* ***something*** *that would make themselves look good. Although, I guess if Salavites were mentioned, people would start asking questions. It's easier to ignore and evade than to risk telling the truth...*

Granted, Darcy didn't know much about the truth when it came to Macbeths and Salavites, but they chose to trust the underdogs.

The surrounding crowd moved forward quite suddenly. Darcy nearly fell over; they restrained a hiss and shuffled along to the back of the museum with everybody else. Somebody in white robes and long platinum-white hair stepped onto the stage, but Darcy was too far away to glean any more details. She turned on a microphone.

"Good day, everyone! Thank you so much for coming here today!"

The audience clapped in response. The person continued. She sounded like a young adult, yet spoke with a grace from beyond her years.

"My name is Libra Macbeth, and I am so happy to speak to you today. I try to give this museum as much attention as possible. It is my mother's pride and joy, and I am so happy to share that joy with the rest of you. Now, shall we begin the exhibition?"

The audience clapped again. Libra pulled something from her robe: a wand of some sort. Darcy wanted to push their way through the crowd, but it was too dense with people—if Darcy wanted to get closer, they would have to go around the crowd and climb along one of the walls, which would be risky.

*Don't get in trouble, Darcy. Don't draw attention to yourself.*

Libra said, "Wands, rods, staves... these are the most common forms of holding spell stones. They help direct the magic so I can do... this!"

She waved her hand in a wide arch. The sunlight above her shifted scattered into rainbows. This rainbow bathed the entire crowd, who now cheered along with the clapping. Libra continued with more light tricks, from changing the color of the room to blocking out the light entirely. At the end of the presentation, she made the light swirl above everyone like a golden hurricane. It dissipated into millions of tiny yellow flecks. The audience applauded.

Libra bowed. "Thank you very much. We wouldn't exist without you. Long live the Macbeths. Long live newstone!"

"Long live nothing!" A voice shouted from the crowd. Someone with bright red hair and a dark red hoodie climbed onto the stage. They tore the microphone away from Libra.

"The Macbeths are frauds! They stole from the Salavites!"

Darcy had to refrain themself from moving.

*Don't get in trouble, don't get in trouble.*

The audience didn't react to this person's shout. Libra delicately put a hand around the microphone. She still spoke in the same pleasant tone, as if this was part of the show.

"Sweetie, we didn't steal anything. We own the mines and we own this land. The newstone *belongs* to us." She put a hand on their shoulder. "Give them a hand, everyone!"

Everyone clapped, but it was the polite, condescending type of clap. The person with the bright red hair pulled themself away from Libra. They stood in place as if contemplating their next move, then leapt at her. The momentum made them both fall over. The person wrestled her for the wand. The microphone only caught a faint portion of their argument.

"Give it back! That's ours!"

Security guards climbed onto the stage, but Libra motioned for them to stay back. She let go of the wand. The person immediately got off her and jumped off the stage. Libra calmly stood up and pulled another wand from her robe. The person tried to push past the crowd, but the crowd pushed back. Now with everyone's focus on the wannabe thief, Darcy took the opportunity to get closer. They ran to the nearest wall and climbed up to get a better view. The people in the front of the crowd held the thief in place.

Libra stepped back to the microphone and said,

"Would everyone like to see one more trick?"

The audience cheered a "yes". Libra pointed at the thief. The wand shot a black beam with white specks. The thief screamed and collapsed. For a horrifying moment, Darcy assumed that they were dead. Instead, an olive-green egg appeared around them. It dissipated to reveal a ruby-red Salavite with light red stripes on their body. The audience gasped.

"It's a member of the Lizardfolk," Said Libra. "They have been jealous of us for a very long time."

The Salavite struggled to get up. Whatever spell Libra had used, it sapped them of their strength. A security guard ripped the wand from their clutches and returned it to her.

"Thank you so much," She said. "Now, the dispel emptied my light wand, so I'll have to recharge it with another spell. Would we like it to have a light spell again?"

The crowd clapped and cheered. Libra lifted the wand into the air, in direct view of the sunlight. The wand shined with light of its own.

"And now I showed you another trick. And it wouldn't have been possible without our *good friend* here." She pointed a hand in the Salavite's direction. "Let's give them one last round of applause."

The security guards restrained the Salavite as the audience clapped. It took all of Darcy's willpower not to intervene.

*Don't break your promise, don't break your promise...*

Still, seeing someone demeaned like this simply wasn't right.

Libra said to the guards, "Take them to the mansion, will you? Scorpio will want a word with them."

*The mansion's at the northeast corner of the city. Maybe I can stop the transfer on the way.*

Darcy climbed along the wall until they reached a clear spot, where they then returned to the floor. Most people stayed away from the guards and their prisoner, but Darcy followed them along from a dozen feet away.

A cop hornet waited outside; Libra likely called it right after the attack. A policeman served as its driver with a second saddle dedicated to prisoners. Like the seats for all flying insects, the saddles had special straps to keep the riders still, but the prisoner saddle was specially designed to minimize a person's movement. Darcy gritted their teeth.

*Shit, I can't catch a hornet! I'll have to stop this **before** they take off!*

The security guards carried the Salavite outside. Upon seeing the hornet, the Salavite struggled against them, but could only weakly push them away. The guards tightened their grip and moved the Salavite towards the hornet's stinger.

*Now. Now!*

Throwing caution to the wind, Darcy jumped onto the scene. They pulled one guard away and threw him at the hornet. The guard hit the hornet's legs and startled the insect, making it fly upward. The second guard pulled out a taser. Darcy grabbed his arm and shoved it upward as quickly as possible. In their panic, they had used too much force and heard a snap. Both the guard and the taser dropped to the ground.

"My arm!" He cried. "My arm!"

"Sorry!"

Darcy used five of their arms to pick up the Salavite and the sixth to grab the taser. The Salavite was bigger and heavier than they were—if not for super strength, Darcy would not have been able to carry them at all.

Darcy heard the drone of beating wings above them. They ran as quickly as they could, but there was no way they could outlast a hornet, and there was always the possibility of the cop calling for backup and driving Darcy into a corner. If they were going to escape, they would have to do it now, not later.

Darcy stopped in an alleyway. The hornet hovered above them. Darcy aimed the taser at its eye. The sting of thousands of volts made the insect drop. Unfortunately, its rider was still rearing to go, as the policeman stood back up. He ordered,

"Put the lizard down and your hands in the air. All of them!"

Darcy assessed the situation. They gently set the Salavite down.

The Salavite whispered, "What are you...?"

"Trust me," Darcy whispered back.

Darcy tossed the taser to the side. The policeman readied some handcuffs and stepped closer. They waited until he was within arm's reach. He said,

"You are under arrest for interfering with-"

"Nope!"

Darcy picked up the policeman, and with their strength, they threw him as far as spiderly possible. They picked the Salavite back up and ran off once more.

"The underground," The Salavite whispered. "Go down..."

"Good idea."

Darcy opened the first manhole they saw and crawled inside. They went downwards, through the levels of the sewers, until they reached Old Newstone. The ancient underground network of tunnels and facilities was officially stated to have been built to expand from the newstone mines, but knowing what they did, Darcy suspected that that wasn't the truth.

They stopped at a large stone gate. Eight circles had been carved into each door. It had no handles, despite being a gate.

"Don't go in," Said the Salavite. "City is dangerous now. But... nobody goes down here. We'll be safe."

"Okay. I'm going to use something that will take us to safety, but no matter what you see, you must promise not to tell other people. Okay?"

The Salavite looked at Darcy. Confusion filled their reddish-pink eyes. Eventually, though, they nodded.

"Alright."

— — —

In Revi's pocket dimension, Oliver tried on the hoodie and pants Revi had fixed for him. Revi had tried to make them red, but they wound up being purple instead. Oliver assured them that it was nothing to get upset over and wore the clothes over his bodysuit. He had been sitting on the couch when he heard the door open.

"Darcy!"

It was indeed Darcy, and with a Salavite that was bigger than they were. Darcy gave a nervous laugh.

"So, uh, remember when I said I wouldn't get into trouble?"

# Chapter 8

Darcy set the Salavite onto their couch to rest.

"...And that's how I met them," They told Oliver. "If I didn't do something, they would've been taken to the Macbeths' mansion."

Worry still painted Oliver's face, but he worked up a smile. "I'm just glad you're okay."

"So how are you doing? Did you have any episodes while I was out?"

"Thankfully, no, but my body didn't appreciate the eggs I ate earlier." He sighed. "Too many nutrients."

"Damn. I'm sorry. We'll figure something out, I promise."

"Thanks, Darcy."

Darcy then whispered, "And by the way, let's not mention anything warlock-related to this person."

"Uh, okay."

After an hour or so, the Salavite gained enough strength to sit up and speak in full sentences.

"My name is Pyrus Kipath," They said. "I come from a trio of clans: Ruby, Sapphire, and Emerald. Together we call ourselves the Trio Clan. We were forced to become nomadic after the Macbeths tried to destroy us."

Oliver said, "Is that the home that Akio talked about?"

Pyrus tilted their head from side to side. "Which Akio? Akio Dubath? Akio Lenath?"

"Um... Akio Ashlath."

Pyrus smiled. "Oh, a member of the Cinnabar Clan, that's great! We thought they were wiped out!"

"Hold up," Said Darcy. "We should bring Akio here before we continue this. Be back in a minute."

Darcy ran to Akio's apartment and knocked on the door.

"Who is it?" Akio asked.

"Darcy."

"Is Revi with you?"

"No, it's just me."

"Great! I'll be right out."

Akio quickly shut the door behind them, but Darcy swore that they caught a glimpse of pillows and blankets in the entryway. They decided that now was not the time to ask little questions and explained everything to Akio. Akio hurried to Darcy's apartment with them.

Upon seeing Akio, Pyrus gave them a weak wave.

"Wow," They said. "I'd never thought I'd see a live Ashlath."

"Same to you," Akio replied. "I thought the Ruby Clan went extinct."

"Not if I can help it." Pyrus leaned forward. "Listen, does your clan have any newstone left?"

Akio shook their head. "'Fraid not. We only have a handful of spell stones at this point."

"But you have dragon warriors, right?"

"Only one, and they're near the end of their life."

Pyrus slapped a hand against the couch cushion. "*Kif*! I came all this way for nothing!"

"Wait," Said Darcy. "Maybe we can still help each other."

"Darcy's right," Said Akio. "If we pool our resources, maybe we'll have enough to make another dragon warrior."

Pyrus's ears lay flat against their skull. Their voice shivered with fear.

"But wouldn't that catch the attention of the Macbeths? Too many Salavites in one place..."

Akio gestured to Darcy and Oliver. "These two have special abilities that aren't dependent on magic. They won't be weakened by the family's dispels."

"Really? And they're willing to help us?"

"Yeah," Darcy answered. "Anything we can do to help."

"So your power isn't caused by some sort of magical mutation?"

"Nope. We've got... secret ingredients."

Pyrus shrugged. "Hah. Well, works for me. I'll go with you to your clan, but I can't make any promises. I'm just a messenger, after all; I don't have any actual political power."

Akio said, "Fair enough."

Darcy put their hands forward. "Wait, hang on. If you're just a messenger, then what were you doing at the magic museum?"

Akio's flicked upward. "You were at the museum?!"

Pyrus replied, "Alright, so I got a little distracted. But I almost got one of Libra's wands!"

Darcy objected, "Then she dispelled you and you got captured."

"I thought the crowd would act like they do in the movies, where a person gives a rousing speech and everybody claps." Pyrus sighed and lay against the couch. "I should've just burned down the museum from the outside. Magma spells would've made it easy."

Darcy asked excitedly, "You can use magic to burn things?"

"Oh yeah."

"Bro, that would've been so cool! Sorry, are you okay with 'bro'?"

Pyrus winked. "Only if you're okay with 'yo.'"

"Totally, yo!"

"Cool, bro."

Oliver stepped in. "Um, let's try to *not* commit arson?"

Akio pinched the space between their eyes. "Okay, time to focus now."

"Right, sorry." Darcy giggled. "So what do we do now?"

"I'll take Pyrus to the council and they will take things from there. Darcy and Oliver, you're coming along, too. It's time that you saw Refugee Clan."

"Sounds like a plan," Said Darcy, "But, uh... Akio, can we speak in private?"

In an adjacent room, Darcy whispered to Akio,

"How are we going to take Pyrus out of here without revealing Patron stuff to them?"

"Did they see anything when you brought them here?"

"They were only semi-conscious, so I don't think so."

"Then we'll give them a blindfold. Also, the pocket dimension drops its users to the last place they've been."

"I've noticed. So won't it drop each of us to different places?"

"Only if you go individually. But if we all go through it at the same time, we'll land in the same location."

"Can we control which location we get? I'm guessing that yours is closer to Refugee Clan."

"It is. I'll lead the group. I'm pretty sure that will determine our destination."

"Sounds good. And one more thing."

"Yeah?"

"How many members of Refugee Clan know English? How easy or hard will it be for us to communicate?"

Akio chuckled. "Oh, don't worry about that. Pizzazz works as a universal translator."

"Holy shit, really?"

"Yeah! Everything you see, hear, and say is translated in real time. It can even detect proper nouns, so you won't get anything like 'Lake Lake' or 'River River'. But I've noticed that words that don't have direct translation are also kept as-is. I guess it's because they're so culturally-specific."

"Oh, wow. It'd be nice if that knowledge was on the contract."

"Well, translation is in all types of pizzazz; it isn't unique to the Patrons. I wouldn't be surprised if they simply forgot that it exists."

"You think they take it for granted?"

"I won't make any assumptions, but I wouldn't be surprised."

"Well, this is good to know. Thanks for telling me."

The two then returned to Pyrus and Oliver. Akio said,

"So first thing's first: we need to cover your eyes."

— — —

The group shuffled awkwardly through the exit of the pocket dimension. Just as Akio predicted, because Akio had led the group, everyone landed in the last place Akio had been: a stone bedroom with every inch of the floor covered in blue blankets. Mounds of blue pillows filled the corners of the room while glowing vines decorated the walls.

Akio took off Pyrus's blinds. "Alright, everyone. Welcome... to the Refugee Clan. Or more accurately, welcome to my bedroom."

Oliver squealed. "It looks so soft!"

"Haha, yeah."

Pyrus said, "Wait, so if we're in Salavite territory, you guys will need to look the part."

"What do you mean?" Darcy asked.

Akio took out their spell stone and returned to Salavite form. They explained,

"Have you ever heard of the phrase, 'You don't know a man until you've walked a mile in his shoes'? Well, a lot of our culture is built off of that idea. When you're with Salavites, you're a Salavite. When you're with humans, you're a human. When you're with Venutians, you're a Venutian. And so on and so forth."

"Oh, I think I get it," Said Darcy. "If I go out there as a non-Salavite, it'll be seen as rude or something, won't it?"

"Exactly. The two of you will have to use transformation spells while you're down here. Darcy, you can borrow mine."

"But doesn't it just make me human?"

"That can be easily changed."

Akio pressed the marble-sized stone against their scales. Its color changed from an olive green to a cinnabar red. Akio tossed the stone to Darcy.

"Place it in your coat pocket."

Darcy did so. A cinnabar-red egg enveloped them, and although Darcy could not see their body at the moment, they felt it alter in shape. When the egg dissipated, they had become a foot taller, although six-foot-two was still not as tall as Akio and Pyrus's Salavite forms. Hell, it wasn't even as tall as Oliver's human form. They pulled back their coat and looked down. Their legs bent in different ways now and their feet ended with five claws each. Darcy put a hand against their head and touched their cone-shaped ears.

*This is weird*, They wanted to say, but they refrained both out of politeness and because they weren't certain how to speak with this new mouth shape. Obviously Akio and Pyrus were proof that verbal speech *was* possible for a Salavite, but the experience was too overwhelming for Darcy to figure it out right away.

"Everything alright?" Akio asked.

Darcy attempted to say something, only to flit a forked tongue at Akio.

Akio chuckled. "C'mon. Let's get you moving."

Pyrus said, "You can hold my hand so you don't fall."

Darcy gratefully took their hand. Even so, their first step was still a wobbly one.

Oliver rubbed his neck as he watched. "You look good, Darcy."

Darcy tried to say "thank you", only to flit their tongue again.

Akio said, "Pyrus, would you mind giving Oliver your transformation spell?"

Pyrus smiled nervously. "I actually lost mine. Libra took it during my little stunt."

"Seriously?"

"It wasn't like I could stop her! She had dispelled me at that point. And she was so arrogant about it, too! And everybody acted like it was the best thing since campfires. Still pisses me off."

"Why were you even there? I thought you were looking for the Refugee Clan."

"Well, I *was*, but I saw the museum and just sort of... went inside. On impulse. Without a plan."

"You could've been killed."

"But I wasn't!" Pyrus lifted up Darcy's hand. "A beautiful spider hero saved me, and I am very grateful for that."

"But you don't have any spell stones on you?"

"Ahahaha... no."

Akio rubbed their face with a sigh.

Oliver said, "It's okay. I can just stay in here. Maybe we can make this work."

Darcy got an idea. They shuffled over to Oliver and pulled out his hand. As a Salavite, they were only an inch shorter than him.

He asked, "What is it, Darcy?"

Darcy placed their stone into his hand. They changed back into being an arachnomorph.

"You use it," They said. "I'll stay here."

"But Darcy..."

"We need to get you to that person who can help you. Besides, if I fight the Macbeths and they use a dispel on me, I'll just return to being an arachnomorph anyways, so what's the point?"

Akio said, "Darcy, the field of battle is different than day-to-day life. Okay, here's what we're going to do: I will take Oliver to Varia, then bring that stone back here and give it to Darcy. Pyrus, you tell the counsel about your situation. Let's all meet at Varia's lab at dinnertime. Until then..." They turned to Darcy. "Don't make a scene."

"Roger that," Darcy replied.

With the plan in motion, Oliver pocketed the transformation stone. The egg surrounded him, but glitched as it did so. Once the change had finished, the egg didn't dissipate with grace like it did for everybody else; bits of it vanished suddenly before the rest of the egg followed suit. Despite the tricky transformation, it succeeded in turning Oliver into a cinnabar Salavite.

"Do you feel alright?" Akio asked.

Oliver gave a reluctant nod. With Akio's help, he left the room.

Pyrus asked Darcy, "What happened to *him*?"

"A dragon warrior used a purification spell on him against his will."

Pyrus' ears shot upward. "Really? The Violet Clan is still active?"

"I guess so. We think they've moved on, though."

"Hm. Well, I wish him luck." Pyrus then tilted their head to the side. "So what's an arachnomorph?"

*Shit, I let that slip, didn't I?*

Darcy rubbed their neck-bristles. "Well, uh... it's a term for spider creatures like me."

"Oh, neat."

Darcy paused. "...You're not going to ask further questions?"

"Would you like me to?"

"Not really."

"Okay, then." Pyrus went to the doorway. "Well, time to see what this clan's council is like."

"Good luck."

Pyrus cheered as they left. "Yes, good luck!"

# Chapter 9

As tempting as it was to sneak out of the room, Darcy stayed put. They were in a foreign culture now, and they didn't want to insult any customs by not following orders. They only went to the stone door to peek out through the crack. It was hardly enough to see any goings-on, so Darcy sat on one of the many pillows in the room and did nothing.

But, of course, their mind began to wander. Darcy observed their body, spidery once again, and thought to themself. They had six arms again. They had chitin again. They once again didn't have bones.

*I was only a Salavite for a minute. I wonder if it would have felt stranger if I was in that body longer. Would the differences truly sink in, then? Or would I adapt too quickly for it to matter? Would I be able to handle it at all?*

Perhaps it would be easy—after all, Darcy had gotten used to being an arachnomorph quickly enough. The only hurdle was the initial realization of what had happened. Perhaps it would be the same for their Salavite form: after initial discomfort, they could break into it like good shoes.

*But maybe being a spider is my "good shoes". Maybe this is the only form I could be good at. I just hope that it's strong enough to fight against any threats...*

Meanwhile, Akio led Oliver through the earthen hallways of Refugee Clan. Each hall split into multiple other ones, turning the area into an underground maze. Simple pillars occasionally lined the walls, with a particular focus on entryways and intersections. The walls themselves housed glowing vines with many flower bulbs. Akio touched a bulb and it opened up, lighting up the area with a six-foot radius. Akio touched the flower again to close it.

"*Levarivan*," They said. "If you ever need to light the way, use these."

In their journey, the duo sometimes passed another Salavite or two; they would share quick greetings before continuing on their way. Oliver stayed quiet for these conversations, both because he was new to this body and out of social anxiety.

"The Macbeths scattered most of the clans," Akio explained. "As I've said before, it all happened before I was born, but I've heard lots of explanations over the years. Disrupting messages, sabotaging supplies, starting infighting between clans... but it all ended the same way. With everyone distracted, the Macbeths attacked in full force, and the capital fell."

The two stopped at an intersection. A symbol had been carved into the floor. Akio stared at it as they spoke.

"But the Platinum Clan held strong. They built this complex and invited all surviving Salavites to come here. Only Iron Clan, Brown Clan, and half of Yellow Clan responded. But still, they came together and created Refugee Clan. *Nonafaniru.*"

Oliver made a hum and nod to show that he understood. A question ate at him, though, so he did his best to speak it.

"Sssss... sssinnn..."

Akio tilted their head. "What are you trying to say?"

"Sina... buh... barrr."

"Cinnabar?"

"Mm-hm."

Akio's ears pointed downward. "My clan lived at an outpost after the capital fell. I was a little kid when it got raided. I saw my family be captured and I... I ran away."

"S-sorry."

"It's not your fault."

Oliver held Akio's hand and gave it a light squeeze. Akio gave him a half-hearted smile.

"Thank you."

Akio stopped at a stone door. They said,

"Varia is from Red Clan. They were on patrol when their clan was attacked. While it happened many years ago, try not to ask them any questions about it. It's a really hard subject for them."

Oliver nodded. Akio continued,

"And also... they're brilliant. Really, they are. They found ways to combine science and magic and it's amazing. But... they get so immersed in their work that when they finally take breaks, they get a little... distracted. So please be patient with them."

"Okay."

Akio opened the door.

Multiple counters and drawers flanked Varia's square-shaped lab. Anything that didn't have machinery on it was covered in paper notes instead. Pencils lay strewn about in random places. A drawer had been so stuffed full of notebooks that it lay permanently open. Home-made schematics and blueprints had been nailed to the wall. Each wall had a door that led somewhere else, with a couple having been left wide open. A red Salavite sat on a sanded wooden stool and wrote down notes in a fervor.

The red Salavite wore old-style laboratory goggles and an unbuttoned lab coat. Their jaw and underbelly glowed like molten lava. Thin lines ran down their back and sides that contained a similar glow. Oliver wondered if the glow would be bright enough to light up a dark room; it was at least enough to illuminate their notes.

"Varia," Akio said. "Hey, Varia."

But Varia was apparently too engrossed in their work to notice. Akio stepped up to them and played with Varia's ear.

"Varia. Variaaaaa."

Varia's ears twitched. They glanced around them.

"Huh? What? Hello?" They turned their head just a little further. "Oh, Akio! When did you get here?"

"Not too long ago. I need to ask a favor."

"Oh, Akio, hang on! I need to return something to you."

Varia stumbled off of their stool and into another room. They shortly came back out and bonked into a countertop.

"Oof! I swear, these things are always jumping out at me."

"The counters can't move, Varia."

"I'm aware, but still."

Varia gave Akio a handheld video game console. It folded open and had two screens.

"Thank you for letting me borrow your GameBoy! It was so much fun."

"Varia, it *isn't* a GameBoy."

Varia patted Akio on the shoulder. "It's okay. Being a gamer is nothing to be ashamed of."

"No, it's literally called a- never mind." Akio pocketed the console. "Did you like it?"

Varia clapped their hands together. "Oh, yes! It was so much fun! The time travel was such an interesting concept. I wish I could do that. I would certainly do things differently the second time around!"

"Wouldn't we all. I'm glad you enjoyed the game."

"Roalen would have enjoyed that game." Varia then finally noticed Oliver. "Oh, hello! Are you one of Akio's friends?"

Oliver nodded. "Hu-hullo."

Akio said, "Oliver is a human, so he's new to Salavite things."

Varia replied, "Ah, I see! Well, don't worry, sweetie, I'll get things ready for you."

Varia ran around the room and closed each door. They cleaned off one of the counters and had Oliver sit on it.

"Now, I'm going to need you to remove all newstone before I run a diagnostic."

"Wait, hang on," Said Akio. "I didn't even say what we need you to do yet."

"Ah, right. What appears to be the problem, Oliver?"

Oliver returned the spell stone to Akio. After another glitchy transformation, he returned to human form. Varia stepped back in response.

"Oh, my! I've never seen a change like that before."

"Um, yeah." Oliver gave a small wave. "Hi."

Akio explained, "Oliver has spider powers. A dragon warrior from the Violet Clan attacked him. They used a purification spell on him without his consent and now he becomes part spider every time he's afraid."

"Really?"

"I know that you'll need newstone before you can actually do anything long-term, but I thought it would be best to let you look at the situation as soon as possible."

"Yes, I would love to run a firsthand analysis! The more I understand how this transformation works, the easier it'll be to formulate a treatment and-or cure." Varia said to Oliver, "But I'll need you to activate this 'part spider' thing at least once. Would you feel comfortable with that?"

Oliver rubbed his arm. "Well, I... it wouldn't be ideal, but if it'll help me return to normal, I can try."

"Fantastic! Then let's begin! It's time for science!"

Akio gave the two a wave. "Good luck. I'll be back at dinnertime."

Varia had returned the wave, but their attention was still directed towards Oliver. They droned to Akio,

"Good luck, stay safe."

The next couple of minutes passed in awkward silence. Oliver watched Varia write into one of their notebooks. Oliver payed with his fingers.

"Um, so... nice to meet you."

"Yes! It's a pleasure. It's been a hot minute since I've last worked alongside a human." Varia made a clicking sound with their tongue. "Alright, I'm going to begin with basic diagnostics. Heart rate, blood pressure, reflexes, et cetera. I will then compare it to the average human of your basic generalized demographic."

"Um, okay."

Despite Varia's upfront nature, Oliver still didn't feel prepared. He couldn't remember the last time he had a medical diagnosis, and the thought of somehow failing it ate away at him.

*What if something terrible happens? What if I'm broken and can't be fixed? What if I don't follow the tests correctly and Varia kicks me out? Can I get a good score? Is there a way to do this right?*

"Oh, that's the 'part spider' that Akio mentioned."

"Huh?" Oliver looked at his now-spidery hands. "Ah! I'm sorry!"

"No, no, it's good to learn. Permission to touch?"

"Um, yeah."

Varia held one of Oliver's hands in their own. They ran their gentle claws across the red chitin.

"Smooth and with a slight polish. Fascinating! Three claws per hand..."

"Does that mean anything?"

"It means you have three claws on each hand. They seem to replace your fingers entirely. Does it hurt when you transform?"

"No, it... it just feels like building pressure. Is it supposed to hurt?"

Varia smiled. "I have no idea!"

"Am I doing well?"

"Indeed!"

Oliver managed a tiny smile and his hands returned to normal.

Varia's ears shot straight up. "Ah, so the transformation appears to be dynamic!" They wrote down notes.

"Um... I guess so. The more afraid I am, the more I change. And apparently the first time I transformed, I was so hungry that I rampaged through the city and tried to eat everything."

Varia looked right at him. "Eating everything?"

Oliver glanced down. "I'm sorry."

"You're not in trouble. Can you tell me why you were so hungry? Was it something you felt before or during the transformation?"

"Well... I guess it was technically before, but not too long. I woke up from a nightmare and it was like I was running on instinct. I was so, so hungry. I think it's because I don't eat enough, to be honest. I'm trying to be better about it, though."

Varia hummed and made more notes. "Are you typically in control of your actions when fully transformed?"

"No."

"So this form..."

"The Night Creature."

"So this Night Creature form runs purely on instinct. That is likely why it has such an incredible focus on food. It could be overcompensating for your lack of calorie intake."

"So... if I eat more, it will be easier to control?"

"There is a decent possibility. There is also your fear to consider. Perhaps your Night Creature form developed as a way to protect your mind and body and that is why you struggle to control it. Oliver, do you have a habit of receding into yourself and trying to avoid the pain in your life?"

Oliver gulped. "Uh... well, I guess I tried to pretend the whole Night Creature thing didn't happen... and before then, I tried to pretend that my anxiety was rational... and before then, I tried to pretend that Harrell only wanted the best for me... and maybe he still does, but then I tried confronting him, and I got hurt." He covered his face with his hands. "Oh, god. I really do deny things."

"...Then perhaps your lack of control is both."

"What do you mean?"

"Perhaps the Night Creature represents your subconscious desires *and* your fears. Perhaps your body transforms to protect you even if the problem is only mental. And because you desire more food, that is one of the Night Creature's desires as well. Theoretically."

Oliver uncovered his face. "So I'm just broken?"

"No, no. Not broken. Everybody deals with trauma differently."

Both Varia and Oliver looked at the latter's hands. They had transformed again. Oliver felt a pit in his stomach, but not from hunger. He wrapped his arms around his waist and looked away.

"Can we not talk about trauma anymore? I... I just wanna fix it. I'm sorry, I just don't wanna get overwhelmed right now."

"...Of course."

The next step was heart rate. Varia readied a stopwatch and placed a stethoscope against Oliver's chest. They wrote down the beats per second, then tested again to record the beats per minute. They squinted at the data.

"Resting heart rate is 120." They added sarcastically, "Little nervous?"

"Little bit," Oliver squeaked. Red fuzz climbed up his arms.

"Sorry. Next up is blood pressure." Varia stared at his arms. "Er..." They tapped on a bicep. "Chitin. We may have trouble there."

"Sorry! So sorry!"

"It's alright. We can still try. Just try to relax... take deep breaths..."

Oliver followed their instructions to the best of his ability. Varia placed a cuff around his bicep.

*What if the chitin keeps them from getting an accurate reading? It* **is** *pretty stiff. What if it doesn't work at all? What if I do something wrong and Varia gets annoyed with me? What if I'm being too much of a burden? What if I'm broken? Too broken to fix?*

"Alright, the cuff is going to apply pressure now. Are you ready?"

He squeezed his eyes shut. "Y-yup."

The cuff pressed into his bicep. It was a gentle action, and an expected one, but as the pressure increased, so did Oliver's fear. It was a primal, instinctual fear.

*Something's attacking me. Something's hurting me! It's just like-*

A memory shot into his mind: Harrell gripping his arm and holding tighter.

"Stop it!"

"Okay. It'll take a second for it to shut down."

His rational mind understood, but it could hardly do anything against the waves of terror that overtook him.

"Just stop it!"

Oliver jumped down from the counter. Varia put a hand on his transforming shoulder.

"Hold on," They said. "I still need to-"

*The hand.* ***His hand.***

"Don't touch me DON'T TOUCH ME!"

Oliver shoved Varia away and tore off the cuff. A pressure erupted in his body and four extra arms sprouted from his sides. The moment he felt the change, he knew what was happening.

"Nonononono!"

Oliver ran with no particular direction in mind. Fear crashed into more fear as he forced open a door. He closed it behind him, only to find that the room he entered was a dead end. It had a simple nest of pillows and a cupboard built into one of the walls.

Oliver crawled under the pillows and tried to become as small as possible. This became increasingly difficult, as the change kept going. Soon, he was full-spider once again and could do nothing but cry.

He couldn't tell how much time passed before Varia entered the room. They had taken off their goggles, revealing their green eyes. They did not touch him again, but instead sat down next to him. They sang him a lullaby:

Little ember
Lost in the forest.
The plants are so big
And there's nowhere to go.

Little ember
Cries for their lost home.
They used to have big fires
But the ashes were buried away.
Little ember
The pinecones heard their cries.
They made a heartful promise
To burn again once more.
Little ember
Had fire once again
And when it died down
A sapling rose with them.

Something about the lullaby awoke Oliver. The fog in his mind became dispersed. He opened his eyes with new clarity.

"Varia."

"Hello, Oliver."

He got up from the makeshift covering of pillows. He looked down at himself only to find that he was still the Night Creature. He said softly,

"I don't understand."

"In the Red Clan, that lullaby was sung to help young Salavites calm down. I suppose it works for other creatures, too."

"But I usually transform back when I regain control."

"Hm. Well, when you're ready, I'll help you figure this out."

Oliver wiped away a stray tear. "Thank you. I'm really sorry for pushing you."

"I accept your apology, and I forgive you."

"Really?"

Varia made a soft smile. "Of course."

This overwhelmed Oliver so much that he cried. "Sorry!"

"Why are you still apologizing?"

"I don't know. I'm sorry."

"It's okay."

"I, uh... can we hug?"

"We can."

Hugging Varia felt like hugging a hot water bottle. Oliver held on to them longer than average, apologized again, and fixed up the nest of pillows. He said quietly,

"They're, um... nice pillows."

"Thank you. Akio gave them to me."

"Really?"

Upon inspection, Oliver realized that each pillow was a different shade of blue.

*Did Akio take them from Revi's pocket dimension?*

Oliver made a mental note to ask Akio later and then returned to the lab with Varia. Due to his size, he was now too big to sit on a chair or counter, so Varia got him a pillow to sit on and joined him on the floor.

Varia said, "Let us take a break from the physical diagnostics and focus on your background. Your name is Oliver?"

"Um, yeah. I made it up myself."

"Really?"

"I'm an orphan."

They gasped. "An orphan?!"

He flinched. "I'm sorry!"

"Ah, I apologize. I shouldn't have yelled. Can you tell me what happened?"

"I was left on a doorstep. I've been in the foster system ever since. People always commented on my olive-green eyes, so I decided to name myself Oliver. It was either that or Red... for my red hair."

"Red is a pretty name. My favorite color is red, actually. Though I suppose that I'm guilty of biases, being of the Red Clan and all. Oliver is so beautiful, though." They put a hand on Oliver's cheek and stared into his many eyes. "That green... so beautiful."

Oliver clicked his claws together. "Gosh, thank you. Your eyes are beautiful, too. And your red scales are really pretty."

"Thank you. Your red setae is gorgeous."

"Setae?"

Varia pointed at the fuzz that covered parts of Oliver's body. "Arthropods have setae instead of hair or fur. It helps them use their senses to better understand their environment."

"That's, um... interesting."

"Unfortunately, my arthropod trivia ends there. My studies focus more on the scientific application of magic for Salavite and human life. With tech knowledge on the side, of course."

Varia gestured to the room around them. They said,

"I built every machine here."

"Oh, wow."

"Yes, I spend every day perfecting my equipment. I hope to someday find a way to make newstone accessible to the modern-day Salavite."

Oliver nodded. "Akio told me that the Macbeths have all the newstone. Or most of it."

"Yes, they took it with no mercy. Akio only has a spell stone because they're a scout."

"Do you think the Macbeths will attack Refugee Clan?"

"They sometimes stop by for 'routine checkups', even though the process has *nothing* to do with medicine *and* the visits are random. I think they simply enjoy scaring us."

*So the Macbeths know where Refugee Clan is already. It's no wonder why Akio wants our help so badly. If the Macbeths wanted to, they could fire a real attack at any time.*

Those thoughts brought fear with them. Oliver did not want to lose himself to panic again, so he distracted himself with something else.

"Thank you again, for helping me."

"Of course."

"Um, can you explain that lullaby to me?"

"I know it from my home clan, but honestly, it's common in all clans that specialize in fire. It's about the nature of forest fires and how there are different kinds of destruction and growth."

"That's... really interesting."

Varia made a light chuckle. "I suppose that it's bittersweet compared to human lullabies."

"Actually, human lullabies are like that, too. We have a lot of songs that sound happy or heartwarming until you pay attention to the words."

"Do you think Venutians have songs like that as well?"

Oliver shrugged. "Maybe? I don't know much about Venutians."

The two continued in low-stakes conversation for another hour. Oliver then looked at himself again. Despite having calmed down considerably, he hadn't changed back yet.

"I swear that usually something would have happened by now. Why am I still...?"

Varia hummed. "How many times have you had a full transformation?"

"This is my third." He put a hand against his head. "Oh, god. What if I was only allowed to change three times? What if that's why I'm not turning back?"

*No. No, I won't panic again. I won't waste anyone's time again. Deep breaths, don't think about it...*

"Sorry," He said. "Um, we should probably continue the diagnostics."

Varia tapped a claw against the countertop. "Yes, but how? Without your human form, we no longer have a control to compare your biology to. I could just jump to the stage of magical analysis, but it involves an invasive process that I'm not certain you're ready for."

Oliver put his claws together. "How invasive is it?"

"It would involve using a combination of spells to scan through your mind and body. It shouldn't hurt on account of being consensual, but the purification spell that is already there will likely complicate things."

"Wait. So the spell is still inside of me? It isn't just... gone?"

"Some spells linger in the target. Fire spells leave burns, poison spells leave toxins, and purification spells leave the target purified. But since you did not consent to it, it had the side effect of affecting your spider powers."

"But... but wait. Hang on." Oliver's breathing quickened. "Isn't magic toxic? Am I dying? What happens if we don't get it out in time?!"

"Easy! Easy." Varia helped Oliver steady his breathing again, then said, "*Newstone* is toxic. Magic is only toxic if you're using poison spells. You're okay. You're okay."

"I'm okay." He exhaled. "So... if we remove the purification spell, then I'll return to normal?"

"Possibly. I will have to run the scan to know anything for certain. But I need to say it again, it is quite invasive. It involves using a telepathy spell to travel through your mindscape. It will be very uncomfortable, especially if you have trauma relating to mental alteration."

Oliver considered this. His trauma had intensified ever since the purification incident. If he couldn't handle a standard diagnostic, then how could he handle a magical one? On the other hand, if he got it over with now, then he and Varia would get to the root of the issue that much sooner; rip off another bandaid.

*Didn't Varia say that avoiding problems is connected to being the Night Creature? If I say "no", then I would just be pushing it away until my situation gets even worse.*

*Do it. Do it before I have a chance to be afraid!*

"Let's do it now," He said.

Varia nodded and put their goggles back on.

"I'm going to have you lay down. That way, you won't fall over during the process."

"That makes sense."

Oliver lay on his stomach and rested his chin on his arms. His two main ones, at least... he didn't know what to do with his four extra ones. Oliver wondered if Darcy ever had this problem.

He closed his eyes. "I'm ready."

"Alright." Judging by Varia's voice, they had sat down in front of him. "I'm going to touch your head. Are you ready?"

"Yes."

Varia's palm rested against Oliver's forehead. Varia said,

"Beginning mental diagnostic in three... two... one."

A power pierced into his mind. It reminded Oliver of the time he went to the dentist and they drilled into one of his teeth. The drilling reverberated throughout his mind and body. Oliver clenched his teeth and curled his fists, and those were the last sensations he felt as his mind sank into depths unknown.

# Chapter 10

Oliver awoke in a black void with a rainbow line forming the horizon. He was human again, but his form was semi-transparent and had a green glow. Varia appeared in front of him, also semi-transparent but lacking any glow.

*Are we in my mind?*

As soon as it crossed his mind, his thought took form as a disembodied voice. Oliver stumbled back.

"Ah!"

"It's alright," Said Varia. "And yes! We're in your mind."

"Is it supposed to be this empty?"

"Think of the mindscape like a computer desktop. Even if you don't have any applications on the desktop itself, that doesn't mean they're not there. We just need to call up the files we need."

"I... I think I understand. So if the purification spell was consensual, then I would've experienced something like this?"

Varia clapped. "Yes, but in violet! You see, I am using a telepathy spell. It's distinguished as black with rainbow lines."

"I... I think I get it."

Varia studied Oliver's glow. "I don't know what the green is, however. No spells with the green coloration would show up in the mindscape."

"Really?" He looked at his hand.

*What if it's my pizzazz?*

The moment the thought announced itself, Oliver knew he made a mistake.

"Ahhhh, don't listen to that! Don't think about it!"

Varia stepped back. "Uh, alright. Easy, now. If it's private, I understand. I simply hope it doesn't interfere with our work."

*Revi said that the spell restored my pizzazz, so it should be fi-*

"Ahhhh, don't listen to that thought, either! Don't listen, don't listen!"

Varia curled their hands around the base of their ears.

They said, "Try to recall the memory of the purification spell!"

"Okay. Okay. Focus, Oliver!"

As soon as Oliver thought of the memory, it appeared around him and Varia like a hologram. In the hologram, the violet dragon curled over Oliver with a hand on his forehead. The real Oliver shivered and held his sides. He stayed close to Varia.

"What now?"

Varia raised a hand. A gray ribbon floated from their hand to the dragon. The ribbon circled around the dragon, then around the memory of Oliver. It made Oliver's brain itch.

"Are you alright so far?" Varia asked.

"I think so." He rubbed his head. "What is the ribbon doing?"

"It's an isolation spell. I'm using it to hone in on the magic in your mind and body."

The gray ribbon then split off into many threads. The threads flew off into multiple directions. Oliver ducked as one of them flew over his head.

"What's happening?"

"The purification spell is intertwined with your feelings and desires. Those desires are, in turn, connected to your memories. Right now, my isolation spell is sticking itself to the purification spell so the latter can be removed. So, if we follow these threads, we can gather up the pieces of purification spell that exist within you. Think of it as gathering up fallen leaves, or rolling up yarn into a ball."

"Will we be able to break the spell once we gather all the threads?"

"We'll have to find out. But I want to ask again: are you alright with me seeing these memories? They're private information."

"Well, I... there are certain things that you aren't allowed to see, but I don't know if I can do this without you. Just, um... try not to get mad if you see anything you don't like."

Varia tilted their head to the side. "Get mad?"

Oliver looked away. *Harrell always got mad...*

The thought projected to the two of them. Oliver covered his face.

"I'm sorry. I'll try to keep my thoughts quiet."

"It's alright. I promise not to comment on anything I see unless you explicitly ask me to. And if you want me to look away from certain memories, I completely understand."

"Thank you."

The duo followed one of the gray threads to a memory of when Oliver was a child. He stood in line at the school cafeteria. One of the cafeteria workers asked him,

"Do you have a lunch pass?"

"Lunch pass? I'm sorry, I'm new to this school."

"Well, this school requires a lunch pass for kids to eat. You can buy one if you like."

"But... I don't have money."

"I'm sorry, dear. Ask your parents to buy you a lunch pass, okay?"

The memory Oliver sat at a random table with his head in his hands. The real Oliver stood next to him and put a hand on his back. He looked up to find a violet cloud hanging over the memory.

"The purification spell..."

A gray thread snaked its way to the cloud. The cloud stuck to the thread like the head of a cotton swab. Varia climbed onto a table and touched the thread. Upon their touch, the thread retreated backwards.

"It's going back to the source, to that first memory we saw. Are you ready to go to the next one?"

Oliver's attention lingered onto his younger self.

"...Yeah," He eventually said. "Let's go."

The next memory depicted a room surrounded by windows—Mike Harrell's office. Harrell sat at his desk with his fingers crossed. His computer had two monitors: one showing footage from Red Arachnid's mask and the other showing various stats. A violet cloud reflected in the windows and monitors.

The mere sight of Harrell made Oliver sick. Or at least, as sick as he could get in this situation.

Oliver mumbled to himself, "It's just a memory. It's just a memory."

Red Arachnid ran into the room, in costume. He had just returned from a patrol around the city and entered Harrell's office. He practically bounced with excitement.

"Mister Harrell, I did it! I stopped some crimes!"

Harrell's eyes stayed glued to the monitors. He gave a disappointed grunt. Oliver looked over his shoulder.

"What is it, sir?"

"When stopping this robbery, you made a joke that wasn't approved by the company. 'What do you call a corvid who brings back the dead? A ne**crow**mancer.'"

Red Arachnid giggled. "I made that one up myself."

"Do you realize how many people die per year? People might take offense to this. Then we'll lose sales."

"Oh. I'm sorry, sir. I didn't think about that."

Harrell glared at him. "No. You didn't."

"I-I'll try better next time."

"Please do. In fact, don't use your own script at all. Too many variables" He handed Red a typed up document. "Read and memorize this. It has all the guidelines on how you should banter when fighting crime."

He skimmed the document. "Um... with all due respect, sir, these examples are kind of... generic. 'I'm all about stopping bad guys'? That doesn't have any character."

"Exactly. We need the audience to be able to project themselves onto you. Appeal to the widest demographic possible. Now memorize your lines."

"But sir, I want Red Arachnid to be relatable."

"Being a blank slate *is* relatable. Everybody loves a hero with no flaws or mistakes."

"I... I don't know."

Harrell stood up. Red cowered back. Harrell smiled.

"Of course, kiddo! I'm right with you. But the company? It's got a very particular image to uphold. We can't just do whatever, right? Right. But don't worry, I understand." He put a hand on Red's shoulder. "You're still new. You're figuring yourself out. You're anxious. Let's get you more treatment. It'll help."

"Uh... okay, sir."

The two figures exited the memory, but the scenery still remained. Oliver sighed.

"I shouldn't have gone with him."

Another gray thread appeared and gathered the cloud. Varia touched it to get it moving.

"The isolation spell is reacting to your behavior. Acknowledging your pain seems to help the process along."

"I... I was taught to repress it."

Oliver's thoughts brought him and Varia to another memory. This memory was in the basement, in the mental recalibration room. Smiling characters had been painted onto the pastel walls. A metal chair sat in the center of the room with a computer monitor nearby.

Varia couldn't help but whisper, "Is this hell?"

Oliver couldn't answer—the sight of the machine alone sent him into a panic. He turned away and leaned against the wall.

"No... no..."

Mike Harrell and Red Arachnid appeared in the room. Red walked alongside Harrell as they spoke.

"...And I was thinking that I could greet people at the gala! Having a superhero there could be great for company publicity. Maybe I could wear a tuxedo over my costume!"

"Actually, Ollie, I don't want you doing that. The gala is meant for civilians only. Having someone with powers there could take attention away from me."

"Oh, right. That's okay! I can stay at the headquarters and-"

Harrell turned to him. "No, aren't you listening? I want you there, but I *don't* want you at the gala."

"I... what? Okay... I can keep guard."

"No!" Harrell pointed a finger against Red. "I don't. Want you. Distracting them." He snapped his fingers. "Stop being difficult."

Red's voice wavered. "I, uh.... That's fine. Then I won't go."

Harrell raised his volume. "Ollie, you are being immature and you know it! Don't you see how hard you're making this for me? I'm the one in control, not you!"

"I don't understand what you want!"

He grabbed Red's wrist. "Then I'll make you understand."

The memory jumped to later that day. Red Arachnid sat cross-legged on his bed, his back to the door. Harrell stepped into the room with a huge smile on his face. The violet cloud followed him.

"That party was *amazing*! We had so much fun, you wouldn't believe it." When Red didn't answer, he said, "Are you *still* moping?"

Red's voice was more hollow than before. He said,

"Sorry. I just... sorry."

Harrell put his hands on his hips. "You better not be guilt-tripping me."

"No, I..." He had to force out the next words. "I'm just... hurting."

"From *what*? What's your problem *now*?"

He turned to face him. "It's just... I think you went too far earlier."

"Please, I was just stating the facts."

"But you..." He gulped. "You hurt me. I'm still hurting."

"So you *are* guilt-tripping me. I knew it. Everyone tries to silence me just because they don't like what I have to say. It's tone-policing, I tell you."

"Sir, I would never lie to you or try to control you. But..." He trembled from fear. "Sometimes... sometimes you take things out of proportion, and you act like hurting people is the only way to make things even."

Red and Harrell both looked each other in the eyes. Red soon broke contact.

"S-sorry."

Harrell's gaze softened. "I'm sorry that you feel that way." He sat next to Red. "It's my trauma. My whole life, I was hyper-criticized by my father. Now, every time somebody criticizes me, it activates my trauma, and I get harsh." He lightened his voice. "So now you know: even all these years alter, I'm still hurting. Ah, I feel like this brought us together."

"Sir... I don't know."

"Right. So I *maybe* hurt you. My bad." He put a hand on Red's shoulder. "But you being so upset makes me feel inadequate as a person. Like I'm not good enough for you. Do you want me to feel that way?"

"No, sir. Of course not."

"Good boy." He tapped his hand against Red's shoulder. "Until next time. Remember, you're like a son to me."

The memory finally stopped. Oliver nearly collapsed from the tears.

"Why did he make me feel that way? Why did he make everything feel wrong? **What did I do wrong?**"

Varia said, "You didn't do anything wrong. That man... he was terrible to you. His feelings aren't your responsibility."

A spark of anger formed. "He said we were family..."

"Family doesn't hurt each other."

A thread gathered the cloud. Oliver simply said, "I know where we could go next."

They arrived in Red Arachnid's room again, but the memory felt a couple years younger than the previous one. The darkness outside indicated night time. Red Arachnid slid open the window and snuck inside. Violet clouds lay across the floor like a carpet.

"You're late."

Red jumped. The lights turned on, revealing Harrell in the room. He sat on Red's bead with his arms crossed. Harrell stood up.

"What have you been doing?"

"Mister Harrell, sir! I, uh, I've just been out patrolling. It took a bit later than I expected, haha."

"Do you think this is a game?"

"No, sir! I'm just, uh, trying to make light of the situation."

Harrell scowled. "I'm getting real tired of your jokes, kid."

"I-I was just..." Red stepped back. "I'll get home earlier tomorrow, I promise. It's just..." He said in a rush, "Sometimes I have nightmares so I procrastinate going home and someone needed help moving and I was right there so I helped carry their furniture." He forced a happy tone. "They even gave me orange slices!"

Harrell took off his sunglasses and pinched the bridge of his nose.

"Ollie, have I told you about my sister?"

"Huh? You... may have mentioned her before."

He put the sunglasses back on. "We were thick as thieves when we were little. We did everything together. But my father didn't like that. He thought every person should only fend for himself. We couldn't share food, space, or even toys. If we did share food, he forced us to throw it back up."

"Oh, god. I'm so sorry."

"Don't interrupt." He readjusted his tie and continued. "So I listened to our father because I wanted to survive, but you know what my sister did?"

"What... did your sister do, sir?"

"She ran away. I didn't see her again until we were both adults. She tore the family apart when she left."

Harrell stepped up to Red until his face was only inches from Red's own. Red instinctively shrunk back.

Harrell said, "Do you want to tear us apart?"

"No, sir."

"Do you want to keep your family?"

"Of course, sir!"

"Then do. What I. Say. Get back on time or never come back at all. I don't want you to be like her. Do you want to hurt me?"

"No. I'll come back on time, sir. I promise."

The memory stopped.

Oliver held his arms close to his chest. "He was all I had. At least... I thought he was. Is what he said normal?"

"No," Said Varia. "I know this kind of relationship. I once had a friend who made me feel like that. She would say horrible things to me on a whim. Then she expected me to get over it as if it never happened. In every fight and every argument, the weight of the relationship was put onto *me*."

"How did you deal with it?"

Varia gave a sad sigh. "I wish I could tell you that one day I realized how awful it was and I left because of that. But to be honest... it was for something selfish instead. Sometimes, I still fantasize about returning to her and everything being good again. But..."

"...But it wasn't good."

Another thread grabbed the cloud. Varia sent it on its way, but Oliver stayed in place. His fists tightened.

"Why do people do things like this?"

"Because they don't want to be responsible for their cruelty. They will never truly apologize. It would mean that they're imperfect."

"That's no excuse!"

The anger in his own voice frightened Oliver. He stepped back with a shiver.

"I'm sorry."

"It's okay. You don't need to repress your emotions."

"But I don't want to hurt anyone. Let's just... keep going."

The next memory was of Oliver as a child again. He peeked out of his bedroom with the door slightly open. Three adults spoke to each other down the hall. Violet clouds covered their faces.

"We just don't know if that's the type of kid we want."

"Please reconsider. Oliver is such a sweet boy."

"We know, but with his anxiety... he's **just too difficult** for us. We were hoping for **a normal child**."

"I... I understand."

The memory paused. The real Oliver wiped away tears.

"It was always something, every time a family rejected me. They always had a reason, but they never told me the real one. Not directly..." He sniffed. "But I always knew. I was always afraid... and that made life harder for everybody else. I was just too inconvenient."

Varia said, "But you were the one who suffered the most from it."

"That didn't matter." Oliver realized what he had just said. "But it should matter, shouldn't it? *I* should matter. I'm a person."

"That's right," Said Varia. "You're a person."

"But if that's true, then... why was I given up?"

Oliver's very first memory appeared in front of the two of them. It lacked detail and was full of haze, like a photo with too many filters applied. A baby wrapped in violet clouds had been left on a doorstep. A tall, robed figure walked away from the scene.

*I wonder if I can...*

Oliver focused and paused the memory. He ran to the robed figure in a vain attempt to see their face. Despite his best efforts, he could not remember what they looked like. They merely remained as a dark, vague shape. No matter how bright the blurred streetlights were, they did not shine upon the person who was once Oliver's parent.

"Who are you?" He begged. "Why wasn't I good enough for you?"

The figure could not respond, but that didn't halt Oliver's desperation.

"Please! Please tell me! Why was I broken?"

He broke down into sobs and buried his head into their chest. He hugged them and wished that someway, somehow, they would come alive and hug him back.

When the tears finally dried up, Oliver backed away from the figure.

"I'm sorry. You... you probably had a good reason. Someone wouldn't carry a child to term just to change their mind." He wiped his eyes with his sleeve. "Wherever you are, I hope you're doing alright. I... I don't hate you. I can't. Goodbye."

He returned to the baby on the doorstep, where Varia waited. The violet cloud had left the baby and collected on a gray thread, but Varia stared at the robed figure in horror.

"What is it?" Oliver asked.

Varia whispered, "How could she do that?"

"I don't know," He admitted. "It could be anything. But it's not like we can go back in time and change it."

A tear rolled down Varia's face. They quickly wiped it away.

"Right," They said. "You're right. I just... a parent should *always* be there for their child."

"I know." He let out a heavy exhale. "Let's keep moving."

The memory disintegrated and the duo returned to the void. Varia said,

"I think the final threads are in that direction, where the other Red Arachnid memories were."

"I think I know why." Oliver explained, "Almond Industries was where I was altered the most."

"What do you mean 'altered'?"

"Remember the chair we saw? It's specially designed to alter the thoughts and behaviors of whoever sits in it. It shoots electrical signals through their brain and the person at the computer controls what kind of thoughts they want the other person to have."

Varia's reaction of horror surprised him. He added,

"You get used to it after the first few sessions."

"*What?*"

"Sorry. I'll just show you."

Just as Varia said, the rest of the threads were in the memories associated with Almond Industries. At first, Oliver tried to gather the clouds with a neutral mindset. After all, he and Varia understood how this process worked at this point and any revelations he made were similar to the ones from earlier memories. But every time he watched himself be manipulated by that man and electrocuted in that chair, more and more resentment built up inside him.

Again and again, no matter how big or small the "betrayal" was, it made Oliver due for more "treatment". In Harrell's eyes, anything could be seen as an act of defiance. Like a battering ram, it never got easier—Oliver simply got used to it occurring. He got so used to it that later on, it was him that offered its use, not Harrell.

It was the last memory to visit.

Red Arachnid simply sat in his room, drawing on a notebook full of violet clouds. Oliver recalled what he was thinking on this day. He had felt that he couldn't do anything without the feeling of eyes judging him. Watching him, staring, just waiting for him to mess up. Those days, the only way he could express himself was through little sketches here and there.

He didn't know why he felt so empty.

The AI voice announced, "Oliver Vermilio, Mike Harrell wishes to see you."

"Understood." He closed the notebook.

"He said to bring your notes."

"Uh... okay."

He held the notebook under his arm and entered Harrell's office. Harrell looked out the glass windows, his back to Red.

"You... asked for me, Mister Harrell?"

Harrell turned around. "Ah, you're here! And you brought the notebook, great."

"Is there something wrong with it, sir?"

"Well, it just seems like a distraction. You should be working."

"With all due respect, sir, I am. I was just taking some time off for myself."

Harrell sighed. "Ollie, have I ever taught you the phrase, 'If you have time to lean, you have time to clean'?"

"I think I might've heard about it before."

"So you know about it. What are your little drawings about?"

He held the notebook close. "They're just... drawings. Little characters going on little adventures."

"Does that help you do patrol?"

"Not... really."

"Does it help you fight crime?"

"No."

"Does it help you design equipment for our engineers?"

"No, but... I... I just like to..." He shut himself down. "I'm sorry, sir. What I'm doing is wrong."

Harrell put a hand out. Red gave him the notebook. Harrell put it into a disposal chute.

"There. No more distractions."

He wanted to cry. But if he did, then Harrell would demand an explanation and then get angry or disappointed at the answer and then give a lecture on how it's bad and then-

And then-

His chest had tightened with a familiar pain. His ribs closed in. His lungs about to collapse. He held his side.

"I need treatment."

Harrell's expression softened. "Then let's go. Maybe it'll help you with your distractions."

Varia hissed. "What a terrible man! He's nobody's father. I'm sorry for commenting, but I just..."

"I know."

Oliver thought over the last sentence Harrell said. He turned it over again and again, the false kindness that an abuser gives to their puppet.

Oliver said in a low voice, "'Maybe'. Of course he would deliver it as a 'maybe'."

"Maybe" Harrell hurt him. "Maybe" Oliver would forget. "Maybe" he would no longer care about whatever caused the problem. "Maybe" he would conveniently become more loyal, more obedient, more faithful to the company.

Fucking *maybe*.

The worst part was that Oliver wasn't the first ambassador for that company. There were others, but they had all vanished or quit for one reason or another.

All the ways Harrell had hurt Oliver and the ambassadors before him, and for what? To make perfection? To sell to the lowest common denominator? Harrell had forgotten them once they became useless and moved on to the next one. And yet, despite this, Harrell still walked free, free as a bird, to influence whoever he liked. He could lie and abuse as much as he wanted to and everyone around him would still treat him like a saint. Because they didn't know and they couldn't know. Or they *did* know and just didn't care.

Oliver didn't know which infuriated him more.

The entire area went dark. The uncomfortable, pervasive feeling burned through his mind and only grew stronger. New thoughts echoed through the darkness.

*He wronged me. He hurt me. All the times he's made me hurt or sad or scared. He twisted me up and turned me into something I'm not. It's all his fault.* ***His fault!***

Oliver's form shifted, but he was too caught up in his awakening anger to care.

*He corrupted me. He changed me against my will! And nobody cares! He's too rich, too charismatic, too influential... or everyone was just too comfortable with the status quo. Our pain is just too inconvenient for them. They didn't care. Nobody cared!*

*So why do* ***I*** *care so much?*

With a primal roar, Oliver struck the ground with all of his hands, now spidery once more. He clawed at the ground and screamed.

"I hate him, I hate him, I hate him! He ruined me! HE RUINED ME!"

Varia ran to his side. "Oliver, your self-image-"

Oliver turned to them, his eight eyes furious.

"HE'S STILL OUT THERE!"

"Listen to me! I know what it's like to escape an abusive relationship! It's like getting out of a bear trap without opening it. But trust me when I say that you don't need that person in your life. *You don't need him!*"

Oliver replayed that sentiment in his mind.

*I don't need him. I don't need him. I don't need him.*

"That's right," Said Varia. "He can't hurt you now."

Oliver closed his eyes. "I'm not... I'm not gonna be hurt by him again. I'm far away. He can't hurt me now. I don't need him."

"You got away. You're so strong. And now, you're going to get stronger. And healthier. And happy. But it's okay if it takes time."

Oliver receded back into human form. He said in a small voice,

"But how long will it take?"

Varia rubbed his back. "As long as it needs to."

Oliver's eyes opened. He said in quiet revelation,

"I'm... I'm free."

Varia smiled at him. "You are."

The final violet cloud had re-formed and floated in front of the duo. A gray thread collected the cloud, and upon Varia's touch, returned skyward. All the threads joined together in a giant ball of gray-and-violet yarn. It floated far above Oliver and Varia. It glowed with ethereal light.

"It's done," Said Varia. "We did it."

"So does that mean... am I cured?"

"We'll still need some newstone to store it in, but for now... it's contained. I will have to check on it daily. But on the bright side, I imagine that you'll be human again when you wake up."

Oliver gave them a hug. "Thank you, Varia. So, so much."

"You're very welcome! It's nice to be able to help someone."

"When we wake up, can we have a hug in the real world?"

"Of course."

# Chapter 11

Darcy stumbled along as they followed Akio. They wanted so badly to explore all of Refugee Clan, but seeing as they still couldn't figure out how to speak as a Salavite, they wouldn't be able to ask for directions if they got lost.

"We're going to make a detour," Said Akio. "I want to check on my teacher first."

Darcy tried to speak again, but instead blew raspberries. Akio laughed.

"We have *got* to get you into a speech class."

Darcy didn't mind the thought of going to classes. The more they understood this situation, the better. After all, it started to sound like they and Oliver would be working with Salavites for the long run. Darcy then internally laughed at the thought.

*Look at me, excited for school. I hated it when I was a kid! I guess opinions really do change as a person gets older.*

Akio led Darcy down the levels of Refugee Clan- Darcy counted five at least- and the lower they went, the less people they saw.

The lowest level opened into a natural underground lake. The light-up flowers grew even down here and congregated on the ceiling. Their shine illuminated the still, clear lake. The floor was made entirely of smooth, flat stones, and the clicks of Darcy and Akio's footsteps echoed through the cave in lonely clarity.

"Teacher," Akio called. "It's me."

A low breath responded. It came from a hole in the wall: a makeshift tunnel. The tunnel was so tall that two basketball players would have to stand on each other's shoulders in order to reach its ceiling, and so wide that it could fit two grizzly bears at once. Scoop-shaped indents lined the wall, as if someone had dug through it by hand. The further down the tunnel they went, the less consistent the indents became.

A dragon rested at the end of the cave. They lay on their side with an eye half-open. Their scales were platinum-white, but had lost whatever shine they may have had. Their limbs and tail had red patterns on them, but lost much of their saturation. Stray dirt clung to their metallic hide. Darcy could not see any wings, but long slits along their back hinted at something just underneath.

"Stay here," Akio whispered.

Akio knelt down next to the dragon's head. The dragon was three times Akio's size, yet the latter spoke to them like an old friend.

"How are you feeling today?"

"Hm? Akio?"

The dragon opened their dark-gray eyes. They forced themself onto four feet and yawned.

"I must have drifted off. Thank you for waking me."

"Aggis, you should take a break. Sleep in a real bed."

"I appreciate your concern, but I am quite alright."

Aggis placed their claws against the wall and carved out a fistful of earth. They held the clump with both hands.

"Hrm... come on..."

A small light appeared, but vanished just as quickly. Aggis opened their hands to find that they still held earth. They looked at Akio's lack of surprise. They made another attempt, but still held nothing but earth. They sighed.

"I am sorry, Akio."

Akio said, "See? This is why you need to rest. Rebuild your strength."

"Perhaps you are right."

Aggis seemed to have finally noticed Darcy, as their ears pointed upward.

"Another member of the Cinnabar Clan?"

"This is Darcy," Said Akio. "They're from the surface."

"Ah, I see. Apologies, I was hopeful."

Aggis trudged towards Darcy on all four feet.

"Pleasure to meet you." They extended an earthy hand to Darcy. "Aggis Theraven, Platinum Clan."

Darcy shook their hand. "Uh, yeah. Pleasure to meet you. Darcy Aran... Spider Clan?"

Aggis tilted their head to the side. "Spider Clan?"

"Yeah. I'm, uh, not exactly human."

"Fascinating! Are you comfortable telling me more?"

Akio interjected. "How about over dinner? After the council meeting."

"Ah, the council meeting. Did I miss its call?"

"Actually, I planned to tell you about it when I... had the... chance..."

As Akio spoke, Aggis strolled right past them as if in a daze. Akio and Darcy followed after them.

Aggis stopped next to the lake and stared into the water. They said,

"Darcy, did Akio tell you yet that this room used to be full of newstone?"

Darcy shook their head. Aggis continued,

"The dragon warriors would compress handfuls of earth and transmute them into newstone. We were the only ones who could. We would sing as we went along. The lake is salt water, so we used it to clean the stones and smooth them out. Oh, we sang so many songs."

Aggis watched the motionless, empty lake. Akio went to their side.

"We should keep moving," Akio said.

"Akio, do you remember when you sat by my side? Right here, on this shoreline. Remember all the stories I told you?"

Akio's tail flicked back and forth in irritation. "Yes, Aggis, I remember. Let's *go*."

Aggis's ears drooped. "Er... yes. Let us go."

Akio said, "Darcy, do you want to watch the meeting or find Oliver? Raise one claw for the first option and two claws for the second."

As much as Darcy wanted to check in on Oliver, they very much wanted to see what a Salavite meeting would be like. They raised a single claw.

— — —

The circular, spacious council room was big enough to hold at least a hundred Salavites. Darcy and Akio sat close to the center of the room, only a few feet away from the council. The council itself sat in a circle and was made up of Aggis and three other Salavites: a brown one with light brown eyes and dark brown horizontal stripes, a gray one with orange eyes and rust-colored limbs, and a yellow one with violet eyes and a shining jaw and underbelly. While the other council members sat cross-legged, Aggis lay with their arms and legs underneath them like a cat would. Pyrus soon entered the room and sat with the council.

Akio whispered to Darcy, "Everyone is invited to meetings, but technically, nobody but the council is required to attend. The person who calls the meeting will sit with the council and explain their request, then everyone gets a say on what they think we should do."

Darcy nodded along as Akio continued,

"See the council member sitting next to Aggis? That's Grisio Kartaniv, Brown Clan. They're in charge of resource management. The one sitting next to *them* is Terio Anuren, Iron Clan. They handle security. The one sitting between Terio and Pyrus is Rivio Rita, Yellow Clan. They're the best at performing first-aid. They manage medical supplies and stuff like that."

Pyrus bowed their head to the council. "Pleasure to meet you. Pyrus Kipath, Ruby Clan."

The council introduced themselves in kind.

Pyrus said, "I come on behalf of the Clans of Ruby, Sapphire, and Emerald. We call ourselves Trio Clan these days."

The council said, "Refugee Clan understands and respects this."

Rivio flicked their tail. Everybody's head turned to watch them.

Rivio said, "Now that the pleasantries are over... what is the meaning of the visit, Pyrus?"

"Trio Clan has dragon warriors, but not enough. We are going through newstone as quickly as we are making it. We heard of Refugee Clan, so I volunteered to journey into Newstone City to meet with you."

Grisio said, "I'm sorry, Pyrus, but we do not have any newstone to share with you, nor a functioning dragon warrior."

Akio flicked their tail and spoke up. "I have a request."

"What is your request?" Asked Rivio.

"We accept Trio Clan into our own. With more numbers, we can better care for each other and maybe even fight off the Macbeths."

Grisio spoke up. "I fear that we don't have the room to house more people. Unless some of them hope to fill the guard barracks..."

"But I just had an idea. What if we reclaimed Salanon? It has hundreds of tunnels and rooms and vast underground farms. If we remove the Macbeths' hold on the city..."

"This again, Akio?" Terio shook their head. "I *told* you, dispels are planted in every room and hallway. We would collapse before even entering the city."

"Yes, but what if we had a secret weapon? What if we had someone who wasn't affected by dispels? What if the Macbeths came around for their routine checkup... and met someone they couldn't intimidate?"

"And do you have an example of this secret weapon?"

Akio whispered to Darcy, "Stand up and take off the transformation spell. Make sure everyone can see you."

Darcy obliged. They removed the spell stone and bowed to the council. The crowd gasped at their arachnid appearance.

Darcy announced, "Darcy Aran, Spider Clan."

The audience spoke among each other in hushed voices.

"A spider creature? What in the world?"

"This feels like a fairy tale."

"Is it a mutation?"

"Looks like something my grandparent would speak of."

The council looked among each other. Grisio asked,

"Where do you hail from?"

"I hail from the surface," Darcy answered. "I was born in Wisconsin, then moved to Newstone City a few years ago."

Aggis peered at Darcy. They observed Darcy with so much intensity that it made Darcy uncomfortable.

"What powers do you wield?" Aggis asked.

"I, uh, have the strength and speed of a spider if it were human-sized. I can cling to any objects, sense vibrations, and even make silk with my spinnerets, although I only did the last part once so far, and not entirely on purpose."

"I see..."

Rivio said, "Akio has incredible strength and speed. They told us they were blessed by the heavens. How did *you* get your powers?"

Darcy considered how they would explain this without revealing the Patrons. They assumed that Akio's cover story was based in Salavite culture; it would be wise for Darcy not to say "blessed by the heavens" until they properly understood the implications. They chose their words carefully.

"I had fallen ill. A stranger found me and nursed me back to health. They used a strange remedy that I don't know the name of. When I woke up, I was like this. The stranger could not change me back."

Terio said, "And this transformation was not done by magic?"

"It was not. I cannot say what it was, but it was not magic. But this means that I am, um, not affected by dispels?"

Akio nodded and motioned for Darcy to sit back down.

"What Darcy means is that they can serve as a guard here. They can protect us from the Macbeths' visits. Maybe they can even remove the dispels from Salanon."

"And what would they expect in return for their help?" Terio addressed Darcy. "I imagine that you won't do this for free."

Darcy tried to sound chipper. "Nothing at all, actually! I'm happy to help."

The council members squinted at Darcy in suspicion.

Grisio said, "Risking their life against the Macbeths for free? Something isn't right here..."

Rivio said, "Perhaps they are a spy or a sellsword. They'll claim to fight alongside us, then stab us in the back and rob us blind."

Akio stood up. "Wait! They misspoke! Darcy is just humble, that's all. In actuality, they want a payment of..."

"Classes," Darcy blurted. "Learning stuff."

Aggis's eyes lit up. "Like history?"

"Yes, history! It fascinates me. I will help fight against the Macbeths, but only if Aggis teaches me things like history."

This seemed to quiet everyone's suspicions, as the council settled back down.

"Very well," Said Terio.

"Indeed," Said Rivio. "Perhaps being in a role that is not physically demanding will help Aggis be useful again."

Grisio said, "Then here is the deal: we shall reserve any trust until Darcy has defended against at least one attack from the Macbeths. If they succeed, then they shall be free to roam about Refugee Clan and have our permission to enter Salanon. If Darcy fails, they must return to the surface and never speak of our kind. Meanwhile, Pyrus shall return to Trio Clan, and upon any future updates, we shall send a messenger to them. Is everyone satisfied with this proposal?"

This was met with many voices in agreement. Rivio announced,

"Then this meeting is disbanded. Gratitude to everyone who attended."

The crowd streamed out of the various exits of the council room. Aggis approached Darcy. Their steps carried a bounce to them.

"When would you like to begin your classes?"

"As soon as you wanna, I guess. But, uh, I gotta warn you, I'm not used to being a Salavite yet. I can't even talk in that form."

"That is alright. I can help you learn."

Darcy put the transformation spell back on and gave Aggis a thumbs-up.

Akio said, "Well, we should get going. We promised some friends that we would meet up at Varia's for dinner."

Aggis's ears perked up. "May I come? I would like to meet your friends. We could spend more time together."

"Uh, I mean... it's pretty high-context. You'll probably be lost."

"I'm sure I can handle it. May I please come along?"

Akio sighed and looked at Darcy. Darcy gave a thumbs-up.

— — —

Darcy, Akio, Aggis, Pyrus, Oliver, and Varia all joined back up in Varia's lab. Varia had cleaned off one of the larger tables that they had and Akio brought their food box.

Darcy gave Oliver a hug. "How are you doing? Have you had any episodes?"

"I feel great, actually," He said. "I feel... lighter." His eyes widened upon seeing Aggis. "Omigosh, who is that?"

"Oh, uh, this is..."

"Aggis Theraven, Platinum Clan." Aggis shook Oliver's hand. "Pleasure to meet you. Tell me, had Akio told any of you about their mystical box yet? It holds the amazing power to conjure food from nothing!"

Darcy and Oliver feigned surprise.

"That's amazing," Said Oliver.

"No way!" Darcy gasped.

"Yes, it is quite the remarkable object. Another gift from the heavens."

Akio used the box to conjure plates full of roots and various isopods.

"This is a pretty standard Salavite dish," They explained. "Roots that have been cooked in an oven and some bugs for extra crunch."

Oliver said, "This looks... delicious... but I think we only have one chair to sit on."

Darcy said, "We could play a really intense game of musical chairs."

"No need, *Uukaniym*," Said Pyrus. "Watch this!"

Pyrus stomped a foot into the earth. The ground glowed a bronze hue and multiple earthen chairs arose from the floor. Akio put a hand against a chair, only for dirt to stick to their palm. They frowned.

"Your terrakinesis could use some work."

"But it's still cool, right?" Pyrus looked to Darcy. Darcy gave them a thumbs-up.

Everyone sat down except for Aggis, who lay down instead to accommodate their size. Each person shared their recent ventures as they ate. Darcy took off their spell stone so they could eat and speak easier. They said to Oliver,

"Wow, so you isolated the purification spell?"

"Yes!" Oliver smiled. "And now I can do this!"

Oliver flexed his hand and made it spidery, then changed it back with ease. The group clapped for him.

Aggis said, "So... you are suffering from some sort of spider-themed ailment?"

"A little bit," Said Oliver. "While I can control it now, I'd like to have the magic out of my body entirely."

Pyrus asked, "Why even cure it at all? That kind of power would be useful in a fight."

"I don't think so. I need regular treatments from Varia to keep it in check. But if we place it into a spell stone, then not only will I finally be free of it, but then *anyone* could use this power."

"Ooo. I see!"

Aggis said, "If I may ask, what would occur if you were dispelled?"

"We don't know," Said Varia. "We would need a spell stone with a dispel before we could try it, and at that point, we may as well just store the purification spell into the stone itself."

Darcy showed Varia the stone Akio had given them. "What about this? Would this work?"

"I'm afraid that that's not big enough. Oliver's arachnid form is larger than a human or Salavite. We would need newstone of at least two inches in diameter in order to store this spell. What you have is barely one inch."

"Aw, man."

Akio told Darcy, "Hang on to that thing. I think you should wear it when we fight the Macbeths."

"Huh? Why?"

"It could give us an element of surprise. Imagine one of the Macbeths coming here for a routine checkup. You fight back as a Salavite and they get all cocky. They pull out a dispel and then..."

"And then I can suckerpunch them," Said Darcy. "Oh, that's genius! Since they'll have the dispel out, it'll be easy to find and take!"

"Exactly!"

"Wait," Said Aggis. "Hold on. Is Darcy our only guard? What of their friend?"

"Oliver's situation isn't quite dependable right now," Akio replied. "But once we cure his ailment, I plan on officially introducing him to the council. I'm sure they won't mind having two guards who are immune to dispels."

"Hm, that is true. And what of you, Pyrus? When will you be off for Trio Clan?"

Pyrus sighed. "I'd love to stay and fight- I mean help- but I'll be leaving as soon as I finish eating. And to be quite honest, I don't know when I'll be able to visit again."

"Why's that?" Darcy asked.

"Trio Clan will be expecting me to give them all the details of my trip, and that includes my little adventure at the museum. I've got a feeling that they won't trust me to be a messenger again."

"Aw, man. So we won't get to set anything on fire together?"

Pyrus put a hand on Darcy's arm. They said in a choked-up voice, "I'm afraid not, bro."

"Aww, I'm gonna miss you, bro."

The two hugged overdramatically.

Akio squinted at them. "You've known each other for only a day."

Everyone continued their meal. The root was dry and lacked crunch, but had a spice to it that made it enjoyable. The isopods reminded Darcy of M&M candies, and while Darcy wasn't experienced in the ways of insect cuisine, they appeared to be lightly roasted.

"Man, these bugs are so good."

Akio replied, "Glad to see you like them. The humans I've talked to get weirded out when they learn about bug foods. They always ask, 'So do you eat Venutians?' And I always have to say..."

Akio, Aggis, Pyrus, and Varia all said in unison,

"It doesn't work like that!"

Pyrus said, "Seriously, what do they think we are? Cannibals? It's more complicated than that!"

Varia said, "Humans have a bad habit of making connections between things that aren't truly connected. If you do one thing, then *surely* you do another thing."

Darcy, meanwhile, turned their attention towards Oliver. He had just finished his root, but left his isopods untouched.

Darcy told him, "You don't have to finish it if you don't want to."

He replied quietly, "I probably should, though."

"You already did great."

"Thanks. Um... do you want them?"

"I'd love some."

He gave Darcy his plate. Darcy munched on the isopods and said,

"So you can even control the Night Creature form?"

"Mm-hm." He looked at them. "Do you... want me to show you?"

"Only if you're comfortable."

"Maybe later, then. Or maybe tomorrow. Don't get me wrong—I'm happy I made this breakthrough. I'm just thinking about the future."

"In what way?"

"Let's... talk about it later."

Darcy finished the plate. They said to Varia,

"Oh, so you're a scientist right?"

"You're correct! Varia Charna, Red Clan."

"Darcy Aran, Spider Clan. So you know how science and testing stuff works, right? Mind if I ask some advice?"

"Indeed! What do you wish to know?"

"Well, I'm trying to run a personal project of mine. It's private, but I'm testing something that will affect my body. Obviously, I don't wanna test on myself 'cuz that would be dangerous, but I don't know where to start when it comes to sampling. Any ideas?"

"Well, you could try blood samples, cheek swabs, scale cells... although in your case, they would be chitin cells."

Darcy scratched their head. "Okay..."

"Do these tests have magic involved?"

"Uh, sure. Theoretically, what would be a good thing to put magic into so it can be reliably tested?"

Akio said, "You could embed the spell stone into a piece of clothing."

"Yes," Said Varia. "I used to have a necklace with a transformation stone inside it. Every time I put it on, the spell would activate. It was an easy way for me to keep a certain form without worrying which pocket I had the stone in."

"Oh, that's a good idea. Okay, I'll try that. Thanks guys!"

"Glad to help!"

Aggis got up. "Well, I believe I have finished with my meal. It was a pleasure to meet you, Oliver."

Oliver nodded. "Same to you, um..."

"Aggis Theraven, Platinum Clan."

He smiled. "Oliver Vermilio, Spider-"

Varia coughed violently. Oliver rubbed their back.

"Ohmigosh! Are you okay?"

Varia wheezed. "Erk. Yes. Just... choked on a root. I'm fine."

"Do you need some water?"

"No, but thank you. I think I'm done for the night."

Varia left the room in the span of two seconds.

Pyrus commented, "Guess their socialization threshold has a hard drop-off."

Darcy said, "Speaking of 'done for the night', I'm gonna check out my room here. From the sound of it, I'll be sleeping in the guard barracks."

"That is correct," Said Aggis. "I can show you where it is if you like."

"Thanks, Aggis."

Oliver glanced in the direction that Varia left in.

"I'll... come with you. Something tells me that Varia wants to be alone tonight."

# Chapter 12

After dinner, Aggis and Akio lead Darcy, Oliver, and Pyrus to the guard barracks, where Terio waited.

The barracks were made up of rectangular rooms with multiple pillow-nests lined against the wall. The wall itself had been decorated with strings and bells.

Terio explained, "This is where our defenses slept... back when we had them."

Darcy said, "I'm going to guess that the Macbeths took them away?"

Akio answered, "Honestly, it was a fifty-fifty chance. The routine checkups either ended in being visited by Libra and getting captured... or being visited by Scorpio and promptly killed."

Pyrus frowned. "I don't envy your situation. This is worse than my council thought."

Terio nodded. "This is a dangerous task. Darcy, your work won't being overlooked, I assure you. We'll be keeping a sharp eye on you."

"Just glad to help."

Aggis pointed at the strings and bells. "We have a security system in case of an attack. These barracks are connected to Refugee Clan's entrance. The strings cross the floor of the entry hall. If someone steps on them, their weight causes the strings to move, jostling the bells."

Darcy said, "Kinda reminds me of a spider web."

"This system was designed by my grandparent. They were actually inspired by spiders and how they worked."

*Interesting.* "Well, thank you very much for allowing us to stay here."

"Yes," Said Oliver. "We promise not to let you down."

Terio's ears twitched. "And who is this?"

"Sorry," Said Akio. "I meant to introduce him when the time was right. Oliver here is similar to Darcy, where he has powers and is immune to dispels. He was suffering from an ailment until tonight, so I waited before telling you all about him."

"...Right. Well, if he assists Darcy in their role, then both will be officially considered guards."

Aggis gave Darcy and Oliver a smile. "I believe in you two. I know you will do your best."

Akio said, "If you need anything, just call. Yell out, 'attack' or something similar. I'll come running."

Darcy nodded. "Thanks, Akio."

"Indeed," Said Terio. "Good luck."

Terio and Aggis left the barracks. Now, it was time for Pyrus to give their farewells.

"It was nice to meet you," Darcy said. "Even if it wasn't for very long."

"Same here," Pyrus replied. "Thank you for saving my life. I literally wouldn't be here if not for you."

"Just try to play it safe from now on, 'kay?"

Pyrus laughed. "Don't worry! I won't be making the same mistake again. After seeing a Macbeth in person, I now know for certain that I can't take them out myself." They held two of Darcy's hands with their own. "But perhaps someday, we can study the art of fire and magma together. Then nobody could stop the fire in our hearts."

"Oh, hell yeah! I'm looking forward to it."

Pyrus pecked Darcy on the cheek. "Until we meet again, *Uukaniym*."

Darcy, Oliver, Akio, and Aggis waved Pyrus off. Once the latter was out of sight, Akio crossed their arms.

"They came onto you rather strongly."

"What do you mean?" Darcy asked.

"Pyrus has a crush on you."

"What? No, no, we were just being dumbasses together."

"In Salavite culture, pecks on the cheek are explicitly romantic *and* 'Uukaniym' means 'small romance'. It's a name you only use when you're flirting with someone."

"...Oh." Darcy slowly looked down. "Ohhhhhh. That's... going to be awkward to explain; I'm aromantic."

"Yeah, have fun with that."

Oliver shrugged. "Maybe Pyrus will understand?"

Darcy scratched the back of their head. "Well... it'll be a hot minute before we see them again, so I guess we just move on and hope that I... never have to talk to them again." They gave a nervous laugh.

Once they were alone, Oliver sat down with Darcy.

"These beds look nice," He said.

"Yeah."

Darcy took off their coat and hat. Oliver looked away.

Darcy said, "Nothing's showing, bud."

"I know. It still feels rude to watch you take off clothes, though."

"Fair enough." Darcy looked at their hat. "Hm... placing it into clothing..."

"Pardon?"

"I have an idea."

They focused on their pizzazz and transferred a bit of it into the hat. Upon activating their pizzazz, the hat glowed blue.

"Yes! Now to try changing it. Oliver, name a spider power. Something simple."

"Uh, joint barbs. They are these large, blade-like barbs that can protract from the elbows and knees. The modern version of the power just has it as a form of equipment that you wear, but apparently it used to be biological."

"Oh, I think I remember hearing about that. Okay, I'll need some quiet so I can focus."

"Um, alright. Good luck."

Darcy shut their eyes and focused purely on the bit of pizzazz within the hat. They felt the powers that existed inside the pizzazz. Each individual power felt like a folder with multiple files inside. The available powers, such as strength and stickiness, were more prominent. In contrast, the unavailable powers, such as joint barbs and form change, were not as noticeable.

*Okay... open joint barbs.*

The "folder" for joint barbs opened like Darcy wanted. The problem was, there were far too many "files" for Darcy to keep track of. Each version of the power had a number assigned to it, and Darcy couldn't parse what these numbers meant, nor the differences between each version. So much data filled their mind that their head hurt.

*Agh... just need to pick one.*

And they did, entirely at random. Joint barbs became prominent like the other available powers and Darcy stopped their focus. They opened their eyes and rubbed their head.

"Ugh..."

"Are you okay?" Oliver asked.

"There were dozens of different versions of just one power. Hell, maybe even hundreds of versions. I think I succeeded, though."

Darcy put on the hat. A familiar jolt ran through their body. Darcy focused on the power of joint barbs. A blade-like barb protracted from one of their elbows. Darcy laughed with excitement.

"Oliver, look! I did it!"

"Darcy, that's amazing! Congratulations!"

Darcy tried to protract barbs for the rest of their arms, but none appeared.

"Hm. Seems like the version I chose only had one barb. Wow. So that means..."

"What is it?"

"Well, if I wanna know what each version does, I think I'm gonna have to test out each one individually." They sighed. "Oh man. Every single version of every single power."

"Oh."

Darcy took off their hat. Their joint-barb automatically retracted back into their arm.

"Well, it was still another step taken. Better than no progress at all."

"Yeah."

The duo chose to share a bed again. Oliver lay on his back while Darcy lay on their side, facing him. Oliver described the full details of his and Varia's journey through his memories.

"It really put things into perspective," He said. "Just how many times I was..." He sighed. "Harrell. I was an easy target for him. That's all I was. He's probably using the Night Creature fiasco for his own benefit. He probably did the same to the other ambassadors, too."

"Will you be okay?" Darcy asked.

"I don't know. It still hurts. But it made me think about the future."

"Yeah?"

"I know that it's a good thing to be away from him... but what am I gonna do when all this is over? What will my purpose be once this magic stuff is out of me? Almond Industries gave me a purpose."

"Well, we promised to help the Salavites..."

"But say that we *do* scare off the Macbeths. Say that everything we do is successful and the Salavites get all the newstone back. What will I do after all of that?"

"Maybe you'll find something new that you'll wanna do."

"But who will I be? I used to be Oliver the orphan, then I became Red Arachnid the ambassador, now I'm Oliver the... the Night Creature. Everything that I've become has been something that happened **to** me, not **because of** me."

"What about controlling your transformations? That's a pretty big step."

"I had help then. It wasn't under my own steam." Frustration entered his voice. "Honestly, with all the support I constantly need, I sometimes don't even feel like a real person."

"Don't say that."

"Am I wrong? Do actual people need this much help? Are real humans this emotionally fragile?"

"Some are. Some aren't. But breaking easily doesn't make you any less of a person."

"I just wish I could be strong on my own. I wish I could be assured and not cloud myself with anxiety and self-loathing. I wish I could be like those heroes who stand on a building with the sun at their back and make everyone who sees them feel safer. I want to be so confident that it gives other people the strength to be confident, too." He faced Darcy. "Like you."

Darcy blinked. "You think *I'm* like that?"

He blushed. "Well... I think so, at least."

Darcy felt warm inside. "If it helps you feel any better, I don't feel like that all the time."

"Really?"

"I may act like I don't care about what other people think, but I honestly do sometimes. I wanna make a good impression on Akio and Aggis, y'know? I wanna prove that I'm an asset to the council. I don't wanna hurt Pyrus' feelings when *that* conversation comes around. And I care about your opinion, too."

"Why?"

"Because you're my friend, and I love my friends. I usually keep my true name hidden for safety, but when it comes to my loved ones... I get legitimately worried that they might reject me."

"But it's your name. It's *you*."

"And it's awesome that you think that, but not everybody does. And if you didn't accept me, then... I honestly don't know what I would have done."

"Oh... I'm sorry."

"No apologies. Luckily for me, that situation is only hypothetical now. I'm so, so grateful to have you by my side."

"I don't bother you at all?"

"Honestly, I can't imagine my life without you."

He made a sheepish smile. "Now you're just saying that."

"I'm not. At a dark time in my life, you gave me hope."

Darcy held Oliver's hand with two of their own. They said,

"I believe that, just like how they can hurt each other, people can make each other stronger. It's okay to have your own strength, but it's also okay to gain strength from others, too." They smiled at him. "You said you want to inspire people, right? So, you and I can inspire each other. After all, we already have been."

Oliver tightened his mouth as if holding in a breath. He rubbed one of Darcy's claws with his thumb.

"So we could... after all this is done... in the future..."

He looked at the ceiling again. He rubbed his head with his free hand with a nervous laugh.

"I don't even know what I'm saying."

Darcy chuckled just as nervously. "It's a bit forward, huh? Sorry 'bout that. I don't even know if there's a platonic term for this relationship."

"No, you're fine. And I mean... platonic partnerships exist, right?"

"Yeah, totally."

"So you're not being *that* forward. I mean... if I make you stronger and you make me stronger, then... being... partners..."

He pulled away from Darcy with a squeak. He covered his face with his hands.

"Gosh, I'm sorry."

Darcy giggled. "You're okay."

"I'm going to think about it first... if that's okay."

"Yeah, absolutely. It *was* a bit sudden."

"Thank you, though."

— — —

Oliver put a hand on Darcy's arm.

"Darcy," He whispered. "Darcy!"

Darcy turned away from him. "Sleepin'..."

"Darcy, wake up! The alarm is going off!"

"Mmm... wha?" Darcy forced themself to sit up. "Who's doing what?"

Oliver pointed at the jingling bells. Long seconds passed before Darcy registered what they meant.

"Aw, shit!"

Darcy jumped to their feet. They smacked their cheeks to wake themself fully.

"Oliver, go get Akio."

"But what about you?"

"I'll be fine. I have a plan, remember?"

Oliver gave a nervous hum, but followed orders. He ran off while Darcy put on their transformation spell. They threw on their coat and placed the stone in a pocket so it couldn't be easily seen or taken. They made unsure steps to the clan's entry hall.

Only a single figure stood in the middle of the long hallway. The light flowers illuminated her white robes and long platinum-blonde hair. She stood about twenty feet away from Darcy.

*Libra.*

"Good evening," Libra sang. "Sorry for the surprise, but we decided that it was necessary to run a checkup. How are you?"

*Is she here because of Pyrus?*

Darcy put a hand against a wall to keep balance. They were not large enough to block the entire entryway, nor agile enough as a Salavite to rush at the woman. Perhaps they could lure her towards them with conversation.

"Sss... ssdo. Ssdoing... goodssss."

Libra smiled. "That's nice. I've been doing quite fine, myself. So, are there any new developments in Refugee Clan? Any newstone made? Any babies born? Any... new members?"

Darcy gulped. They answered to the best of their ability.

"Fi... fi... fine. We... fine. No... new... pe... peee...pollll."

Irritation entered her faux-friendly tone. "Can you speak a little faster, please?"

Darcy's ears pointed backwards, reflecting their own anger. Libra closed the gap between them.

"A lizardfolk tried to take my newstone earlier today. It would be wonderful if you told us where they were."

"Duh-don't... don't nnnnn... know."

She snapped, "Are you developmentally challenged?"

Her tone alone made Darcy hiss. They bared their fangs at her.

Libra stepped back with a forced smile. "Apologies! That was unprofessional of me. I can't expect reptiles to think like humans. What I mean to say is, does **this** interest you?"

Libra pulled a sphere of newstone from her robe. It was the size of an orange and perfectly clear. She held it out for Darcy to see, mere inches from their grasp.

"The lizard we're looking for is from the Ruby Clan. If you bring them to us, this stone will be yours. No strings attached."

*With a stone that size, we could contain Oliver's magic situation. Maybe I should try to take it now, while it's in sight. She could still pull out a dispel, but if I surprise her...*

Too late—Libra hid the sphere back within her robe. She said,

"Think about it. Your clan has little resources as it is. If you help us, you will have more to your name *and* have one less mouth to feed. Everybody wins."

Even if Pyrus was still around, the thought of betraying someone made Darcy sick.

They growled and gave out a hearty, "No!"

Libra's smile vanished. "Then I suppose we'll do this the hard way."

She pulled out a wand and pointed it at Darcy. The wand's spell stone was black with white speckles.

*Perfect!*

Darcy feigned terror and put their hands forward.

"W-wait!"

"Too late. You made your choice."

A dark beam shot out of the wand and hit Darcy. Nothing hurt, but their body tingled as the transformation spell came undone. Darcy returned to spider form and fell forward as if unconscious. They focused on the vibrations around them as Libra stepped closer to them.

"What in the world?" She placed a hand against Darcy's fuzzy head. "Some sort of... spider?"

Darcy's arms short upward. One pair of hands kept Libra's arms pinned together while another pair of hands grabbed the wand.

"Surprise."

With their third pair of arms, Darcy pulled Libra close. Darcy kneed her in the diaphragm. She collapsed inward. Darcy set her onto the ground and rummaged through her robes for the rest of her newstone. A part of Darcy felt guilty to be essentially robbing someone of their belongings, but they reasoned to themself that if they hadn't, then Libra would have done something far worse.

"Darcy!" Akio's voice echoed through the hallway.

Akio ran up to them. Before Akio could say anything, Darcy handed them the wand and the newstone sphere.

"Here. This is what I've found."

"Wow. Nicely done!"

"I don't think she has any more."

"She must've been counting on just the dispel wand. In any case, we should get her out of here."

"Wait, why? Why not imprison her? She could be a bargaining chip."

"If we keep her here, it'll only give the Macbeths a reason to attack us in full force."

"What makes you think they won't do that anyways?"

"They won't," Libra said in a weak voice. "A deal.... If you let me go free... I won't attack."

Darcy marched over to Libra and put a foot against her back. Their super strength kept Libra pinned down, but Darcy made certain not to place too much pressure onto her.

"How will we know that you'll keep your word?"

"We have information," Libra replied. "Another dragon warrior... in the city."

Akio's ears shot upward. "What?!"

"We had been watching her... making sure she didn't cause trouble. She would be an asset to you... right? Set me free... and I won't attack... *and* I will tell you where she lives. You win in this situation."

Darcy and Akio looked at each other. Akio looked back to Libra.

"It's a deal."

But Darcy didn't let go of her. They said,

"Akio, you sure about this?"

Akio nodded. "We need another dragon warrior."

Darcy stepped away from Libra. She stood back up with a hand against her diaphragm.

"You're powerful," She said.

Darcy didn't answer her.

Libra continued, "The dragon warrior lives in a warehouse with two others: one lizard, one human."

She told them the address, then retreated back down the hallway. Darcy stood alert, though, so much that Akio had to pull them back to the guard barracks.

Oliver waited there close to the doorway. Akio said to him,

"Hey, guess what: you don't need to be backup. We handled it."

"Oh, thank goodness!" Oliver hugged Darcy. "Are you alright? She didn't hurt you, did she?"

Darcy returned the hug. "No, thankfully. And now we have two more spell stones."

"Really? That's fantastic!"

Akio said, "I'm calling a council meeting. I can explain everything to them if you two want to go back to sleep."

"Thanks, but I think I'll keep watch in case she comes back."

"Fair enough. Good night, Darcy."

Darcy sat up in bed with Oliver next to them.

Oliver said, "Sorry I wasn't more help."

"You're fine. You did what I told you."

"Sounds like you captured Libra pretty well. That's really cool."

"Thanks."

"Um... are you okay?"

"Yeah. Go to sleep."

Oliver eventually fell asleep, but Darcy kept an eye on the doorway. They watched the little bells, waiting for them to move. They listened for even the smallest sign of alarm. They pulled their hat close just in case they needed the extra power, just in case.

*Imagine if I had even more power, though...*

# Chapter 13

Darcy awoke the next morning to find Oliver pacing about in spider form. He hummed in discomfort as he went back and forth through the guard barracks.

*I must've nodded off.*

"Hey, bud. You okay?"

Oliver jumped upon hearing Darcy's voice. He whirled to face them.

"Darcy! You're awake."

"Yeah. Everything okay?"

"Sorry. I-I just keep worrying. What if this doesn't work? What if we move the spell into the sphere and I'm still stuck like this? And I..."

Oliver covered his face and took deep breaths.

"I can feel the yarn beginning to unravel."

"Better get to Varia's, then."

"But people are gonna notice me!"

"I'm sorry, but unless you can change yourself back, we'll have to do this as spiders."

"Right. Right. You're right. Let's move quickly."

Darcy put on their transformation spell, but just as they guessed, the dispel from last night's conflict had completely wiped the stone—it was now colorless. Darcy pocketed the stone and got moving.

Darcy and Oliver hugged the wall as they went along the hallways. Darcy stood in front of Oliver as if they could somehow hide his huge frame with their tiny body.

A sleepy Salavite stepped into the same hallway as them. They caught sight of the duo.

"Good morning- ah!"

"Sorry," Said Oliver. "Sorry!"

The Salavite averted their gaze and shielded their eyes with a hand.

"You two, um, must be the new guards. You look, er, interesting."

"Sorry," Said Darcy. "We don't have transformation spells."

"It's alright," They replied. "We all know the feeling. Er... have a healthy day!" They shuffled off.

Thankfully, the early morning meant that not many people were up and about, but the ones who did see Darcy and Oliver covered their eyes or looked away. The duo gave out quick apologies to anyone who happened to see them.

*It's like we're running around naked!*

Thankfully, Oliver's skill with vibration senses helped the two quickly make their way to Varia's lab. Thanks to the equipment and machinery, the area reflected vibrations differently than the rest of Refugee Clan, making it easy to find.

Darcy and Oliver shut the lab door behind them. Varia sat at a counter engrossed in some notes.

"Sorry to bother you so early," Said Darcy.

Varia didn't look up. Oliver stepped over to stand beside them.

"Um, Varia... I'm sorry to bother you, but..."

Varia still didn't respond. Oliver put a hand on their shoulder.

"Um... Varia..."

"Huh?" Varia looked at him. "Oh! Oliver! When did you get here?"

"Just a minute ago. So, um... we have news."

"Oh, yes! What is it?"

Darchy said, "We were visited by one of the Macbeths last night. Thankfully, things went well."

Varia's ears pointed upward. "You shared breathing space with a Macbeth? You *fought* one of them? And you *survived*?"

"Yeah. Not having a body that runs on magic really gave me the advantage. Er, no offense."

Varia jumped out of their seat. "Wow! Fantastic! Amazing! Stupendous! This..." They placed a hand against their forehead. "This changes everything."

A tear formed in Varia's eye. They promptly wiped it away and continued to smile.

"Akio mentioned getting some stones... oh, this is simply fantastic."

"Yeah, a wand and a stone the size of an orange. Is Akio still with the council?"

"Oh, yes! I considered going to the meeting, but I am not at my best in large crowds. However! I *did* give Akio some talking points."

"Damn, Akio went to call a meeting last night. It's been hours since then. Has it really been going on that long?"

Varia nodded. "It's a matter of newstone. With a resource that precious, there will be a lot of arguments about the best way to use it. But hopefully, Akio will help us gain custody of the larger stone."

Oliver stepped back. "Wait... so there's a chance that we won't get to use the stone?"

"I'm afraid so."

Darcy crossed their arms. "Well, that's not fair at all. Hell, I was the one who got the stones, so I should be the one choosing what to do with 'em."

"I don't think that would go over well for your public reception. But don't worry! I have faith in Akio. They will succeed, I'm sure of it. In the meantime..." They said to Oliver, "Shall we start your treatment?"

"Treatment?" Oliver's eyes widened. His breathing quickened. He backed into a counter and yelped. His eyes became unfocused, almost wild. He covered his head in his hands.

"No!"

"I'm sorry. Wrong choice of words."

Oliver sat onto the floor with his back against a counter and his eyes squeezed shut. Darcy ran to his side.

"Just a memory..." He muttered. "Just a memory..."

Varia asked, "Should I-"

Oliver hissed. "Shh!"

Both Varia and Darcy stepped back. Eventually, Oliver's breathing slowed back down. He made a heavy exhale.

"Sorry for hissing. I just needed..."

His sentence trailed off. When he eventually spoke again, he sounded drained.

"Should we... can you...?"

Varia nodded. "It should only take a moment."

Varia placed their head against Oliver's. Darcy leaned forward as they watched, as if getting closer would somehow help. But from the outside, it only looked like the two were embracing and nothing more.

Minutes later, the two separated from the embrace. Varia stepped back. Oliver put his hands together and closed his eyes again, this time in peace. Magic covered his body and he shifted back into human form. He sighed with relief.

"That's much better. I'm sorry for panicking."

"No apologies," Varia replied. "It happens to the best of us."

Darcy said, "So that's what you need to do to keep your condition in check? That mind-meld thing?"

"Basically," Said Oliver. "If I don't, the purification spell will get tangled up in my mind again. It's... hard to describe."

Oliver's stomach then audibly growled. He flinched in response.

"Ah... I'm sorry."

"You're good," Said Darcy. "I'll get us some food from-" They remembered the Varia wasn't a warlock. "...I'll just get some food. Be right back."

They went back into the halls and checked for any bystanders. They then pulled out the crystal heart and teleported back to Revi's pocket dimension.

Darcy grabbed their food box and passed by the Wraith Lodge on their way out. They considered visiting the Wraiths, but surmised that now wasn't the time. They exited the pocket dimension and returned to the lab.

"Okay, so you know how Akio has a mystical, amazing box?"

Varia gasped. "You have one as well? Astounding!"

Darcy placed it on a table. "What're you guys up for?"

"Oh, it has been forever since I've last had *echavelo*. And with *dandaveloviym*!"

Darcy stared at them in confusion. "I... uh... don't know how to spell those."

"*Echavelo* is fish that has been cooked over a flame. The flame can be at any strength. *Dandaveloviym* is mushrooms that have been cooked with a flame, specifically of medium strength. Personally, I believe that medium-cooked mushrooms are the best."

"Gotcha."

Darcy wrote down the food descriptions and handed Varia their serving. Varia had a bite and sang with delight.

"This is fantastic! Thank you very much, Darcy!"

Darcy smiled. "Happy to help."

Darcy had never eaten mushrooms before. They didn't know what to expect, but to them, the texture and warmth of the mushrooms reminded them of meat. They liked it.

Darcy kept an eye on Oliver to make sure he ate as well. He ate his serving one piece at a time, but smiled all the same.

"This really is good," He said.

Varia said, "Roalen and I used to collect mushrooms together. We would use fire spells to try different strengths of heat. There was a time that we even burnt the mushrooms into charcoal!"

Varia laughed at the memory, but their voice had been tinted with sadness.

"I would tuck them into bed and we would make plans on what we would try the next time we found mushrooms. We would..."

Their smile had completely vanished. Their ears hung limp. They didn't stare at the table, but past it. They shook their head.

"I'm sorry. Old memories."

"You're okay," Said Darcy.

Oliver said, "I'm sorry if we reminded you of anything."

Varia waved a hand. "No, no. I was the one who brought it up. It was my own responsibility."

Varia only had one mushroom left to eat. They held it up between two claws.

"I think Roalen would be happy if they learned that you won against a Macbeth. They would be so excited to meet you... both of you."

Oliver said, "I'd love to meet them, too."

Varia made a tearful smile.

After everyone had finished eating, they sat at a counter where Varia kept a pile of fresh notes.

"So- and this is assuming we gain custody of the sphere- I will use the same magical technique that I've already been doing with you, Oliver. But instead of merely keeping the purification spell isolated in your mind and body, I will move it into the newstone sphere. You should probably be in human form when we do so to prevent any complications."

"Understood. Is there anything else I can do to help?"

"Be as calm as you can. Think neutral thoughts. Actually, it may be most efficient if we perform this process while you are unconscious."

"Okay. Um, Darcy, would it be alright if you stayed close when-or-if we do this? I feel safest when you're around."

"Of course, bud." Darcy asked Varia, "So your notes were about the spell process?"

"Er, no." Varia sorted the notes into a stack. "These are for... something else. I'll put them away."

The lab door opened, capturing everyone's attention. Akio entered the room, their slow steps portraying exhaustion.

Varia jumped from their seat. "What is the news?"

Akio replied sarcastically, "Well, it was one of the longest meetings I've ever been in, so that was fun. It took us forever just to decide what to do with the dispel wand. We decided to clear out the spell and replace it with the spell for light solidification."

Darcy asked, "You can remove dispels?"

"Yeah. You touch it and clear it out just like any other spell. Now as for the wand, Rivio and the other medical workers will be using it to form hard-light sutures and thread."

"I see," Said Varia. "The wand would make the creation of such small objects child's play. And you could use the wand to guide them with ease. And once the wound has finished healing, they will dissipate with ease."

"Exactly. Taking care of injuries will be much easier now. As for the newstone sphere..." Akio pulled it from their jacket pocket. "Varia can use it as they please."

Everyone cheered, "Yes!"

Oliver had to grip the counter to keep from falling over. He giggled with relief.

"Sorry. I just... yes. Oh my gosh. It'll be over. I can't wait!"

Akio handed Varia the sphere. They then said,

"By the way, the council said that Oliver is also officially welcome as a guard as long as his situation proves to be stable. Which means that he'll still be spending time with Varia."

For just a moment, Varia's ears sank. They sprang back up just as quickly.

"I would love to have him with me!"

"Good. Now if anyone needs me, I'll be taking a quick nap. Then I'm headed to the address that Libra gave us. I want to find that dragon warrior as soon as I can."

Darcy said, "I'll come with you in case it's a trap."

"No. Oliver will be vulnerable while the spell is getting transferred. That means that you will be the only defense during that time. You need to stay here."

"But are you sure you'll be safe on your own?"

"I'm a scout, Darcy—moving around safely is my entire job."

Darcy gave Akio a handshake. "Well then, good luck. Let's hope this dragon warrior is the real deal."

"Same here. If she truly is a dragon warrior and willing to help us, it would change everything. We could make newstone again!"

"Then let's hope for the best."

# Chapter 14

Varia had Oliver lie in their bed so he could fall asleep. They sat next to him and readied the newstone sphere. Darcy watched from the side.

Darcy held their breath as Varia placed the sphere against Oliver's chest. After a moment's delay, the sphere glowed. It swirled with violet and gray hues. Varia put their free hand against Oliver's forehead, then pulled away from it. Ethereal violet and gray ribbons left Oliver's body. Varia guided the ribbons into the sphere.

The sphere shined brightly and made a chiming sound. Varia's ears pointed straight up in response. They pulled the sphere close to their face to look. The sphere's color had now become a singular hue: vibrant cherry-red.

Darcy said, "What's going on?"

Varia said in a whisper, "Wake him up."

Darcy did so by nudging Oliver back and forth. His eyes opened.

"Did... did it work?"

Varia motioned for him to sit up. They showed him the sphere.

"We did it."

"Really?" He ran a hand through his hair. "It... you succeeded?"

"Well, try shifting to spider form."

Oliver looked at his hands. Moments passed, but nothing happened. He looked back up.

"Nothing. I don't feel it."

Varia smiled. They placed the sphere into Oliver's hands.

"Try it now."

This time, his hands shifted. Oliver then transformed his entire body to the spider form. He then placed the sphere down; the moment it left his person, he shifted back into human form.

"Woah. It... it worked." He laughed with relief. "It worked! I'm me again!"

He and Darcy hugged. Darcy said,

"I'm so happy for you! Congrats!"

"I already feel so much better!"

Varia picked the sphere back up. "And I have even better news. Have you two noticed that the sphere changed color?"

Darcy replied, "Oh, yeah, it's red now."

"Yes! Do you know what that means?"

Oliver said, "That... it's a nice color?"

"No. Well, yes, this is a very lovely shade of red. But no! You see, each spell is a specific color. For example, magma spells are ruby-red. While there are other spells that are red, none of them are *ruby*-red. When new spells are discovered or created, they are borne in a new color." Varia hugged the sphere. "My friends! No other spells are cherry-red!"

"Woah," Said Darcy. "So you made a brand-new spell?"

"*We* made a new spell! And we made history!" Varia twirled around. "Oh, this is stupendous! And so fascinating, too! A spider-themed spell. What could it mean? Is this a one-time occurrence? What other spells could we craft this way? Granted, this was the result of many variables, but still!"

Varia ran into the lab with Darcy and Oliver close behind. They put the spell stone onto a stand and looked at it from different angles.

"Fascinating! Just fascinating!"

Darcy asked Varia, "Think we can use it against the Macbeths?"

"I'm afraid that it's just as vulnerable to a dispel as any other spell is."

"So it's useless."

Varia gasped. "Don't say that! This will increase our understanding of magic even more!"

"But no matter how much we understand, it's useless against people who can cancel out magic."

"Well... yes... but still. The expansion of knowledge is important."

"I guess so. On the bright side, we can finally put the Night Creature business behind us. Well, I promised Aggis that I'd take their history lessons, so I'll be with them if anyone needs me."

"They'll likely be in the underground lake," Varia explained, "Do you know the way there?"

"I'm pretty sure I can find my way. Oh, that reminds me." Darcy gave Varia their spell stone. "This got dispelled in the fight against Libra. Can you turn it back into a transformation spell?"

"Sure thing."

Varia placed the stone against their palm. The stone became a basic red. Varia returned it to Darcy.

"Hope you're alright with looking like a member of the Red Clan."

"I'm not picky." Darcy pocketed the stone and transformed into a red Salavite. "Th-thaaaankssss."

Varia nodded. "Enjoy your lesson. Oliver, will you be joining them?"

Oliver rubbed his arm. "Well, Akio said the council wants to be certain that my situation is stable, so..."

"Ah, right."

"So I suppose I could stay here and study the new spell with you? I'm actually really curious on how this process works."

"Yes, yes, I'd love to have you! The more, the merrier. Here, I'll give you an official tour of the lab..."

Darcy stopped at the doorway and looked back at Varia and Oliver. They didn't know if it was because he was eating more or because the magic was finally out of his system, but he already looked healthier, and they could watch him smile for days. Darcy smiled themself and stepped out the door.

*You deserve the best, Oliver.*

Oliver, meanwhile, followed Varia around with delight. He didn't have any scientific knowledge, so he didn't understand anything they said, but he simply enjoyed spending time with them.

"Where did you get all this equipment?" He asked.

"I found most of the materials at junkyards and then fixed them up, but a couple of these machines are from a... previous workplace." Varia cleared their throat. "But anyway, they have a focus on combining magic and science together. Unfortunately, without newstone, all these machines can do is collect dust."

"What would they do if they *did* work? Um, sorry for asking."

"It's alright. If everything worked as intended, then this machine here would change a person's species without them having to wear a spell stone. That machine over there would show a projection of all the spells a person knows, and that machine would allow a non-Salavite to digest newstone."

"That's amazing!"

"They would be... if they worked." Varia scratched their head. "As it stands, their functions are only theoretical. Perhaps that's for the best. After all, many Salavites have a lot of pride in being the only creatures capable of consuming newstone."

"Oh, that's true. I suppose that magic is very important to Salavite culture, huh." He rubbed the back of his neck. "Maybe I *should* join Aggis's class with Darcy."

"You can if you want to." Varia held the cherry-red stone in their hand. "I'm going to study this if you would like to join me, though."

"...Well, I'm sure they wouldn't miss me for a few more hours."

Varia showed him a sheet full of data. "I wrote this down when I did your diagnostics."

"Oh, I remember that. So are you planning on comparing the data from before and after storing the spell?"

"Yes! And since the spell is no longer in your body, I would like to perform another diagnostic on you, if that is alright. I'd like to see just what kind of changes this spell does to a person."

"That makes sense. Um, I promise not to panic so hard this time."

Varia smiled at him. "You'll be okay."

Oliver didn't know if it was because he knew what to expect or if it was because he trusted Varia, but the analysis went much more smoothly this time. Varia showed him the resulting data.

"Huge difference in heart rate and blood pressure. Stress levels are the same as a normal human of your demographic."

"Well, I *do* have a lot more reasons to be calm this time around."

"This gives strength to the hypothesis that the purification spell intensifies emotions." Varia wrote down notes. "Now to see if this new spell does the same." They looked up at Oliver. "If you're not comfortable, I can try it and compare it to Salavite information."

"It's okay. I think I can handle it."

Oliver held the stone in his hands and activated the spell. He couldn't get over just how smooth the transformation was now. It felt so natural, so easy, and it only took a second to happen. Before, his transformations had felt like a pressure erupting from within, but now, it felt like putting on a sweater that had just come out of the dryer.

"How does it feel?" Varia asked.

"Really, really nice." Oliver opened and closed his claws. "Wow. Are all transformation spells supposed to feel like this?"

"Yes! Like putting on a new coat."

"Incredible."

Oliver continued the analysis with new confidence. He and Varia compared the resulting data together.

"Fantastic! Your Night Creature form is exactly the same as before we removed the spell! Oh, this is excellent news."

"So we were able to perfectly translate it?"

"Yes, and into a new spell at that!" Varia tapped their claws against the countertop. "I wonder if it is because of your spider powers. How did you get them, again?"

"Oh, um... it's private. I'm sorry, that's all I can say."

"Hm. Well, I have a theory that they may be the key to crafting new spells. A spider theme..."

Oliver sighed and removed the Night Creature spell. "I'm really sorry, but I honestly can't tell you more about my powers."

"Hm." Varia quickly hid their disappointment. "Well, any step forward is a big one in the world of science."

— — —

Just as Varia had predicted, Darcy had found Aggis at the underground lake. Aggis sat up straight and alert at the lakeshore.

"Good morning, Darcy," They chirped.

"Morn... mornin'." Darcy took off their transformation spell. "Sorry. Still figuring out how to talk as a Salavite."

"If you like, I can give you some tips on how to talk easier."

"That'd be appreciated, thank you."

Darcy put the spell back on. Aggis moved closer to them.

"Alright. First off, I imagine that you are already used to speaking as a spider creature, yes?"

Darcy nodded. Aggis said,

"Your spider form does not appear to have flexible lips, so you have to make certain sounds a different way than you would as a human. Am I wrong?"

Darcy realized that Aggis was indeed correct. From the second they awoke as an arachnomorph, they had been able to speak with the same competence that they had as a human. It had come so naturally for them despite being so different. So why was it hard for their Salavite form?

Aggis said, "Salavites are quite similar in that aspect. For example, we do not place our teeth against our lips to make 'F' or 'V' sounds; instead, we we open our mouths just enough for air to pass through. 'V' is soft air while 'F' is hard air. Does your spider mouth work a similar way?"

Darcy realized that it did; they had never considered that. Instead of comparing their Salavite mouth to their spider one, they had been comparing it to their human one. This didn't apply to the shape of the head and tongue, though. Darcy pointed at their open mouth to declare this.

Aggis said, "Yes, thanks to the shape of our mouth and jaw, certain sounds must be mimicked with our tongues rather than perfectly reproduced. To make 'R' sounds, we don't move our lips or mouth. Instead, we move the top of the tongue slightly backwards when speaking. The 'S' sound is similar. Instead of trying to place your tongue against your teeth, try placing it close to the roof of your mouth. To make the 'TH' sound, do the same thing, but let your tongue touch the roof."

Darcy did so. Making these sounds became much easier with these methods. Aggis continued,

"Alright, next are the hiss sounds. 'SH' is the soft hiss. It involves opening the mouth slightly and pushing the air through. Moving the tongue is not required. 'SCH' is the sharp hiss. It requires more force, but otherwise works the same way. And then there are the 'CH' and 'J' sounds. 'CH' and 'J' are the same for Salavites. 'CH/J' involves hissing while also touching the roof of the mouth with your tongue."

Aggis also explained other sounds, like how 'U' was created with the throat rather than the lips. 'M', 'B', and 'P' all involved closing the mouth, then opening it again to make the sound, each requiring different levels of air being pushed. 'L' was made by pressing the tongue against the roof of the mouth, then sliding the tongue backwards. Like 'CH' and 'J', 'S' and 'Z' were seen as the same sound.

Darcy memorized these instructions and practiced until they could work out a sentence without hesitation.

"Words. Many. Talking. Words."

"Yes, that sounds good."

"Aggis. Darcy. Oliver. Varia."

"Very good!"

"One big long sentence." Darcy giggled. "I'm doing it!"

"Yes! Nicely done!"

"Thank you so much."

"It is no problem at all. I am glad to help someone learn."

"Sorry to derail the lesson, though."

"Actually, language and history are quite intertwined with each other. Languages reflect the cultures around them and can shape future cultures."

"Really?"

Aggis nodded. "For Salavites, it brings us together. In the beginning, there were only eight Salavite clans, and each spoke a different language. When they united, they crafted a new language together. We still use that language today: Yanavite."

"Wow. How many clans are there now?"

"Four for each element. And we have eight elements, so that makes..."

"Oh, god, I'm terrible at math."

"The answer is thirty-two."

"Wow, that's a lot! How was each clan made?"

"Well, do you know how spells are made?"

"Um... I know that new spells *can* be made. They each have a certain color."

"Correct, and the same goes for Salavites. A spell for hydrokinesis will always be sapphire in color. Similarly, a Salavite who specializes in hydrokinesis will always take on the appearance of sapphire. The two are linked."

"So each clan is based on a different spell?"

"Precisely. When a Salavite changes which spell they specialize in, their appearance changes to reflect this. Transformation is baked into our very existence."

"So which clans were the first ones?"

"The ones based on the simplest spell for each element. For example, magma is an element in our culture, so magmakinesis is considered the simplest spell for that."

"What were the elements?"

"There are nine in total: one 'parent element' and eight 'child elements'. Earth is the 'parent element', something that every Salavite has. The eight 'child elements' are magma, water, poison, roots, metal, glass, light, and sky."

Darcy nodded. "Okay, so the first eight clans used magma spells and water spells and so on."

"Yes, exactly. Ruby Clan with magmakinesis. Sapphire Clan with hydrokinesis. White Clan with toxikinesis. Brown Clan with earth fertility. Platinum Clan with ferrokinesis. Tourmaline Clan with telepathy. Black Clan with photokinesis. Finally, Emerald Clan with aerokinesis."

"And you're Platinum Clan, right?"

"Yes, although my parent and grandparent used to be of Silicon Clan."

"Which spell does Silicon specialize in?"

"Silicon does magma transmutation. They can transform their bodies into magma."

"Woah! That's cool as hell!"

"Yes, but not always practical." Aggis chuckled. "My parent once told me about the time they got into a fight in the middle of a forest. They realized too late that the area was experiencing a drought. They became magma and..."

"Oh no."

"'Oh no' indeed. Thankfully, they knew a water spell and was able to stop the fire before it spread too far, but it was quite a wake-up call for them. The magma element may be powerful, but power can be dangerous."

"No kidding."

"But power can also breed creativity. Or rather, you can use creativity to create new kinds of power. That's what my grandparent and their partner specialized in."

Darcy leaned forward. "Oh yeah?"

"Yes!" Aggis smiled. "They were utterly fascinated by spiders."

"You mentioned that they designed the security system that you use."

"Yes, that is the one. I studied Silicon Clan's security back when Refugee Clan was being built. The system of attaching bells to weblines is one of the most advanced in all the clans."

"It sounds like each clan was in a different location or something."

"Correct. We had underground cities all across the American continent. But the largest city by far was our capital, Salanon."

Aggis put a hand over the earthen floor and it glowed a bronze hue. A scale model of a city rose from the ground. It had dozens of levels, with each level having over a hundred rooms and hallways. The hallways twisted, turned, and journeyed in every direction imaginable like a maze.

"At first, the clans fought among each other over who was 'the best'. Eventually, they realized how petty these rivalries were and began to see their differences as strengths instead of threats. When that occurred, they all joined together to build Salanon. And every time a new clan formed, they built an addition to the city."

"Oh, wow."

Darcy bowed close to the ground to see the scale model better.

"So there was a point where every Salavite lived here?"

"Many of them. From what my parent told me, some preferred lives away from the city. But... yes. For thousands of years, Salanon was the heart of our civilization."

Darcy was nearly too afraid to ask the next question.

"Did the Macbeths destroy it?"

Aggis's ears lowered. "No, but... it would be best if I showed you what they did."

Aggis led Darcy to the outskirts of Refugee Clan. They passed through an underground tunnel and arrived at a huge stone door.

"Oh," Said Darcy. "I saw a doorway like this before."

"Salanon has many entrances." Aggis ran their claws along the creases of the doors. "These doors can only be opened with an earth spell. Once upon a time, only a Salavite could enter."

"May I ask what happened?"

"The Macbeths. They got newstone from their mines. They threw the doors open and attacked with dispels. The clans were already weakened from miscommunication and infighting. And in the end, everyone was forced to retreat. The survivors fled to outposts and other cities. But, as the years passed, the Macbeths found those as well. One by one, they fell."

"I'm so sorry."

"The day I became a dragon warrior, I tried to take back the city. I thought I could serve as a one-person army. A hero, if you will. But the second I stepped foot in this place, I lost my magic and collapsed."

"A dispel?"

Aggis nodded. "The Macbeths had lined the walls and floors of the city with dispel stones. I had to drag myself out of their range before I could even begin to regain my strength."

Darcy hummed in thought. They took off their spell stone-changing back to spider- and activated vibration senses. They tapped a claw against the stone in their hand and memorized the kind of vibrations it gave off. They then gave Aggis their stone

"Hold this."

"Darcy, what are you doing?"

"I have an idea."

Darcy placed their hands against the earthen floor. They knocked and focused on the resulting vibrations. They detected pings similar to their stone: one of them was embedded only a few feet away, on the other side of the doors.

"Can you open the doors for me, Aggis?"

"Are you certain?"

"Yeah. I don't run on magic, remember?"

"If you insist. Step back."

Darcy moved out of the way. Aggis pointed a hand in the doors' direction. Bronze ribbons danced from their arm and blanketed the doors. The doors slid open with nary a sound.

"That was incredible," Said Darcy. "You're so cool!"

Aggis beamed in response. "Now hurry, before we potentially draw attention to ourselves."

"Right!"

Darcy immediately scurried to the ping they had detected. A stone the size of a tennis ball lay half-buried in the floor. It had a black hue with white speckles.

*A dispel stone.*

"Yes! Hey, Aggis, mind if I dig into the floor a little?"

"Er... just don't cause too much damage."

Darcy clawed at the earth around the stone. Once they could put their entire hands around it, they used a combo of sticky power and super strength. The stone leapt out of the ground, taking some dirt with it. Darcy quickly looked it over to make sure they didn't break or crack it.

*Still good. Perfect!*

Darcy glanced around at the area around them. They stood in an entryway similar to the one for Refugee Clan, but this one had a much wider hallway and much more elaborate column designs. Just as Aggis described, dispel stones had been embedded into the walls and floor, each a few feet away from each other. Darcy smirked to Aggis.

"I got another idea."

"Oh, dear."

Darcy placed their current stone into their drawstring bag. They went to the next stone in the floor, took it out, and bagged it. They continued this pattern until they had grabbed the wall-stones closest to the doors.

"Darcy, please hurry," Aggis said. "I have concerns."

"Right, sorry. Got caught up in the excitement."

"Before you come closer, can you check on the stones? Do they still glow? If they're still active..."

*That's right. I wouldn't want to accidentally weaken Aggis.*

Darcy pulled a stone back out. Its center glowed with white light.

"Yeah, it's still glowing."

"You need to clear the dispels, then. Do you know how to do that?"

"Uh... no."

"No worries, it is the same as clearing out regular spells. Do you know how to do that?

"Sorry, but no."

"Simply touch the stone and extend your will. Set the stone to rest."

"Like putting a kid to sleep?"

"Yes, like that!"

Darcy imagined that the stone was a child. They imagined tucking them in, kissing them goodnight, and turning off the bedroom light. The stone stopped glowing and lost its coloration.

"Well done," Said Aggis. "Now do the same with the others."

Darcy did so. Once all the stones had been cleared out, Darcy returned to Aggis's side. Aggis used terrakinesis to fill up the holes and shut the doors. The duo then checked Darcy's bag.

"Six stones!" Said Aggis. "This is fantastic news! Let us share this news with the council."

"Yeah!"

Aggis rambled on the way back.

"Oh, this is simply wonderful! Akio spoke to me about getting non-magical help. Now I understand the potential of this idea! Oh, if only there were more of you."

"Can I ask a question, though?" Said Darcy. "Why were these stones still on? From what I've seen, when a spell gets separated from their wielder, they just... turn off."

"You're correct, but dispels are unique in that aspect. If you turn one on, then it will stay on indefinitely, and aren't affected by other dispels. They can only be deactivated manually."

"Oh, I see."

"Also, here." Aggis returned Darcy their transformation spell. "For when you enter the clan proper."

"Oh yeah." Darcy shifted to Salavite form. "Sorry again for derailing the lesson."

"No apologies. We gained something quite valuable out of this."

"Can I keep learning from you, though? I wanna learn more about Salavites. Like, which clans were made after the first eight? Which ones are the newest ones? Were new spells discovered on accident or by organized efforts? How are dragon warriors made?"

Aggis smiled so brightly that it could be mistaken for the sun.

"I would be delighted to teach you more."

"Ohh, I can't wait!"

# Chapter 15

Since Akio had given Darcy their spell stone, they didn't have a transformation spell that they could reliably use. They would have to make sure not to draw any attention to themself—no fights, no arguments, no announcements. Should be simple enough.

A scout's role is to go to the surface and gather resources for the clan. This included food, tools, intel, and the recruitment of new clan members. Ever since Aggis's health declined, Akio began working as a scout. It had been years now and Akio could traverse the surface with ease.

Still, they couldn't help but worry. Libra may have given her word, but she could have easily created a loophole. She promised not to target Refugee Clan any more but Akio was no longer in the boundaries of Refugee Clan. If the Macbeths had ambushed them at this moment, Libra would still technically be keeping her word.

*Maybe I should have brought Darcy or Oliver along.*

Well, it was too late to turn back now—Akio had arrived at the address that Libra had given them. It was a warehouse that had been converted into a living space. Akio held their breath, knocked on the door, and readied themself for anything.

A pearlesque white dragon warrior with red eyes opened the door. They wore a mage robe with holes cut for their wings. Their ears shot upward upon seeing Akio.

"Another Salavite!"

"A member of the Pearl Clan! I never thought I'd see one!"

"Come inside."

Another Salavite- a gold one with a red face and silver eyes- sat on the couch in the main room. This one was not a dragon warrior, but still caught Akio's attention.

The pearl Salavite asked, "Would you like any tea before we talk?"

"No, thank you. I want to keep this brief." They quickly bowed their head. "Akio Ashlath, Cinnabar Clan."

The two other Salavites mimicked the gesture.

"Auvia Andronus, Pearl Clan."

"Adiren Adinen, Gold Clan."

Akio asked, "What in the world happened to your clans?"

Auvia answered, "Pearl Clan and Gold Clan were both scattered during the evacuation of Salanon. My family moved to an outpost with some members of Gold Clan. Adiren and I are cousins."

"Wow. Is the outpost in the city? Is it possible to reach them? Do they have more dragon warriors?"

Adiren said, "Sorry, but we don't know you enough to trust you with that information. We've only survived for this long because our families stayed hidden."

"But if we combined resources, we could help each other."

"I'm sorry, but I don't think you can help us at this point."

"Why not?"

"Our friend Lorenzo had been... under the weather. I asked Almond Industries for help. At first, they turned me down, but then the Night Creature appeared."

Auvia pulled an ID card from her robe. It was white with the beige Almond Industries logo in the corner. Adiren pulled out a matching card.

Auvia said, "I am officially on call in case the creature ever appears again. That is my role now."

Akio's ears fell at the sight of them.

"But the Night Creature isn't dangerous," They argued. "Heck, it may never even appear again!"

"Yes, but a spider creature was also spotted in the magic museum. They kidnapped a Salavite and attacked the police. Mister Harrell is certain that they are in league with each other."

"But that isn't right. I mean, yes, it's true that the spiders are helping us, but not in the way that you think! They would never truly hurt anyone."

Adiren crossed their arms. "How do you know this?"

"Because I met them. They're just trying to live their lives and help people. And we can help you, too. Where is your friend Lorenzo?"

Both Auvia and Adiren averted their gaze.

Auvia said, "They took him. He's in the Almond Industries headquarters now."

"Why?"

"It was one of their machines that made him this way. So, they're trying to use their machines to reverse it."

Akio studied the two's expressions. With Auvia and Adiren's level of hopelessness, Akio doubted that they could arouse them with a speech or a promise. So, they elected to simply be honest.

"Auvia, Adiren, I understand that you are hurting right now. You've had to make sacrifices and I feel for you. But if you could join Refugee Clan, it would be a huge help. We need more dragon warriors."

Adiren replied, "We're sorry, Akio, but we can't help you. We have a different loyalty now."

Auvia added, "Out of respect for our species, I won't tell Almond Industries about you, nor what you've said about the spiders. But please... do not come back here again."

Akio hid their disappointment with a smile. "Well, it was a pleasure meeting the two of you. I wish you good health."

"Same to you," Said Adiren. "Good luck out there."

Akio trudged back home.

*No wonder Libra was so willing to share this address; she knew that Auvia and Adiren were tied up with Almond Industries. At least those two are reasonably safe now—I doubt that the Macbeths would want to risk catching Mike Harrell's attention. Still... if only we could make more newstone.*

— — —

Akio found the halls of Refugee Clan strangely empty. No guards in the barracks, nobody strolling along, not even a child wandering around.

*Oh no. Did the Macbeths attack while I was gone?*

Akio rushed to the safe room. A Salavite of the Iron Clan stocked the shelves with emergency rations. They said,

"Hey, Akio. Welcome back."

"Where is everyone?!"

"In the council room. A big announcement was made. I just wanted to finish up this chore before I went over."

"So... so we weren't attacked?"

"Thank Envir, no. Aggis and one of the new guards returned from a trip. They have exciting news, apparently."

"Really?"

Akio didn't wait for them to respond. They ran to the council room as quickly as their feet could carry them.

The council room was as full as it had ever been. Everyone in Refugee Clan had joined to hear the news. Salavites sat elbow to elbow. Some flicked their tails with excitement, which bothered the people behind them. Hundreds of cone-shaped ears pointed at the ceiling as everybody paid attention. Akio couldn't even enter the room without stepping on someone.

The council itself sat in its usual circle, with Darcy next to Aggis. Aggis held everyone's attention.

"And so, that is how we acquired these spell stones. Theoretically, with Darcy and Oliver's help, we could gather enough newstone to make someone into a dragon warrior. With enough time and effort, we may even be able to remove every last dispel from Salanon."

The crowd cheered in response. Someone asked,

"Who will be the dragon warrior? Will it be a vote?"

"Yes, we shall vote on it."

Rivio said, "Let us not be too hasty. Yes, we *could* make another dragon warrior, but that doesn't necessarily mean that we *should*. I believe we should focus on carving these spell stones into multiple, smaller stones. That way, we will have more transformation spells for scouts to use. Hiding underground will only do so much, after all."

Grisio said, "If I may argue, how often do we truly need to go to the surface? We have our underground gardens and Akio's mystic box conjures any extra food that we need. What we are missing is newstone to supplement the food."

"What good will that do?"

"Rivio, our children need to develop magic. If newstone isn't a part of their diet, they will never gain that power. We will lose our way of life within a single generation."

Rivio argued, "We already did when the Macbeths stole everything."

Aggis said, "And that is why I believe that this newstone is best-suited for creating a dragon warrior. With them, we will be able to make more newstone to suit our other needs."

"We wouldn't *need* another dragon warrior if you were competent."

The crowd gasped in response.

Rivio recoiled. "Er, my apologies. It slipped out."

Darcy stood up. "Aggis is plenty competent! They're intelligent, wise, and just cool in general. Not to mention that I wouldn't have been able to get these stones without their help! And yeah, sure, they're up in their years, but that's no reason to disrespect someone! Hell, living that long deserves tons of respect! So there."

Akio was tempted to add to Darcy's point, but restrained themself. Once upon a time, they were that defensive of Aggis's honor, but that was years ago. Now, Akio couldn't think of anything to say that wasn't untrue.

Someone in the crowd asked, "If we use the newstone to create a dragon warrior, how long will the process take?"

Aggis answered, "If they are already physically powerful, then it will take no time at all."

A child raised their hand. "What if we made Darcy a dragon warrior?"

Darcy coughed. "'Xcuse me?!"

"Yeah, 'cuz you're strong!"

"Well, I'm super-flattered, but if I become a dragon warrior, won't I become magical like everybody else? Then I would be weak to dispels."

"Oh yeah..."

Aggis said, "Personally, I believe we should choose Akio. They have incredible strength just as Darcy does, with a good head on their shoulders as well."

Someone else said, "Oh, yes! Akio would be a wonderful choice!"

Another person said, "Wait, shouldn't it be Terio? They're the head of security, after all—they have more than enough strength."

The entire room filled with chatter as various people voiced their opinions, but Akio couldn't help but feel ashamed. They turned tail and left the council room.

In their bedroom, Akio rested their back against the wall. They slid into a sitting position with their knees close to their chest. Their ears drooped and brushed against their neck.

Someone knocked. "Hey, it's me Darcy. Can I come in?"

"Sure."

Darcy entered and sat down next to them. "I saw you leave the council room. What's up?"

"I feel awful."

"Why is that?"

"Well... Aggis has... they and I..."

Akio sighed. They hugged their knees.

"After I lost my clan, it was Aggis who found me. They brought me to Refugee Clan and raised me like I was their own child. They promised me that one day, they would train me as a dragon warrior. I was so excited."

"What happened?"

"It started hopeful, but Aggis was... they just... were old. Their body had slowed down. They slept more. They often got caught up in old memories. And they stopped being able to make newstone. So, my training ended before it could really get anywhere."

"But you can become a dragon warrior now."

"That isn't the problem." Akio looked them in the eyes. "Darcy, I resented Aggis for getting older. I hated seeing them deteriorate. There were some days where I avoided seeing them entirely. I just couldn't handle it. When Revival Patron approached me, I felt relieved. With spider powers, I could at least have *something* similar to being a dragon warrior. From then on, I stopped hoping the best for Aggis. I didn't care anymore. But Aggis never gave up on me. They still loved me no matter how distant I became."

Akio dug their face into their knees and sobbed.

"I'm a horrible person."

Darcy rubbed Akio's back. "Yeah, that kinda sucks. But I wouldn't say that it makes you *horrible*. You're just a person like everybody else."

"But I don't deserve to be a dragon warrior. They're supposed to be noble and loyal."

"Well, think of it this way: the most practical thing right now is to turn a strong Salavite into a dragon warrior so they can start making more newstone as soon as possible. Being a warlock means that you're already strong and you seem pretty popular. And if you talk with Aggis, I'm sure that they will understand your feelings about everything."

"Even if Aggis forgives me, how could I forgive myself?"

Darcy tapped a claw against their chin. "Well... it starts with behavior, right? Change yourself for the better. Try not to make the same mistakes. Do good by others." They shrugged. "And sure, you're not perfect, but is anybody? What good comes from setting impossibly-high standards for yourself?"

"I just don't know. I don't think I can face them again."

"And what would happen if you didn't? What would happen if you never looked at or spoke to Aggis ever again? Would it help Aggis feel better?"

"...No."

"Would calling yourself a horrible person make your relationship with Aggis any healthier?"

"No."

"So what would help right now?"

"...Talking to Aggis. But... maybe not today." Akio wiped away their tears. "I need time to think of what to say."

"That's valid. I'll tell Aggis that you need time to think it over."

"Thank you, Darcy."

# Chapter 16

Darcy spent the next morning with Oliver in Revi's pocket dimension. They had convinced him to help them grab some of the infinite blankets and pillows from their apartment. Darcy conversed as they went along.

"There's got to be a way to use that spider spell without magic."

Oliver said, "Didn't Revi say that the purification spell tapped into warlock abilities?"

"Yeah, something like that. And then you and Varia isolated that spell. And then you transferred it into newstone. And then it became a whole new spell." Darcy hummed with thought. "Maybe there's a way to copy the spell onto pizzazz? I'm gonna ask Aggis more about magic later today. I'll let you know if I figure something out."

"Can I come with you?"

"You wanna?"

"Yeah. Maybe if we put our heads together, we'll figure something out. Plus... I feel like I let down Varia yesterday. I wish I could tell them about pizzazz."

"Yeah, but unless the Patrons agree to make them a warlock, we can't tell them anything."

"Maybe we can ask one of them to give Varia the test?"

"Salavites eat bugs, don't they?"

"Yes, but we can tell Varia not to eat the spider. Although I guess that would interfere with the test results..." He sighed. "I don't know."

The duo left Darcy's apartment with arms full of blankets and pillows. Darcy bumped into someone in the hallway.

"Shit, sorry. Hard to see with all the stuff I'm carrying."

The other person replied, "Darcy?"

"Wait, Akio?"

Darcy leaned backwards so they could see. Akio also carried a number of pillows and blankets.

Darcy chuckled. "Guess we had the same idea that you did."

"Hey, the Refugee Clan could always use more, right?"

"Right."

The three exited together. Darcy said,

"Hey, so are you gonna accept being a dragon warrior today?"

Akio's face fell. "I don't know. I still haven't spoken with Aggis yet. And besides, when- or if- I do accept that role, it'll still take a few days to get ready for the ceremony."

"Well, sooner is better than later, right?"

"I suppose." They sighed. "I just wish I could have recruited that dragon warrior from the city, but she's been tasked with finding the Night Creature. What would Almond Industries even want from it at this point?"

A flash of anger crossed Oliver's face.

"I can't believe Harrel is manipulating people like this. And he's still doing it!"

Darcy said to him, "It's not your fault."

He replied in a spiteful tone, "Never said it was."

Akio asked, "Is everything alright, Oliver?"

"I'm just... frustrated. Sorry."

The trio passed through the portal and arrived back in Refugee Clan. Akio led them to the supply room. It had a long, rectangle shape that stretched backwards for at least a hundred yards, yet appeared empty.

Akio explained, "The storage units can only be opened with terrakinesis. I'll take the blankets and pillows off your hands—I know where everything goes."

"Thanks, Akio." Darcy then said to Oliver, "Ready to visit Aggis?"

Oliver had balled his hands into fists and his gaze stayed downward.

"Yeah," He answered.

"Will you be alright?"

"I'm fine. I just need to think."

"Just let me know if you want to talk about it."

"Yeah."

Darcy and Oliver met with Aggis at the underground lake once more. Aggis sat up straight and their tail rapidly swayed side to side.

"Good morning, Darcy! Oh, and you brought your friend!"

"Mornin', Aggis. How'd you sleep?"

"I slept quite well, actually. Yesterday's victory led to good rest, it seems."

"Hey, that's great to hear. I hope you don't mind having a second student today."

"Not at all! Welcome to the class, Oliver."

Oliver simply nodded. He and Darcy sat down facing Aggis.

Darcy asked, "So I was wondering if we could learn more about magic today. There's something I'm trying to figure out."

"Yes, of course! What would you like to learn?"

"How are new spells made?"

"Well, you typically start with an already-existing spell. Let us take water, for example."

Aggis stepped into a shallow portion of the lake, where the water only reached their knees. Sapphire-colored spheres formed in the water. Balls of water rose up from the surface and floated around in the air around Darcy and Oliver.

"This is hydrokinesis—water spells. Now, what are the different states that water can be in?"

"Liquid, solid, and gas. But you can only get those by making the water hotter or colder, right?"

"Yes, that is right. You can cool the water spell until..."

A white, pearly color covered the balls of water until they froze. They still floated in the air and Darcy tapped on one. It was pure ice all the way to the center.

"Oh, wow."

"And that is how cryokinesis was discovered—ice spells."

"And when some Salavites specialized in ice spells, they became a new clan?"

"Yes, precisely! Those who studied cryokinesis became the Pearl Clan. Of course, making a new spell is not always as simple as heating something up or cooling it down. Take magma and fire, for example. The two are often associated with each other, but they are not necessarily related, as magma is molten rock and fire is simply a reaction. Magma can cause fires, but fire does not become magma."

"So how did people figure out fire spells?"

"Give me a moment."

Aggis changed the balls of ice back into water and set them back into the lake. Aggis then stepped out of the water and led Darcy and Oliver to an open area on the shoreline. Aggis put a hand over the floor.

A ruby circle glowed in the ground. It changed into magma, and although Darcy sat a couple feet away, the heat that rose from it could be felt even from there. They were tempted to put their hands over it as if it were a campfire.

Aggis said, "Now, do you have anything flammable?"

Darcy dug through their drawstring bag for something they could use. They pulled out a small scrap of paper.

"This good?"

"That will work. Drop it into the magma. Be sure not to touch it."

Darcy followed their instruction. The paper scrap landed in the magma circle and set alight.

"And now..." Aggis guided the flame with their hand. It grew bigger, smaller, and even split in two. The second flame danced around Darcy.

Darcy couldn't stop smiling. "This is incredible! So... so fire spells were made when people understood how magma spells burnt things."

"Exactly. With pyrokinesis, the Red Clan learned how to conjure fire out of thin air."

With another spell, Aggis changed the magma back into regular earth.

"And sometimes," They said, "Connections are made out of complete accident. Take the element of roots, for example. Its first known spell was earth fertility, but all the spells following it weren't so literal."

"Really?"

"Yes. Oliver, would you like to try guessing what other element has non-literal spells?"

Oliver thought for a moment. "I don't know. I'm sorry."

"Are you alright? You have been quiet thus far."

"Sorry. I'm just... thinking. Can you tell me the answer?"

"Well... I suppose. The two elements that lean towards metaphor are roots and glass. The glass element's first spell is telepathy, seeing into the minds of others as if using a looking glass. Another spell of the glass element is the magic sphere, which can encase a spell or object as if holding it in a glass container."

"That's wild," Said Darcy.

Oliver said, "So Varia used spells of the glass element to help me."

"Yes."

Darcy scratched their head. "But Oliver, you didn't describe it like a sphere. I thought you said it was like a bunch of threads being balled up into... well, a sphere. Ah." Darcy chuckled. "Never mind."

Aggis continued, "The roots element is arguably the most difficult to create new spells from. Earth fertility is obvious- what with plant roots needing fertile soil- but purification is a bit trickier."

Oliver leaned forward. "Purification is the roots element?"

"Yes. It was discovered when a Salavite found that their source of water had been tainted. They purified it and realized that this technique could be used for anything. Soil, plants, a person's mind.... Although I should note that only dragon warriors are powerful enough to use this spell on the mind. The inner workings of the brain are much more complex than removing toxins from food, after all."

"So... dragon warriors can do powerful versions of spells?"

"Yes. To become a dragon warrior, a Salavite must train their body and consume much more newstone than usual. Then, when they are ready, a ceremony is held. In the Platinum Clan, we would have an elder dragon warrior give a word to them. Then we protect them while they transform. When they are finished, they have become as powerful as, well, dragons."

Darcy nodded along. "So becoming a dragon warrior gives you the strength to cast powerful spells."

"Yes. A regular member of the Red Clan can create and manipulate fire. Meanwhile, a dragon warrior of the Red Clan can do that as well as emitting a mighty laser. This laser can set fire to anything it touches and erupts in a blazing explosion. Or so I've heard."

"That sounds awesome!"

Aggis gave a nervous chuckle. "Forgive me, but I would not trust you with that level of fire."

"Fair enough. Okay, so if I wanted to create a new spell, there are a lot of different ways I could go about it."

"Essentially. What kind of spell are you thinking of?"

Darcy and Oliver looked at each other.

Oliver said, "Maybe we shouldn't..."

Darcy said, "I'm just thinkin' about how to make similar spells. How being spidery relates to magic and vice versa."

Aggis's ears twitched. "May I ask why?"

"Well..." Darcy looked out to the still lake. "Do you think the Macbeths will keep their word? Will they really stop their 'visits'?"

Aggis followed Darcy's gaze. "The optimistic answer would be yes. The pessimistic answer would be that they are merely biding their time. Making deals, forming plans, figuring out a way to deal with this complication. And when they do, they will likely send Scorpio."

"What's Scorpio like?"

"Imagine a tall, powerful human wearing armor made of dispel newstone."

Oliver's brow furrowed. "He wears dispels?"

Aggis nodded. "Nobody has been able to get close, and if a far-range spell were shot at him, it would fizzle out before even touching him."

Darcy said, "But that would mean he can't use any spells of his own, right? 'Cuz his armor would dispel them."

"That is correct, but a man like Scorpio does not need magic. He has so much physical strength that he dwarfs most humans. I once heard a rumor that he even wrestled a grizzly bear into submission."

They gulped. "How did he get that strong?"

"The Macbeths have never made an official statement. This implies that whatever they did, it was not something to brag about."

"Think he uses steroids?"

"No. They have too much pride for something so simple. I believe the Macbeths would do something much more unique."

"Like what?" Oliver asked.

Aggis stared into space for a good while. Eventually, however, they merely shook their head.

"Just more rumors. Simple speculation. Nothing concrete."

"Maybe he has superpowers."

"Perhaps. It is difficult to say."

Darcy shuddered in discomfort.

*I may have powers myself, but if I fought Socrpio... god, I would be so fucked. Being a little spider just wouldn't be enough.*

They said, "Aggis, when Varia placed Oliver's purification spell into newstone, it became a cherry-red spell."

"Really?"

Oliver added, "It became a spell for spider transformation."

"That is incredible! An all-new spell!" Aggis's ears fell. "Ah... but even if you used that, it would be powerless against the dispels."

Darcy said, "But what if there was a way to make my powers mimic these spells? What if I could make myself as big and strong as the Night Creature? I could fight Scorpio then, right?"

"I suppose." Aggis put a claw to their chin. "I must admit, all of this is starting to sound like something my grandparent would know."

"The one who was fascinated with spiders?"

"Yes. In fact, I have something of theirs that may be of use to you. Follow me."

As they walked, Aggis asked,

"Darcy, Oliver, have you two had an official tour of Refugee Clan yet?"

"We haven't! Do you wanna show us?"

"Yes, I can show you everything on the way to my room. Except for the nursery. For safety reasons, newcomers aren't allowed to know its location."

"That makes sense."

Aggis flicked a tail in the direction of the lake. "First off is the underground lake, which you already know of. The next level up is reserved for storage. The safe room and Varia's laboratory are also there."

"I saw one of the storage rooms. It's pretty cool how people use magic to store things there."

Aggis led Darcy up to the next level after that, which had a long hallway circling around multiple underground farms. Some Salavites tended to root-based plants like tubers and carrots. Others cared for the various mushrooms that grew in the earth. Spell stones the size of ping-pong balls had been placed into the ceiling and glowed like tiny suns. Darcy recognized one of the Salavites as Grisio, a council member. Grisio gave Aggis, Darcy, and Oliver a wave and the trio waved back.

Aggis said, "Akio's special box may have an unlimited source of food, but it is always good to have rations just in case."

"That's a good idea," Said Oliver. "I used to have a special box, too, but I lost it years ago."

The trio continued upward, to the social level. This contained multiple large rooms: a room dedicated to casual conversation, a room for social eating, another for social bathing, and finally the meeting room.

"So does that mean that there are private baths and eating places?"

"Of course. Different people have different social needs, and crowded rooms can get too loud for some people. I believe that Varia has a private bathing room next to their lab."

Darcy was also aware of the restrooms that existed at every level. They had used one a couple times—they had used a hole, then went to the opposite side of the restrooms to wash their hands. Pebble-sized spell stones had each formed a water bubble upon activation. Darcy had placed their hands into the bubble and washed as one does. While Darcy was curious on where the restroom holes went, they weren't desperate for an answer in this particular subject.

The next level had the bedrooms, including the guard barracks. The hallways of this level connected to a central room, but when Darcy entered, they found that it lacked the lighting that the rest of the clan had.

Aggis said, "This was the nap room. Spell stones would beam rays of sunlight onto large, flat rocks. People would rest here to rejuvenate themselves. But when I stopped being able to... be useful... we had to decide which stones were important and which ones were not."

"But if we grabbed more stones from Salanon, then people could use this room again."

"That would be nice, but we have higher priorities at the moment."

The two exited the room, but something scurried in the darkness. Darcy's ears pricked up and they turned to find the source.

"Hello?"

A giggle echoed from the darkness. Darcy stepped towards it.

"Don't bother trying to use a dispel."

The giggle grew louder. A small creature pounced onto Darcy's chest. Darcy fell backward. Oliver caught them before they hit the floor. Aggis plucked the creature and brought them to the light of the hallway.

A small Salavite, only three feet tall. Aggis easily held their torso with a single hand. This child's silver scales complemented their golden eyes, but the face itself was actually cornflower blue. This blue coloring decorated their throat as well. The child's silver ears wiggled with excitement.

"I got you!" They cheered. "I got Darcy!"

Darcy chuckled and got to their feet. "How do you know it's me? I could be any Salavite."

"Because I know that Darcy is learning from Aggis. And also you're the only one with that coat."

"Ah. Right."

Aggis spoke in a tone that was stern, but gentle. "Kibo, it is not polite to pounce on people."

"It's Kifo now."

"Well, Kifo, would you like it if somebody attacked you without warning?"

"Yes!"

Aggis rolled their eyes. "Still, please ask people before you playfight with them."

Kifo crossed their arms in silence.

"Kifo," Said Aggis, "Asking for permission is important. So is apologizing after doing something wrong."

"Ugh, fiiiiiiiiiine. Sorry that I pounced on you, Darcy."

"Apology accepted," Darcy replied.

Aggis set Kifo down.

Darcy asked, "So you said your name was Kifo?"

"Yeah! It was originally Kibo, but I wanted to sound tougher, so I changed one of the sounds!"

Aggis explained, "Salavite language uses a lot of building blocks and has special uses for certain sounds. 'V' sounds are positive, 'B' sounds are neutral, and 'F' sounds are negative. 'Kibo' is based on 'kib', the word for fortune and luck."

"I think I get it." Darcy knelt down to be Kifo's height. "So by changing from Kibo to Kifo, your name means 'bad luck' now."

"Yes!" Kifo nodded. "I'm gonna be bad luck for the Macbeths!"

Darcy smiled. "I believe in you."

"Can I help you fight them?"

"I'm sorry, but you can't." Upon Kifo's disappointment, Darcy added, "Because you'll be busy protecting the other kids."

"Really?"

Aggis caught on. "Indeed. The nursery needs a strong fighter to defend it, and you have proven yourself."

"Does that mean I can become a dragon warrior?"

"One day, when you're old enough."

"Okay!" Kifo sprinted off. "I'm gonna train real hard! You'll see!"

Once Kifo was out of earshot, Darcy squealed, "That was so cute! Gosh, I always forget what kids are like."

"They can be quite adorable... when they want to be."

"What do you think, Oliver?"

Oliver had stood off to the side in silence. He watched the direction where Kifo had run off to. He held a tight hand against his chest.

Darcy held Oliver's other hand. "Hey. You okay?"

"Huh?" He shook his head. "Sorry. Just thinking again."

"Will you be okay?"

"I... I don't know." He sighed. "I'm sorry. I'm just out of it. We can keep going. Sorry to hold you up."

The group continued on their way.

Darcy asked, "So Salavites can change their names just like that?"

"Well, yes and no. When a Salavite hatches, they are given a baby name until they come of age. Then they pick an adult name."

"Is there a difference in naming styles?"

"Baby names are typically small and simple, while adult names can be of any length. Both baby and adult names are based on words in Yanavite with an ending attached. For example, my name is based on *aggi*, which means 'unflinching' or 'immovable'. I then gave it the ending '*is*', combining them to make Aggis."

"That's so cool. I wonder what my name would be? In Yanavite, I mean."

"Well, what does 'Darcy' mean?"

Darcy thought for a moment. "I have no idea. I just kinda liked the sound of it. It felt like it fit me, y'know?"

"That is fine. Yanavite names can be based on appearance as well. Your name could be based on *ranle-* 'white', or *anan-* 'spider'. Then, we would choose an ending to make it unique. Or, if you are feeling particularly fanciful, you could name yourself Ranlenan, a combination of those words."

"Oh, so that name would mean 'white spider'?"

"Wellllllll, technically it would mean 'white of spider'. Yanavite grammar is picky when it comes to the order of description. The subject is always placed first and the adjectives are always placed second. So if you wanted to say, 'white spider', you wouldn't say *ranlenan*, you would say *ananranle*. It specifically means 'spider of white'."

"Ah, I think I get it. So if I wanted to say, 'metal of platinum'..."

"You would use *veralli* for metal and *theraven* for platinum."

"Oh gosh, those are big words. So 'metal of platinum' would be, uh... *verallitheraven*?"

"Yes, precisely!"

Oliver then blurted, "What does Roalen mean?"

Aggis thought for a moment. "*Roa* means 'ball' and 'orb' while *len* is short for *lenath*, 'emerald'. It is used to refer to objects that are both round and green."

"Oh. Interesting."

"Actually, sorry, I misremembered. *Roatham* is more common when referring to objects since *thamo* means 'green'. *Roalen* is strictly used as a baby name. It refers to people with green eyes."

"Green eyes?"

Aggis smiled. "Yes, it is quite common in the clans that have green eyes: Gray Clan and Red Clan. Your eyes would fit as well!"

Oliver's face went pale. "Oh..."

"Are you alright?"

"Sorry. I- never mind."

Darcy put a hand on his back. "Do you need to take a break?"

"Sorry. My thoughts are just running away from me. Um, Aggis, can you tell us more about Yanavite?"

Even Aggis seemed concerned, but they continued as requested. "Well, as a tip for combining words, you can connect a noun and an adjective freely, but if you want to combine two nouns, then you are expected to place an 'A' sound between them. So if you want to take *sal*, meaning 'center' and 'core', and combine it with *vite*, 'magic', then you would need to use the 'A' connector. Put them together and you get..."

"*Salavite*," Said Oliver. "'Core of magic'."

"Yes, well done!"

The trio entered Aggis's room. Darcy had expected it to be larger due to Aggis's size, but it was the same size as Akio's room. If Aggis touched their face against the far wall, then their tail would trail out into the hallway. Despite this, Aggis navigated the room with ease.

Their belongings were few and far-between. Darcy had noticed that Salavites made nests to sleep in, but Aggis had none. As if sensing their thought, Aggis said,

"I prefer not to take resources from storage. Someone else likely needs it more."

"We could always get more, though."

"It is fine. Really. I will survive without bedding."

"If you say so."

Aggis used an earth spell on a far corner of the room. A shallow hole opened up and Aggis pulled an old book out of it.

The book had a leatherbound cover and pages made from thick, sturdy paper. The front cover had the name "Nionne Verifen" with a spider symbol above it. Aggis explained,

"This was my grandparent's journal. It had been passed down to my parent and then passed down to me. Unfortunately, it is written in code, but perhaps with our combined efforts, we can crack it."

Aggis opened the book for Darcy and Oliver to see. The ink letters appeared to have been written in modern English. Darcy read it aloud.

"The year is 1580. I had just made a fascinating and wonderful friend. We share many similarities! So many that our combined studies have resulted in a new technique of magic. I decided to record our creations and any future ones that we may stumble upon. But I must write it in code, as our studies delve into the hidden world of life, death, and revival."

Darcy thought, *Life, death, and revival... this person was fascinated with spiders... and they felt the need to hide this information....*

"Holy shit," Darcy whispered. They and Oliver looked at each other in combined surprise.

Aggis's ears pointed upward. "You can read it?"

Darcy answered, "Well, yeah... it's in English."

Aggis tilted their head to the side. "I know English. These symbols do not match it at all."

*Symbols? But- wait. Pizzazz doubles as a universal translator. That must be why it looks like English to Oliver and me!*

Oliver played with his fingers. "Um, Aggis, we have some good news and bad news."

"Oh?"

Darcy said, "Good news: we can decipher this code."

"Really? That is stupendous! How so?"

"That's the bad news," Said Oliver. "We... can't tell you how. And we can't tell you the contents of this journal, either."

"What? Can you please tell me why not?"

"The... gift that gave us our powers also require us to keep it a secret. We can't share anything with you. I'm so sorry."

"So... it must remain a mystery?"

Darcy and Oliver nodded.

Aggis's ears fell. "Oh."

Oliver returned the journal. "I'm really sorry."

"We should probably go," Said Darcy. "Meet you at the regular place tomorrow?"

"Yes, I will... be there."

"Sorry again."

Darcy and Oliver headed straight to the guard barracks, then used the crystal heart and teleported to Revi's pocket dimension. The moment they arrived, Darcy stomped their foot.

"Man! Can't tell Varia, can't tell Aggis, can't tell anyone! This would be so much easier if we could just... *grah*!" They kicked the grass.

"Yeah," Said Oliver. "But we need to remember that even if we went against the rules and told them, then if the Macbeths ever interrogated them or entered their minds..."

"I know, but still." They called, "Revival Patron!"

Revi appeared in front of the duo. "Hi! How're you doing?"

"Revi, can we *please* tell the Salavites about warlock stuff? It would make things so much easier."

"Haha! Nope!"

"What if we only told two of them?"

"I'm sorry, but no."

Oliver said, "Revi, I understand that the rules are important for Patrons, but if the Salavites had the full support of the warlocks, then the Macbeths would not be as much of a threat. And if we defeat the Macbeths together, then you would never have to worry about them capturing a warlock or Patron. This would benefit everyone."

Revi put their claws together. "Yeah, but it isn't just up to me. Trust me, I think it would be awesomesauce if we worked together, and I'm sure Death would be chill with it, too, but Life... oh, gosh, if they found out about this collusion, they would lose it."

Darcy said, "I don't understand. What does Life have against-"

Darcy then remembered their conversation with Revi after the former had become a warlock.

*Revi mentioned that Life had once been captured by a family that tried to use their power.*

"Oh... I think I get it. It was the Macbeths, wasn't it?"

Revi made a slow nod. "A hundred years ago, Life met Ophelia Macbeth. She agreed to become a warlock. She asked Life if she could tell the rest of her family and she assured them that her family would be... good."

"But they weren't."

Revi shook their head. "And ever since then, Life has been... hurt. Not physically, but..."

"Emotionally," Said Oliver. "I know how that feels."

"Mm-hm. So you can't tell the Salavites anything. I'm super sorry."

# Chapter 17

Oliver had returned to Refugee Clan, as he needed to talk to someone, but Darcy elected to stay in Revi's pocket dimension a little longer. They entered the bar of the Wraith Lodge, also hoping to have a conversation.

Perci worked as the bartender again. Dusk sat in the exact same place as before. Sky sat next to them and had been rattling off her thoughts.

<...And that's why I think the musical *Cats* is actually about criticizing the elitist behaviors of modern Christianity. It's no mistake that 'jellicle cat' sounds close to 'evangelical Christian'. Plus, everyone is obsessed with getting onto the balloon that symbolizes death, which mirrors the Christian obsession with getting into heaven! One of the characters is even named Mistoffelees, which sounds like Mephistopheles!>

Dusk stared at Sky in silence for a good, long minute.

<...Sky, what the fuck are you even talking about?>

<Do I need to explain what musicals are first?>

<Oh, uh...> Dusk pointed at Darcy. <Would you look at that, someone else I can have a conversation with. I suppose you and I need to stop talking now.> They turned to face Darcy. <Please tell me you need something.>

"Uh, am I interrupting anything?"

<Absolutely not.>

Sky said, <I need to go anyways.> She chirped to Darcy, <Nice seeing you again!>

"Actually, I'd like to ask both of you this question." Darcy took off their transformation spell. "A friend of mine has a journal written by a Salavite who used to be a warlock. I want to read more, but I don't understand magic that well yet, and to be honest, I don't want to leave my friend out of it, either. But they're not a warlock, y'know?

And Revi doesn't seem to wanna hire more Salavites." They sighed. "I guess I was just hoping you guys would have some wisdom I could use."

Dusk asked, <How old is this journal?>

"I think it was written in like... the fifteen-hundreds? I didn't look at the year for too long."

<Hm. Recent, then. Too recent for me to know.>

Sky said, <A Salavite who was a warlock? Did you catch their name?>

"Ni... Nionne... Verifen! Yeah, Nionne Verifen."

Sky's expression saddened. <Oh. I don't recognize it.>

"Did you know any Salavites from back then?"

<It's a little complicated. When I was alive, I was a Salavite warlock.>

Darcy gasped. "Really?"

Sky nodded. <I was a member of one of the clans with the sky element. I can't recall which. In Yanavite, I think my name was... Omviira, but I liked Sky more because of how it sounded.> She tapped a shadowy claw against her head as she thought. <I grew up in an outpost. It was underneath modern-day England. An empire was invading... Romans. Yes, the Roman Empire. After I became a warlock, I met someone who was rebelling against the empire. They were a spider like you.>

"An arachnomorph?"

<Yes! They were a bright, golden color that reminded me of the sun. I can't remember which one of us came up with the nickname, but they were called Sunny. I helped them fight against the empire. Never anything grand, but enough to help keep the local humans alive.>

"Why are you telling me this?"

<Because I think warlocks, Salavites, and arachnomorphs are all intertwined with each other. I think there is something deeper in

our relationship, something lost to time. And I think if you can find more information in that journal, you should do everything in your power to do just that.>

Darcy glanced away. "I don't know. It feels skeevy to use Aggis for information like that. Don't they deserve to know this stuff, too?"

<Well, unless you can think of a really good argument to say to Revi, I'm afraid that you'll have to keep secrets, even from your friend.>

Darcy looked down with a sigh. "I was afraid you'd say that."

<If I remember more information, I'll be sure to tell you.>

"Thank you. Any help is appreciated. Dusk, are you sure you don't have anything to add?"

<Not when it comes to magic and Salavites. Apologies.>

"Hm. Okay. Have a nice day you guys."

<Good luck.>

— — —

Oliver still retained some anger towards Mike Harrell, but subdued it for Varia's sake. After all, studying something made Varia so happy, and Oliver didn't want to taint that with his personal feelings. Varia may have helped him in the mindscape, but it still felt like overstepping boundaries if he asked them to help him again, even if certain questions ate away at him. He entered the laboratory with a smile.

"Hello, Varia."

"Hello, Oliver!"

Varia sat at a counter with a notebook and the spider transformation spell. They wrote something down as they spoke.

"You're just in time! I'm about to test this spell on myself."

"On yourself, are you sure?"

Varia giggled. "Whether I'm sure has nothing to do with it. It must be done! After all, it may be safe for human use, but is it also safe for Salavites? It's important to know these things."

"Is there a reason it would be dangerous?"

"Not entirely, but as a scientist, I must have recorded proof. I have already recorded my biological stats to use as the control. Next, I will use the spider transformation spell, which I've dubbed the Night Creature spell. Then, I will record the bio-stats of my Night Creature form and compare them against the control. I will then compare them to *your* Night Creature data. Would you like to be my assistant?"

"I'd love to." Oliver picked up a pencil and opened to a fresh page. "Let me know when you're ready."

"Fantastic!"

Varia put on their goggles, then placed the stone into their lab coat pocket. A cherry-red egg enclosed around them, and when it dissipated, they had shifted into a large, red, monstrous spider, nearly matching Oliver's in design. The spell had altered Varia's coat and goggles to suit multiple arms and eyes, respectively. Varia spun around with glee.

"Fantastic! Simply fantastic!"

"How do you feel? Are you in control?"

"Yes, very much so! It feels exactly the same as any other transformation spell."

"No animal instincts or anything?"

"None at all."

Oliver jotted down this information. "That's good. Even if we can't use this spell against the Macbeths, this is still kind of exciting."

"Yes, exactly! Knowledge for the sake of knowledge. Although I *could* do without the increased hunger."

"Really? The hunger is still there?"

"That would make sense, actually. After all, larger bodies require a larger calorie input. Salavites eat more than humans and dragon warriors eat more than Salavites."

Oliver furrowed his brow. "But food isn't... it's not..."

Varia ruffled Oliver's hair. "Food is energy, Oliver. That's all there is to it. Without food, we'll shrivel up and die."

"Yeah, I guess so." Oliver smiled. "I'll keep that in mind."

Varia smiled back at him. "Now, I need you to take a sample of my blood. The needle is in that drawer there."

"Okay. I'll try."

"Just make sure to place the needle into one of the joints. My body is the softest there."

"But won't that hurt you?"

"With a body this size, a little pinprick won't do much. After all, we took a sample of your blood when you were in Night Creature form."

"Yeah, but it's okay when I'm getting hurt. I know what I can handle."

Varia tilted their head to the side. "And I don't?"

"I-" He blinked. "Ah. Sorry. I should trust your abilities more."

"It's alright. Now, once you've taken my blood sample, I'll need you to inject the blood into a test tube, then place it into that machine against the wall. My claws are too big for those actions right now."

"Understood."

Oliver still worried about harming Varia, so he put all his focus into the task at hand. After he placed the blood sample into the machine, he asked,

"So did you design all of these machines yourself?"

"Yes! I spent a good portion of my life studying technology, how to combine it with magic, and how the two influence biology. I suppose you could call my field of science 'bio-magitech'. All of the machines here are powered by batteries that I charge with lightning spells. Some of them are designed with newstone in mind, but alas... until we get more, that tech is useless, and some never worked at all. Such is the way of science."

"Seems like you know a lot of different spells."

"Oh, yes! Learning a wide range of spells was important for my work. I wish I could go to the surface to collect materials myself, but I lack a transformation spell. Akio has been a huge help in that endeavor, but I still wish I could journey upward myself."

"Is it possible to use a transformation spell without a newstone?"

"Unfortunately, that is not viable."

"Why not?"

"It's... a tricky thing. Us Salavites have magic in our bodies, which is why we can use spells without stones. But non-Salavite creatures don't have magic naturally. So in a theoretical situation, if a Salavite *did* use transformation without a stone, they wouldn't be able to change back. They'd be stuck in whatever form they've taken. It's just not viable."

Varia put a hand against a machine in the corner. It was one of the larger ones and had two mechanical prongs jutting out.

"I invented this one to induce transformation into others. If you placed a transformation stone into its inner chamber and then pointed the prongs at someone, it would change that person permanently. I named it the Gene Cleaver."

Oliver gulped. "Did you ever use it?"

Varia stood in silence, their back to Oliver.

"...Sometimes, I would consider using this machine on myself. I would fantasize about stealing a transformation spell from one of the scouts, making myself human, and going to the surface to start a whole new life there. I could raise a family then."

"But what about Roalen?"

Varia removed the stone from their pocket and looked at it in their hand. As the Night Creature, the stone easily fit in their palm.

Varia removed the stone and shifted back to Salavite form, but didn't move for a good while. They then turned to look at Oliver.

Oliver stepped towards them. "Varia? Are you okay?"

Varia looked back to the spell stone, then to the Gene Cleaver.

"...I don't know."

Grisio knocked on the door and entered the lab. "Hello, Varia."

"Ah! Hello, Grisio. Is there an occasion?"

"We ran the calculations, and we will need more newstone before we can turn someone into a dragon warrior. Oliver, we would like for you to venture to Salanon and retrieve more stones."

"I can do that. Um, but I'll need someone to lead my way."

"I will," Said Varia.

Grisio nodded. "Inform us upon your return."

Once Grisio left, Varia placed the stone back into their pocket and changed back into a Night Creature. They marched out of the room.

"Let's go."

"Wait, you're taking the stone with you? But Salanon has dispels."

"I'll stay out of their range." They spoke with a new intensity in their voice. "There's something I have to show you. I'm strong enough now."

— — —

Varia led Oliver out of Refugee Clan and into the tunnels of Old Newstone. They arrived at an entrance with two enormous doors steeped in rubble. A tunnel in the right wall had collapsed, seemingly the source of the rubble. Varia stepped towards the tunnel entrance.

Oliver commented, "This looks like the place Darcy described when they went to Salanon with Aggis. They didn't mention the rubble, though."

"This is a different entrance to the city. It's the entrance to Red Clan. Oliver, can you tell me what powers the Night Creature has?"

"Huh? Um... all the same as my regular spider powers, but stronger, I guess. Strength, stickiness, vibration senses, agility... actually, I don't know if that specific form is more agile..."

Varia placed a hand against the wall. "Hm. I don't understand the information I'm feeling. Can you help me?"

"Sure. What are you looking for?"

"I need to know how sound this tunnel is. If my guess is correct, only the entrance caved in. The rest of the tunnel should be safe to go through."

"Let me check." Oliver knocked on the wall and focused on the vibrations. "You're right, the rest of the tunnel is still standing." He squinted as if that would help. "There is also... some sort of... metal? Deep into the tunnel is lots of metal, like the hole place is made of it." He knocked again. "Yeah, I'm sure of it."

"Good. Now stand back."

Oliver stepped back and Varia shifted to Salavite form. They placed both hands against the rubble and made it glow with a bronze light. The earth shifted itself back into place, reversing the collapse and recreating the entrance to both the city and the tunnel.

"Nice work," Said Oliver. "Now it'll be easier to gather up the stones."

While Oliver did so, Varia stared into the right tunnel's shadowy depths. Its metallic intestines echoed with oblivion.

"Never wanted to return to this place unless I truly had to."

"What do you mean?" Oliver asked. "What's down there?"

Varia shifted into the Night Creature. "I'll show you."

The further down the tunnel they went, the more metal the tunnel had. The two of them stopped at sliding doors made of steel. A keypad had been attached to the left of the doors, but it didn't respond to Oliver's touch.

"I think these doors are dead," He said.

"That's no problem," Varia replied. "I have strength now."

Varia placed all six arms along the seam of the doors. They grunted from the exertion, but managed to open the doors enough for them and Oliver to step through.

"Be careful," They warned him. "What you'll see in this place will be... not the best."

Oliver gulped and entered.

Dim lights flickered in the ceiling, showing glimpses of the metallic room. Counters held devices and samples, all broken beyond repair. Larger equipment lay strewn about in a similar state. Oliver didn't know about the sciences to identify the machinery, but their style matched the ones in Varia's lab.

A doorway led to an adjoining room, this one with an operating table in the center. A counter held surgery equipment and a framed photograph that had fallen over. Oliver couldn't tell if the stains on the operating table were from blood or dirt. He looked to the back of the room and found another doorway.

Glass containers lined the walls of this room, all of them broken and empty. A single, large container went all the way up to the ceiling. Many tubes connected to this cylinder-shaped container, but Oliver's attention was on the interior. Shards of glass lay at the bottom of the container.

"Something broke into this," He whispered.

He found Varia in the room with him. They stared at the container, their goggles hiding their expression. Oliver quietly asked them,

"Varia... why did you bring us here?"

"Because... I used to work here." They looked to another door. "There were more rooms, more parts of this lab, but I spent most of my time in these three. I loved working here."

"What made you stop?"

Varia held back a sob. "Roalen. I lost Roalen. I- I made them stay at home because I thought they were safer there. I would spend the morning with Roalen, then go to the lab, then come back to feed them supper. I was worried that if my lab partners saw them, they would be in danger."

The sob transformed into a growl. Varia's claws clenched and they bared their fangs.

"The Macbeths. The Macbeths took Roalen from me! They attacked and I wasn't... I wasn't..." They screamed, "**I wasn't there!**"

Varia smashed their fists against the metal flooring. They stayed there in silence.

Oliver went to Varia's side and put a hand on their back.

"I'm sorry," He said. "I can't pretend to know what that feels like. Thank you for trusting me with this."

Varia took off their goggles and sat cross-legged on the floor. They wiped away tears, but new ones kept forming.

"I spent so much time trying to undo my mistake. I was willing to do *anything* to bring Roalen back. But it didn't work." They covered their face with their claws. "Not even combining magic and science can bring back the dead. Revival is impossible."

Oliver cried out of empathy. He hugged one of Varia's arms.

"I'm so sorry. I am so, so sorry."

Varia looked at him. "Why are you apologizing?"

"Because I want you to know that I'm here for you."

Varia hugged Oliver and wept. Oliver hugged back and rested his head against their chest. Varia stroked his hair with a claw. Eventually, their emotions neutralized and Varia gave out a heavy exhale.

"Thank you."

"Mm-hm. I'm glad I can help."

Varia shakily stood up. "I think I'm ready to leave now; I'm emotionally-exhausted. I'll be at the entrance."

"Okay. I'll be right with you."

When Oliver entered through the room with the operating table, he went to the counter to look at the photograph.

The photo depicted two women standing next to each other, both wearing lab coats and gloves. The woman on the left wore a bird mask that completely covered her head. The woman on the right had auburn-red hair with bangs and a small ponytail, and she held an infant baby in her arms. Her green eyes matched Varia's own. Writing at the back of the photo said, "New life! December 8, 1996."

Oliver's blood ran cold. He hid the photo into his hoodie pocket and returned to Varia.

*Darcy needs to hear about this.*

# Chapter 18

Darcy had been busy. In their frustration from not being allowed to share information with Aggis or Varia, they had left Refugee Clan and to another entrance to Salanon. They pulled out the newstone there and removed the dispels from the stones. They ran into Oliver and Varia on their way back.

"Darcy?" Oliver blinked. "What are you doing out here? And... where did you get that newstone?"

"Uh, hey! I'm gonna be useful by giving these to the council!"

"Darcy, *we* were asked to get more newstone. While I'm glad to see you, doesn't this mean that you left the clan unguarded?"

Darcy gave a nervous laugh. "...Oh no."

The trio found Grisio, Terio, and Akio conversing in the council room. Darcy stepped forward, but Varia put a hand on their shoulder, stopping them, and motioning for them to listen first.

"I'm sorry," Said Akio, "But I just don't feel like I deserve it."

Grisio replied, "We understand. We'll find another someone else for this role."

"What about Terio? The people support them as well, and they would make a perfect dragon warrior."

Terio hummed in thought. "Well, I wouldn't refuse such an offer, but I'm confused. You're young and full of life, Akio; why wouldn't you want to become a warrior?"

"I just don't feel worthy. I still want to contribute to the clan, but if I became a warrior now, I would never shake the guilt."

Grisio said, "If Terio is becoming one, then I have another idea in store for you, Akio."

"Really?"

They nodded. "The Macbeths are an ever-present threat. Their attacks had taken our homes, our families, and our resources. The fear of more loss has been the primary reason why the surviving clans have limited contact with us. But our guards' victory against Libra could be just the push we need to reestablish a relationship with the others."

Terio's ears perked. They turned their head in the direction of the trio.

"Speaking of the guards, here they are now."

Darcy gave them a wave. "Uh, hi. Sorry to listen in."

"No apologies. Is there something you need?"

Darcy gave Grisio the newstone. "Here. I know that being near Salanon is dangerous, but I really wanted to help."

Terio furrowed their brow. "You left your post without informing someone?"

"I didn't know that Oliver was already asked to-"

"Even if he wasn't, you cannot just leave the clan borders without speaking to one of us first."

Darcy looked to the floor. "I'm sorry."

Grisio asked, "Oliver, how many stones were you able to gather?"

"About five."

He and Varia set the stones down at the center of the council circle.

"Very good. You two may leave if you wish. As for Darcy..."

Terio rubbed their forehead with a sigh. "Luckily for Darcy, nothing went wrong in the time they were gone. But!" They looked Darcy in the eyes. "I feel the need to remind you that as a guard, protecting the clan should be your top priority. Do whatever you like when not in battle, but you cannot simply leave on rogue missions."

Darcy nodded. "I'm sorry. I'll keep the clan's safety in mind from now on, I promise."

"Good." Terio said to Grisio, "Inform Rivio and Aggis that I will undergo the dragon warrior ceremony. In the meantime, Akio will deliver a message to the Trio Clan. Akio, tell them about the guards and the resources we're gaining. See if you can schedule a meeting between that clan and ours."

Akio saluted in excitement. "Yes, sir! I won't let you down. I'll leave as soon as I'm able."

"Good. By the time you return, the ceremony should be ready. Does anybody object to these plans?"

Grisio shook their head. "No objections from me. I will inform you if Rivio or Aggis have anything to say against it."

Terio nodded to them.

Darcy said to Grisio, "Hey, can I come along with you? I want to talk to Aggis about something."

"My steps are your steps, Darcy. Follow away."

Darcy looked down at themself and realized that they weren't wearing the said transformation spell. They pulled out their stone and found that it had been dispelled while they were collecting newstone earlier.

"Wait, hang on," They said. "Varia, can you recharge my stone again?"

"Gladly." The stone became red once more.

"Thank you. Hey, Oliver, wanna come with me and Grisio?"

Oliver pursed his lips. "Um... actually, I need to think about something first. I'll meet you in the guard barracks."

"Sounds good."

Grisio dropped off the newstone in the storage room, then stopped by Rivio in the infirmary. Darcy stayed at the entrance as the two spoke.

Rivio said, "If we have leftover newstone after the ceremony, I believe we should use a couple as transformation spells."

"Yes, it would be nice for our guards to fit in easier, especially if they feel the need to linger in doorways."

Darcy gingerly entered the room. "Sorry."

"Apologies are accepted as long as you do your part."

"Yeah." An awkward pause. "Uh, so... how many patients do you usually see?"

"Not many, thankfully. Most days, the only visitors are people with minor injuries or illnesses. I have a scout going to the surface for supplies, but the wand has been a huge help."

"Akio isn't the only scout?"

"Far from it! But since you're still new to the clan, you're not permitted to know their identities nor the routes they take."

"Ah, yeah... understandable."

Next, Darcy and Grisio visited Aggis in the latter's bedroom. Grisio knocked on the doorway.

"Is now a bad time?"

Aggis raised their head and opened their eyes. "Hm? Is it tomorrow already?"

"It's nearing evening. May we speak with you over council matters?"

"Certainly."

Grisio updated Aggis on all the decisions thus far. Aggis tilted their head to the side.

"I am confused. Why would Akio turn down the opportunity to become a dragon warrior?"

"In their words, they don't feel worthy of it."

"But they would make a wonderful warrior."

"It is their decision alone to make. A Salavite must be prepared both in mind and body."

"...Yes." Aggis let out a sigh. "Well, as a member of the council, I approve of these choices. If Akio does not stop by before they leave, please tell them that I wish them good luck."

"I will."

Once Grisio had left, Darcy sat down in front of Aggis.

"Sorry," They said.

"What are you apologizing for?"

"There is... so much I can't say. It's unfair. I wish I could just crack open the truth and be fully honest with you on what I know." They looked towards the ceiling. "But the truth isn't mine to give."

Aggis formed a wistful smile. "You sound just like my grandparent."

Aggis stood up and removed the journal from the floor. They held it in front of Darcy.

"Here. Take it."

Darcy hesitated. "But... you want to learn this stuff too. I won't be able to share these secrets."

"If that is the way it must be, then I must live with that. If this journal has knowledge that can help you defend our clan, then that is what is important. *That* is what matters."

Darcy held the journal close to their chest. They bowed to Aggis.

"Thank you so much for trusting me with this." Their voice wobbled. "I promise not to let you down."

Aggis smiled and stroked their head. "I believe in you."

Darcy gave them a salute before leaving. As they stepped away, they wiped stray tears from their eyes.

— — —

By the time Darcy made it to the guard barracks, their emotions had settled back down. They carefully set the journal next to their bed.

"Aggis let you have it?" Oliver asked.

"Yeah. To help the clan." They took off their transformation spell. "What did you wanna talk about?"

"Um... well..." Oliver pulled a photo out of his hoodie pocket. "I found something that, um... I-I think it's my birthday."

Oliver showed Darcy the photo and date on the back. Darcy peered at this information.

"'New life', huh? And that's your month and birthyear... but I thought your birthday was on the twenty-seventh?"

"That was the day I was found. But I was told that I was about two weeks old at that point. So I would have been born on the eighth, or at least around that time."

"So you think the red-haired woman in the picture is your mom?"

"I... I think so. She *does* resemble me."

"Do you think she's still alive?"

"I want to hope so." Oliver gazed at the photo. "But there was another thing I learned... Varia worked in that lab."

"What?"

"The style of equipment is exactly the same as the machines Varia built. And they spoke about trying to use a mix of science and magic to bring Roalen back."

"*What*?"

"Yeah, but I don't think they... I don't think they succeeded." His expression saddened. "You can't bring back the dead."

"I see." Darcy thought for a moment. "Wait. Hang on. Does that mean Varia could be your birth parent?"

"Or they worked with my mother. Either way, I think Varia knows about my past."

"Have you asked them directly?"

Oliver rubbed his arm. "No. I haven't figured out how I want to go about it. Plus, I'm just... scared."

"Why are you scared?"

"What if my mother wasn't a good person? What if she's dead and I never get to meet her? And what if... what if she's like Harrell?"

Darcy held his hand. "If she's anything like him, then I'll beat some sense into her. Then we'll get you a new mom."

Oliver smiled. "Darcy, you can't just pick up moms at a store."

"No, but families are chosen. Like, sure, you might be blood-related to someone, but you still need to *choose* to foster that relationship. Even if you're someone's parent, you still need to be worthy of being considered family. If my mom didn't put in the work of raising and caring for me, then she wouldn't be my mom."

"I... I guess so."

Sensing that he was still uncertain, Darcy put more of their hands around Oliver's own. They looked him in the eyes.

"Listen. If we do find your mom, you two won't have a relationship immediately. I just want you to be prepared for that. Developing a familial bond will take time, and it'll take work. If you two don't connect right away, don't be too hard on yourself. Okay?"

Oliver nodded. "Okay." He hugged them. "Thank you, Darcy. I'm glad I can talk about this with you."

"Yeah. I'm glad I'm able to help."

# Chapter 19

The next morning, Darcy and Oliver wished Akio farewell as the latter passed through the guard barracks.

"Stay safe out there," Said Darcy.

"Good luck," Said Oliver.

Akio smiled. "Thanks. I'll tell Pyrus you two said hello. Darcy, do you want me to...?"

"Thanks, but I'm an adult—I'll handle it myself. Thanks, though."

Oliver asked, "Are you sure you don't want to say goodbye to Aggis in person?"

Akio clutched their duffle bag. "I don't know... they're probably disappointed that I turned down the offer to become a dragon warrior."

Darcy said, "You're being too hard on yourself. If there's anything I learned about Aggis, it's that they're understanding."

Akio's ears fell as they looked down. "Then I suppose the shame is self-inflicted. Either way, I should get going. I'll see you guys in a few days."

"Okay. Stay safe."

"Yeah."

Darcy and Oliver watched Akio leave. Once they were out of sight, Darcy sat down with Nionne's journal.

"Okay, let's crack this bad boy open."

Oliver sat down next to them as Darcy read the journal aloud.

"For my entire life up to this point, I have lived peacefully and without experiencing any events of note. The object of my excitement was preparing to become a dragon warrior, but that was hardly a surprise for anyone. After all, Silicon Clan already had ten dragon warriors—my addition was superfluous. And yet, I was so curious towards its power that I could not help but put in the work and build up my strength.

"But today... today, something else occurred. I had been a dragon warrior for only a fortnight. I was patrolling the halls of Salanon, searching for something to relieve me of boredom. I then found a small spider hanging from a thread. In my fascination, I watched its descent. Just before it could reach the floor, a random Salavite happened to pass by. They noticed the spider with excitement and prepared to eat it. I admit, I was slightly selfish when I rescued the small arachnid. I had become emotionally attached in the short time I knew it. I plucked the spider from the stranger's grasp and returned to my bedroom.

"Then, this morning, a strange and magnificent creature appeared. It stood on two legs like humans and most Salavites, yet its body resembled an arachnid. It gazed upon my form with its eight green eyes and spoke to me with quiet grace. 'The spider was a test', they explained. I had passed the test and could now become part of a larger universe. I jumped at this call. This could be just what I need!

"Even though this journal is written in a code of my own design, I still cannot help but hide certain words. So, I shall call my new role *ananarkos*, my full role being *ananarkos laschi*."

Darcy tapped a claw against their cheek. "Hm. I wonder why those terms weren't translated?"

"Maybe it's because they are used in the context of culture, what a Salavite would call these things."

"Hm." Darcy continued to read the journal aloud. The next few entries were about Nionne's new life as a warlock. They were peaceful in nature, simply describing times when they helped people.

"...And now five years have passed. I can scarcely believe it. Although becoming an *ananarkos laschi* initially filled me with excitement, I once again find myself in the midst of boredom. The peace of Salanon is too much to bear. Tomorrow, I shall call upon my *Salarivochro* and request some excitement."

Darcy commented, "'*Sal*' means 'center'. Hm..."

Oliver said, "The context implies that that could be the term for the Patrons."

"Oh, I think you're right." Darcy continued reading,

"And excitement they brought! My *Salarivochro* told me that a sibling of theirs had an accident, as it were. They witnessed a human fall ill and apparently used their incredible powers to rescue them. As an unfortunate consequence, this human had been transformed into a spider-like creature."

Oliver gasped. "An arachnomorph!"

Darcy said, "A Salavite and an arachnomorph as friends..." They continued reading the entry,

"The word the Patrons have for spider-like beings does not have a direct translation in Yanavite, so I shall create one with similar meaning: *teranan*."

Oliver cooed. "That sounds so cute!"

"Yeah. I wish I knew the specific meaning. Heh, I guess that's all the more reason to study the language. Okay, so by the sound of it, this arachnomorph's name was Onofre. He got sick with influenza and his family didn't want to get infected, so they abandoned him. Revi saved him and turned him into an arachnomorph, then he chose to become a life warlock. Then Life introduced him to Nionne and the two became friends."

The next portion in particular caught Darcy's attention:

"Onofre and I have been working together for ten days continuously. Despite this, our energy is boundless and our imagination refuses to tire. I had crafted a spell stone to demonstrate how magic works. Onofre asked if charging spell stones was not limited to just Salavites. Curious, I asked his meaning. He reasoned that if a Salavite can charge a stone with transformation, then surely the same is true for a *teranan*. And so, I gave him a stone, and to my surprise, he charged it! The stone became a shade of red I had never seen before."

Oliver looked at Darcy. "A spider spell?"

Darcy continued reading the entry with excitement:

"I placed the stone against my body and transformed into a *teranan* myself. I could hardly believe it! This gave Onofre another idea. If magic can mimic the actions of *grisiarivochro*, then is the reverse also possible? Of course, we first had to think of a unique ability to theorize with. We looked back to magic and studied the methods of new spell creation."

Oliver said, "So they were on the same path that you were, Darcy! But these two were alive centuries ago; if they found anything, then it would be a part of Salavite history, wouldn't it?"

"Not necessarily. The existence of pizzazz is a secret, so if they discovered anything that required it, they wouldn't be able to share that information to the public." Darcy smiled. "Which means the answer could be just inside this journal!"

Just then, Terio entered the room with plates of food.

"Guards, I brought dinner."

Darcy stood up. "Holy crap, is it suppertime already?"

Oliver got up as well. "I guess time flies when you're with a good book. Thank you for the food, Terio."

Terio nodded and gave them their meals: baked potatoes with a side of carrots.

"Varia actually helped us cook tonight," Terio said.

"Really?" Oliver asked.

"Yes, I was surprised as well. But when mealtime rolled around, Varia volunteered with fire magic. They seemed energetic, happy even."

"Huh.... Well, um, thanks again for the meal."

"Yes, and thank you for your continued work."

As the duo ate, Darcy picked up a potato and bit into it as if it were an apple. They said,

"Oh, man. This is some good stuff."

Oliver frowned. "I heard that potatoes are starchy."

"That's not all bad."

"I know, I just..." He closed his eyes and shook his head. "Stop it, Oliver! Food is energy!"

He took a bite.

Darcy asked, "Do you like it?"

He swallowed and thought for a moment. "Could use some salt."

"Oh, good choice." Darcy conjured salt with their food box. "And I'll get some butter for myself. Hey, did you know that potatoes and dairy products have all the nutrients a person could ever need?"

"Are you sure? That sounds like an urban myth."

"Well, I believe it. Dairy is awesome and potatoes are awesome, so of course they're the best thing ever when combined! Smack some cheese onto the- ooo, Oliver, have you ever had twice-baked potatoes?"

"I can't say I have."

"Oh, man, they're so good! My family would make them every Thanksgiving. We would bake 'em, cut 'em in half, then bake 'em again, and ooo, the toppings! Butter, shredded cheese, diced onions, bacon bits! Oh, man, I'm droolin' just thinkin' about it!"

"Well, maybe someday we can make some together."

"I'd have to ask my mom for the recipe, but yeah!"

As the duo ate, Oliver's gaze drifted towards the hallway that led into Refugee Clan. He shifted in his seat.

"What is it?" Darcy asked.

"I'm curious about Varia."

"You wanna ask them about... the stuff you learned?"

"I don't wanna just leave you, though."

"It's okay, I'll still be here."

"Still, I think it would be best if we built up more trust with the council. If they see us consistently do what we're told, then we'll be granted more leniency in the future, when it will truly matter."

"Good point. You're smart!"

Oliver blushed. "Aww... I just... thank you. But at the end of the day, I think it's for the best that I don't confront Varia at the moment. I don't want to make any assumptions just yet."

"Yeah, but you won't learn anything without asking questions."

"...I know..."

After the meal, Darcy read more from Nionne's journal.

"Unfortunately, we may have discovered a dead-end in our studies. We attempted to translate a magma spell into Onofre's *grisiarivochro*, but it rejected the process. It appears that *grisiarivochro* has some sort of barrier protecting it from alteration. I shall ask my Patron what this could be.

"It is the next day and my *Salarivochro* brought bad news: *grisiarivochro* does indeed have a barrier. My *Salarivochro* explained that this barrier exists to prevent a process called corruption. This means that the *ananarkos* never have to fear losing control of their powers, but can never truly experiment with them, either. While we can translate our spider abilities into spells, I am afraid that the opposite may never come to pass. Not in a way that is safe."

Darcy set the book down with a frown. "Oh. Well, translating pizzazz powers into spells is still really cool..."

Oliver said, "Darcy, didn't you figure out how to isolate bits of your pizzazz?"

Darcy blinked. They looked over at their hat. Their jaw dropped.

"Holy... wait a minute! Holy shit, you're right!"

They grabbed their coat. "I place little pieces of my pizzazz into an object, then I can tap into its power to make it do a certain thing. With the help of a spell, I can make the power do **that specific thing** so I won't have to browse through an infinite list." They raised a claw. "But! I wanna test this with something before trying it with the Night Creature jazz."

Darcy pulled out their transformation stone. They held the stone in one hand and the coat in another. They placed a bit of pizzazz into the coat. Then, while still focusing on the pizzazz, they placed the stone against the coat. They squeezed their eyes shut.

"I... I think I feel it... maybe..."

They felt the pizzazz inside of the jacket and the information stored within the spell stone. They ordered the pizzazz to copy the data in the stone. An error appeared.

<ERROR: Unverified species detected. Only associated abilities will be copied over. Proceed?>

*Unverified species? Guess that means the Salavite transformation. But what does it mean by "associated abilities"? Well, only one way to find out!*

Darcy proceeded. They felt a shift of power in the coat, yet it appeared the same. Darcy readied the coat.

"Alright, Oliver, wish me luck!"

"Good luck!"

Darcy put it on. Their body changed in color, but not in shape nor size. They looked down and found that their setae had changed from white to red. Their chitin glowed like fire and their claws resembled red-hot metal. Darcy made a fiendish grin.

"Ohohohoho... now this I like!"

Oliver asked, "Darcy, you look incredible! How do you feel?"

"Hot."

"Like a fever?"

"No, like... like there's a fire in my body. I can feel it in my pizzazz."

Darcy faced a palm upward and activated their power. A small plume of fire appeared. Darcy's smile grew.

"YES!"

"Holy cow, that's amazing! You're like the spider version of a Red Clan Salavite!"

Darcy jumped up and down. "Yes! Yes! Fire! YES!"

In their excitement, their coat caught fire. Darcy jumped back.

"Ah! I thought it became fireproof!"

"Turn off the fire!" Oliver yelled.

Darcy waved their arms up and down. "I don't know how!"

"Then take off the coat!"

Darcy threw it off. They returned to normal, but the coat was still on fire. They tried to stamp it out.

"Ow! Ow! Hot hot hot!"

"I'll get Varia!"

After Oliver ran out, Darcy grabbed their hat and tried beating the flames. Unfortunately for them, this only caused the hat to catch fire as well.

"Nononono, SHIT!"

By the time Oliver returned with Varia, the hat became ashes, most of the coat had burned away, and smoke hugged the ceiling. With a wave of their hand, Varia made the fire die down until not even a spark remained. They picked up the coat and herded Darcy and Oliver into a hall with clean air.

"Darcy, what in the world did you do?"

Darcy answered sheepishly, "I... got excited. Sorry. But I figured out a new thing with my powers!"

They tried to put on the coat, but the sleeves fell off and all the seams had separated. Darcy may as well had been wearing strips of cloth. They didn't even feel the pizzazz in the coat anymore.

They sighed. "Never mind."

Oliver looked Darcy over. "Are you okay? Are you burnt?"

"No, I'm fine. Just a little singed."

Varia asked, "May I ask again: what in the world were you doing?"

Oliver explained, "We were hoping to try something that would allow us to become the Night Creature without magic. We tested it on something else first, and..."

Varia's ears stood upright. "You gave yourself fire powers? Fascinating!" They looked back towards the barracks. "Well... unfortunately, your living space will be unlivable until we can clear out its air, and that may take a while. Oliver, you stay here while I talk to the council. Darcy, I'm afraid you'll have to come with me to explain yourself."

Darcy gulped. "Well, before we do, can I check on the room? I wanna make sure I didn't burn anything else."

"Certainly."

Darcy hurried into the room and looked for the journal.

*Everything else is replaceable, but what about-?*

When their coat had caught fire, they had thrown it off and away from them. It landed a few feet away from the book, but the edges had gotten singed and smoke stained the cover. Darcy picked it up.

*Oh man... this was pristine when Aggis was taking care of it. Darcy, you idiot.*

— — —

It wasn't a surprise that the council members were nonplussed by the situation. Most of them had just gotten into bed, only to be woken up again by this call to meeting, Terio especially.

Darcy looked down. "Sorry, Terio."

"I'm not angry- just disappointed. I was hoping for something more responsible than this."

"But-but I created fire without magic. That could help us against the Macbeths."

Rivio argued, "But that power is meaningless if you can't control it! What would have happened if the fire spread? If the smoke choked out the entire clan?"

Aggis said, "Rivio, with all due respect, those events did not occur. I believe we must focus on what *did* happen rather than what *did not*."

"Very well. What *did* happen is that Darcy caused damage to the guard barracks, the only location dedicated to defense within the clan. What *did* happen was our only guards putting themselves in danger."

Grisio said, "I believe I am with Rivio for this one. Cleaning out the barracks will take time and resources away from preparing for the dragon warrior ceremony *and* our meeting with Trio Clan. We do not have time to deal with Darcy's... *issues*."

That one hurt. Darcy had experienced this kind of talk before, back when they were in school. Books would be too hard to read, so Darcy would kick their feet and be "distracting". Lectures would be too monotone to listen to, so Darcy would tap their fingers against the desk and be "disrespectful". The one time they *were* invested in a lesson, they jumped up and yelled about it so bombastically that they "disrupted the entire class".

"Sorry," Darcy said.

"Sorry isn't good enough," Said Rivio. "How are we going to fix this?"

"Maybe a purification spell could clean the air?"

"If we had one of those on hand, this wouldn't be a problem at all."

Varia stepped forward. "If I may, I believe I may have a solution that can work for all of us."

"Share it."

"If I understand Darcy correctly, they have found an evolution in their fantastical abilities, one that allows them to copy Salavite powers. All it takes is a charged spell stone and a single article of clothing." They asked Darcy, "Am I correct?"

Darcy said quietly, "Yeah, that's right."

"So, all we would need to do is charge a stone with a wind spell, then give it to Darcy. It would not be as ideal as using a purification spell, but having them clean up their own mess would result in a zero sum, correct?"

Terio said, "That would be true, but the question still stands: can Darcy control this power?"

Both Aggis and Varia said, "I will help them."

The two looked at each other in confusion.

Grisio said, "My apologies, Aggis, but you will be needed for the preparations of the ceremony."

"Ah..."

Darcy went up to Aggis. "Um, but here." They returned the journal to Aggis. "It's safer with you."

"Did you learn what you needed to?"

"I think so."

Terio said, "Then I suppose it's settled. Varia will oversee Darcy's cleaning of the guard barracks. If Darcy can prove that they can control this new power of theirs, then all past transgressions will be considered moot."

"Moot?" Rivio asked. "Are you certain?"

"I am uncertain as you are, but this ability would be useful when appealing to the other clans. Imagine telling them that we have someone who is not only immune to dispels, but can attack just like a Salavite."

Grisio nodded. "I see. Yes, that would give us a great deal of diplomatic leverage. Very well, I agree to this decision."

"As do I," Said Aggis. "Darcy is a good student. I know they will fulfill their potential."

Darcy nearly teared up. *Aww, Aggis...*

"Fine then," Said Rivio. "But Darcy will be responsible for any injuries that might occur during this training. I hope you know what you're doing, Varia."

Varia nodded. "We won't let you down, council members. We'll begin immediately."

— — —

Grisio sent a scout to the surface to charge a spell stone. Darcy waited in Varia's lab with Varia and Oliver until the scout returned.

Varia said, "So you've found a way to translate spells into your special power. That is outright incredible! So does that mean you can do the same for the Night Creature spell?"

"Hopefully," Darcy replied. "It would be really cool if I can. Being so big and strong..."

"Well, if you would like to, you can use the spell while we wait for the scout to return."

"Sure, but I'd need something to attach it to, first."

Varia thought for a moment, then clapped their hands. "Idea! Before they left, Akio lent me their cute little Gameboy again. The game inside was a sequel to the one I tried before. It's all about masks and the power they hold. We can carve a mask while we wait!"

Darcy shrugged. "Sure, we can do that. Maybe in the meantime, you can tell me how Salavite powers work."

"Ah, fantastic! Oliver, would you like to join us?"

"Of course."

Varia opened a drawer and pulled out a small plank of wood.

"You'll never know when you might need some good wood!"

"I... I suppose."

"Do you have a creature in mind?"

Darcy managed a laugh. "I suppose a spider!"

The trio placed the wood onto a counter. Darcy and Oliver worked together to cut out the shape of the mask while Varia handled the details. It mimicked the appearance of the Night Creature, with large chelicerae and tiny eyes. As they worked, Varia explained,

"Magic is a part of Salavites, so using spells feels natural for us, even moreso for the spells we specialize in. When I use fire magic, I can feel everything that I burn as if it's a part of me."

Oliver asked, "Does it hurt when someone takes out the fire?"

"No, no! It's simply like... a sixth sense. And when I put out a fire, it's like setting it to sleep."

Darcy said, "But I didn't 'feel' the fire I made. Though I guess I wasn't using the power for very long..."

"Then first, we'll have to get you connected to the element in question! Let's throw you into a pit of fire!"

Oliver squeaked. "What?!"

"Joking! Only joking. Let's get you settled on wind. The sooner we can get that smoke out of the barracks, the better."

"Connected to wind, huh?" Darcy hummed with thought. "Well, that'll definitely be safer than using fire."

"Precisely."

The scout- a Platinum Clan Salavite- stopped by with an emerald-green stone.

"Wow, that was fast," Said Varia. "Nicely done."

"I was lucky," They replied. "It was windy on the surface."

"Well, thank you!"

"*Kiv*. See you."

Varia showed the stone to Darcy. "First, let's get you used to using it as regular magic."

"Sounds good."

Varia placed the stone into one of Darcy's hands. They guided the arm so that it pointed against the wall.

"Focus on the air in the room. Think about your breathing. Air is a substance that fills every container that it's in. It's always around us, within us. For Earthlings, death is a vacuum."

"Okay... I think I got it."

"When you're ready, imagine pushing the air towards that wall."

Darcy took a deep breath and did just that. A slight breeze moved past them. Darcy exhaled.

"Uh... was that me, or...?"

"Well, we *are* underground. Wind isn't too common down here."

"So... so I did magic?" They asked more excitedly, "I did magic?"

"Yes! Now try to get used to that feeling you had. Try to recreate it."

Darcy did it again. They made another breeze, but it had slightly more pressure this time. With every attempt, Darcy's wind became a little stronger, more controlled. By the time morning came, Darcy could create a gust of wind with enough force to shove a paper cup off of the counter.

"Fantastic," Varia cheered. "Simply fantastic! This'll be enough to ventilate the guard barracks."

"Awesome." Darcy yawned. "Then we can..." They yawned again. "Oh man. I'm not built for all-nighters."

"Understandable. You can nap in my bed for an hour or two. I have some notes to take."

"Thanks. Oliver, what about you?"

Oliver had already fallen asleep. He sat in a chair and leaned against the counter, his head in his arms. Varia placed a blanket over him with a smile.

"Rest well, Oliver."

Despite how tired Darcy was, a question ate away at their mind.

"Varia... how do you feel about Oliver?"

"Oh, he's a wonderful and intelligent young man. And he's so compassionate and soft-spoken."

Varia's smile became bittersweet. They added quietly,

"I'd be proud of him... if I were his mother."

"And what would you do if you were?"

Varia glanced at Darcy in confusion. "What gave you this idea?"

"Nothing in particular. You just seem fond of him."

The smile completely vanished. "Being a hypothetical mother would be one thing, but being a literal mother would be another. If I were the one who left him on that doorstep... I'd never be worthy of his love." They looked away.

"Rest well, Darcy."

— — —

Darcy didn't sleep for long, but apparently it was long enough for Varia to carve another mask. This one resembled Darcy's face.

"I made this one for the wind spell. If I had paint, I would make it resemble the Emerald Clan. They specialize in aerokinesis."

"That looks amazing, Varia. Have you made masks before?"

"Oh no no. Trust me, a professionally-made mask would look much better than this. But may I ask something about your special power?"

"Depends on what the question is."

"So you gained fire powers by copying the Red Clan transformation spell. Why didn't you become a Salavite? And how in the world did you do this without magic?"

"I think I didn't become a Salavite because whatever made me this was was spider-themed. They can't make people into Salavites, humans, or Venutians. Just spiders. But it still copied whatever powers it could, even if the resulting powers weren't sourced in magic."

"Ah, I see. So it's like the reverse version of mimicry in nature: instead of looking like another creature without its powers, you can mimic the powers but not the appearance."

"Uh... sure?"

*What I can't tell them is that warlock pizzazz has so much history and iterations that I'm not surprised that elemental powers were a part of it at some point. Maybe back when warlocks and Salavites worked more closely together?*

*God, but by the sound of Nionne's journal, the two worlds were separated even centuries ago. Dusk made it sound like they stopped contact even thousands of years ago. Just how far back does this go?*

"Should we wake up Oliver?" Varia asked.

"...No. Leave him a note and let him rest."

Darcy decided to multitask by applying the pizzazz to the mask while on the way to the barracks. They then copied the spell to the mask.

"Alright, done. Once I put this on, I should gain wind powers."

"Fantastic!"

Darcy put on the mask and felt a rush of energy. Somehow, the mask stayed on their face even though it didn't have a string, and to Darcy's surprise, their body didn't change colors this time.

"Right. Last time, it was a transformation spell. This time, it's just a regular spell."

"You changed colors last time?"

"Yeah, it actually looked pretty cool. I was all red and glowy, like you."

"Ooo. Fascinating!"

Darcy and Varia lined up at the entrance to the guard barracks. The stench of smoke remained just as potent as the night before.

Varia clutched the wind stone in their hand. "Alright, you focus on pushing the wind out and I'll handle anything that comes this way."

"Sounds good."

Activating the wind felt just like it did while practicing. Darcy had to admit that having such control felt pretty good, even if their stance was incredibly basic. Their progress was slow, but steady, and after a couple hours or so, they had pushed it into the entryway, then further and further. The larger the hallway became, the thinner the smoke was.

After another hour, Darcy sat down with a cough.

"Are we good?"

"Well, it isn't perfect, but unless we find a purification spell, it's the best situation on-hand. Nicely-done, Darcy."

"Heh. Thanks. It was all you, though. You and Aggis are such good teachers."

"You're also a good student."

"I wouldn't say that." Darcy curled a knee close to their chin and hugged it. "I can't never seem to focus."

"You focused just fine when I was teaching you."

"Yeah, but when you and Aggis do it, it's so... I dunno. Easy? It didn't make me feel stupid at all."

"I don't believe that you're stupid." Varia sat down next to them. "Darcy, have you considered that your brain simply works differently?"

"*Tch*. Trust me, I have."

"That isn't what I mean. You went to schools on the surface, right? Public schools with desks and chalkboards and books?"

"Yeah?"

"And the information was given to you as a list? Something projected and memorized?"

"I guess so. I always sucked during the tests. And don't even get me started on the SATs. No matter how many times I read the questions, my brain just wouldn't tell me what they meant. Thankfully, it was all multiple-choice, so I just filled in random bubbles."

"Hm, I see."

Darcy quickly added, "But it's not like I *don't* like reading! Hell, Oliver and I spent the entire day reading that journal! That was nothing but words yet I absorbed that knowledge like nobody's business! I didn't get up or eat or use the bathroom or..." They paused. "Wait, that's not normal."

"'Normal' is subjective. What's important is what works for you. Darcy, I don't believe you're stupid or whatever your schools may have told you. I think you just need a proper outlet to learn things. You need the right structure to help your brain flourish."

Darcy looked at Varia, skeptical. "Ya really think so?"

"Of course I do."

Darcy managed a smile. "Well it would be nice... not feeling like an idiot."

"And we have the next few days to learn as much as we can."

— — —

And for the next few days, they did. While it was too dangerous for Darcy to practice anything fire-related, Varia helped them with other elements. Varia placed the spell stone against a metal tool to charge it with ferrokinesis.

"Wait," Said Darcy. "That was our wind spell. If we want to get another one, wouldn't we have to send another scout up to the surface?"

"We only needed to do that because the surface had wind. But because your mask can create wind, then re-charging the stone with that spell will be no trouble at all."

Oliver added, "Plus, all we'd have to do is touch the stone against the mask to copy its properties, like how we turned the Night Creature form into a spell."

"Oh yeah!" Darcy looked at the Night Creature mask on the counter. "I'd really like to try that form soon."

Varia said, "We will as soon as you have a couple more spells under your belt. We want the council to be impressed."

"But wouldn't they be impressed by a super-strong spider? Something that can go toe-to-toe against Scorpio?"

"The more bases we can cover, the better. But I promise, as soon as we have a handle on the basics for metal and water, we'll take on the Night Creature next."

Oliver asked, "Varia, why these elements in particular?"

"Well, to be honest, they're the safest ones. If a beginner lost control, then air would only make the room a little gustier. Metal wouldn't move at all, and water would simply make everything damp. I'm afraid I'm out of wood, so our masks will have to be paper plates from now on. Oliver, would you like to make the masks?"

"Sure thing. Um... Darcy, is there anything in particular you'd want me to put on them?"

"Do whatever you want, bud. Let your inner artist be free."

Oliver couldn't hide his glee. "Okay!"

Oliver made the masks while Darcy practiced with the stone. Varia had placed metal utensils on the floor and had Darcy use ferrokinesis to pick them up.

"Call the metal to you," Varia said.

Darcy could only move them slowly, and one at a time, but the joy they got from raising up a fork was unmistakable.

"I'm like a Jedi!"

Varia giggled. "Sure!"

"This is so cool. I wonder if I can use this to eat cereal hands-free."

"Let's not get too ahead of ourselves. Using a fork or spoon for its intended purpose takes a lot of balancing and micro-actions. Let's simply focus on calling objects to you."

"Fair enough. I think it would be cool to have this one be a transformation spell, though. When I put it into the mask, I mean. I wonder what colors I would become?"

"Well, the Platinum Clan specializes in ferrokinesis, so you would be white and red."

"Ooo. Wait, isn't Aggis a member of Platinum Clan? Can we visit them?"

"I don't see why not. Oliver, would you like to come along?"

Oliver, however, was deeply entrenched in his mask-making. He poked his tongue out as he cut up the eye holes.

"Oliver?"

"Huh?" He looked up. "Oh, um, I'm almost done with this one. Go on without me, I'll be here."

"Alright. We'll be back soon."

His attention already turned back to his work. "Okay, have fun."

Darcy smiled as they walked. "It's nice to see him happy."

Varia nodded. "Yes, his mental health seems to improve with every passing day. Already, the frightened spider that entered my lab feels like a distant memory."

The two walked in silence for a bit, then Varia asked, "How would he react if he met his biological mother?"

"I think he'd be excited. He really wants a familial relationship."

Varia's ears fell. "I doubt they could still be considered family. She was never there for his birthdays or holidays, victories or losses. She didn't patch up his injuries or hold him when he was scared."

"True. They'd have to work for it and catch up on all those things. But Oliver is going to be twenty-five this year. Do you think his mother would want him to go another twenty-five without her?"

"No!" Varia quickly lowered their volume. "I mean... no."

Darcy stood in place. Varia took a few steps before they realized that Darcy stopped; the former looked back to the latter.

Darcy said, "He was discovered on the twenty-seventh of December, but he was born two weeks before. He suspects on the eighth."

Varia's eyes widened in both realization and fear. They quickly turned away with a hand over their mouth. They couldn't stop shivering.

Darcy approached Varia and put a hand on Varia's arm.

"What happened?"

Varia didn't look them in the eyes. "I... there was a human scientist named Demeter Vermilio. She created new life that day. But the laboratory did not allow infants to be cared for on the premises. Too much cross-contamination, especially for newborns. So she ran away. The laboratory never discovered her true nature- she hid it because she was afraid of what they would say, how they would react."

Darcy said softly, "She used a transformation stone."

Varia shut their eyes. "But she lost it during the escape. So then she- or they- were a Salavite on the surface with a human infant. They couldn't join a homeless shelter because they only accepted humans and Venutians. A Salavite with a human child drew too much suspicion. But they had no ID, no way to secure a home or job. They didn't have anything."

Varia's shoulders shook.

"After two weeks, he fell ill. I couldn't treat it. I had to make a choice. I... I..."

Varia fell to their knees with a sob. Darcy knelt down next to them and rubbed their back.

"He hates me," Varia wept. "He hates me, I know it."

"He doesn't hate you. If you explain what happened, he'll understand."

Varia trembled. "I... I can't. I'm too scared. I'm too scared..."

"We don't have to. But I think the responsible thing would be to at least tell him the truth. He deserves to know."

Varia let out a heavy exhale. "...You're right. I'll tell him... after the dragon warrior ceremony. Once things have calmed down."

"Sounds good."

The two continued down to the underground lake. Lights had been set up along the walls, making the lake sparkle. Terio and Aggis conversed on the lakeside with a pile of newstone between them.

Aggis said, "And after you have consumed the newstone, I will guide you into that tunnel and protect your body during the metamorphosis. When you awaken and exit, the ceremony will be over. Afterwards, everybody shall move to the food hall to celebrate."

"I understand," Terio replied. "And thank you for overseeing this. This ceremony just wouldn't feel the same without the guidance of a senior dragon warrior."

Aggis nodded. "It is an honor."

Darcy stepped up to them with a wave. "Uh... hi."

Terio's ears immediately pointed backwards in irritation. "Please don't tell me you caused a cave-in or something."

"No, no! I've actually been getting pretty good! I just needed Aggis for something."

"Yes?" Aggis asked.

"Is it okay if I charge a spell stone with your, uh... Platinum Clan jazz?"

"Pardon?"

Varia stepped in. "They mean that they would like to create a transformation spell based on Platinum Clan."

"Oh! Yes, of course. Simply press the stone against one of my scales and charge it."

"Thank you."

Darcy did so and the stone became platinum-white.

"Thanks," Darcy chirped. "See you at the ceremony!"

Terio said, "Actually, while you're here, I'd like to give you your orders for that event."

"Hit me."

"Oliver will stay stationed at the guard barracks while you keep watch over the underground lake."

Darcy beamed. "I get to see the ceremony?"

"See it? Yes. Participate? No. All of your attention *must* be on security. No conversing or resting until the event is over. You are allowed to eat, but any distractions must be limited. Do you understand?"

"Yes, sir. But... why me? This seems like a big responsibility and you don't seem to, uh... think I'm trustworthy."

"Because guarding the clan entrance is more important and I know that Oliver will do his job."

Darcy glanced down. "Oh."

Varia said, "If I may, Darcy has already cleared out the barracks of smoke and is making decent progress on some basic spells. They're a hard worker, Terio. They mean the best."

Terio's gaze softened. "Show me proof of that before the ceremony and I will believe it. And... if nothing goes wrong during the ceremony itself, I will reevaluate my opinion on you."

"Thank you," Said Darcy. "I promise not to let you down."

"For both of your sake and mine, I hope you succeed."

— — —

As Darcy and Varia neared the lab, Darcy asked,

"So why Demeter? The name seems a bit on-the-nose."

"I actually chose it before I lost... everything." Varia explained, "I had a phase where I read a lot of Greek mythology, and Demeter was my favorite of the gods. I admired her love and strength as a mother. I had told myself, 'If I have a child, I want to be devoted to protecting them as Demeter is.' But just like in Greek mythology, fate enjoys being cruel."

"Oh. I'm sorry."

Varia gave a weary sigh. "Let's please not speak of this again."

Back in Varia's lab, Oliver waved to the returning duo.

"Welcome back! How was it?"

Varia returned the wave, albeit slowly and awkwardly.

Darcy said, "It was alright. Terio has our orders for the dragon warrior ceremony. You're covering the barracks while I watch over the ceremony."

"Oh, wow, congratulations! They must really trust you now."

"Uh... that's one way to look at it..."

Oliver showed Darcy the paper plate masks. "Ta-da! What do you think?"

Oliver had used a pencil to sketch in the details on the masks. Each one resembled Darcy's face and the backs had a label for which spell it was based on.

"As soon as I get colored pencils, I'm going to make these look so pretty!"

"Wow, I can't wait to see it!"

Darcy picked up one of the masks and placed a bit of pizzazz into it, then copied the transformation spell into the mask.

"Alright, we ready?"

Varia grabbed their notebook. "Absolutely ready!"

When Darcy put on the mask, their setae became platinum-white and their chitin became dark red with large, lighter-red dots running along them. Their claws were now a metallic, silvery color.

Varia's eyes widened. "That is... incredible! But where did the mask go?"

"What do you mean?"

To Darcy's surprise, their mask was no longer on their face, but it wasn't on the floor, either. Darcy put their claws to their face.

"Wait, but I still feel the changes in pizzazz. It's still attached. I think I just gotta..."

Darcy focused on the specific pizzazz that was within the mask. They felt its invisible presence on their face. They grabbed its edges and pulled it away. The mask reappeared, now separated once again. Darcy had returned to normal.

"Woah. That didn't happen with the fire spell."

Varia asked, "Could it have something to do with masks in particular?"

"But I could still tell that I was wearing a mask with the wind power."

Oliver said, "Maybe it's because it's a mask with a transformation spell? Maybe masks are special because they already imply transformation."

"That could be," Said Varia. "Let's do more practice with ferrokinesis, then run a test with another paper plate mask. We'll copy a typical water spell onto it- not a transformation spell- and see what happens."

Darcy went along with the exercises of practicing ferrokinesis, but their attention was no longer on the task at hand. As a result, they kept dropping the utensils. After the fifth or sixth drop, they took off the mask with a sigh.

"Sorry, Varia, but I just can't focus. I can't stop thinking about this mask stuff."

"You're completely fine. Tell you what, let's copy the Night Creature form onto that first wooden mask we made. You can try using that while I go charge the spell stone with water."

Darcy jumped up. "Really? Holy shit, I am *so* ready!"

Oliver said, "Um, Darcy. Just as a warning, when my powers caused me to transform, the instincts were... overwhelming. They become stronger with stress. Varia didn't feel those instincts when using magic to transform, but since you'll be using our... special powers, you'll likely feel them."

"I understand."

Darcy said that, but they were so caught up in their own excitement that they didn't fully register what this meant. All they could think about was the idea of being big and strong.

*My entire life, I've felt tiny and weak. Well, not anymore!*

Once Varia left, Darcy placed the stone with the Night Creature spell against the mask.

"It's done. The spell is copied into the pizzazz."

"Good luck," Wished Oliver.

*This will be the first time I use a pizzazz transformation that's actually related to spiders. I wonder how different it will feel?*

The moment Darcy put on the mask, their chest became tight with energy. It felt as if something new had formed in their body and now was trying desperately to get out. Darcy's limbs trembled. They put one shaking hand onto another in an attempt to steady it. Huge claws burst out of their tiny ones. Their chitin broke along the seams as a new exoskeleton formed underneath. Their limbs, their head, their torso, their abdomen—every part of them grew simultaneously. Their old exoskeleton fell to the floor in pieces.

Darcy grabbed a counter top with a large hand. Their sudden growth made them lose their balance. The dizzying sensation didn't seem to go away- in fact, Darcy felt a pressure in their head.

*Tired.*

Making coherent thoughts was like grabbing smoke. The feelings were there, but Darcy couldn't put words to them. Instead, their mind was driven by simple feelings.

*Hungry.*

Everything looked so small now. A red-haired human stood next to them. He seemed familiar, but his name was just out of reach.

*Hungry.*

They could swallow his head whole. They could eat one of his arms with a single bite. They could inject him with venom and liquefy his insides, making him perfect to cut and break and digest.

And Darcy was so very hungry.

"Darcy? Is everything okay?"

Darcy growled. They turned to fully face him.

The human backed away. "Darcy. You... you remember me. I'm Oliver. I'm your friend."

Recognition flashed in their mind. Darcy understood "Oliver" and "friend". They realized that they did not want to eat this prey, but they were so very hungry.

Darcy turned away with their hands against their head. They sifted through their memories and scraps of usable language to recall what speech was. It felt like turning through the pages of a waterlogged book.

"F-food," They mumbled. "**Food**."

"Food. Right! I'll go get the food box and be right back!"

Oliver sprinted out of the room.

Darcy sat down as they waited for him to return. They shut their eyes and focused on whatever memories they could. Their hunger pushed against them like a tidal wave.

Darcy didn't know if Oliver actually returned in a minute or if it only felt that way, but he carried a familiar box with him. He opened it to reveal an entire roast turkey.

"I don't know if this is the best thing, but..."

Darcy grabbed the turkey and shredded it with their teeth. It vanished into their mouth so quickly that it may as well have not existed at all.

With a full belly, Darcy sighed with relief. Everything seemed to settle down now and became sensical.

"Oliver," They said.

He smiled. "You remember."

"I do now. Oh man, my head..."

"Yeah. Being the Night Creature is, um... it's a doozy."

"I think I'm in control now, though."

"That's good." Oliver sat down next to them. "How do you feel?"

"Big." Darcy looked at one of their hands. "Strong."

To Darcy's surprise, however, they weren't red like Oliver was when he was the Night Creature. They still had white setae with cobalt-blue chitin and black joints. Their neck bristles remained as tough and spiny as ever. Darcy opened and closed their azure-blue claws.

"Oliver... I can reach high places now."

"I didn't know that was a problem."

Darcy laughed. "That's because you've never been short."

Varia returned with the spell stone. "Here's water! How are you feeling, Darcy?"

"Better now. Kind of lost control earlier, though."

"Oh my. Was it anxiety?"

Darcy shook their head. "Just hunger."

"That is the calories burnt during the transformation. The body uses a lot of energy during the change, and now that it's much larger, it needs even more energy to keep going. A calorie debt is created, so your instincts enter crisis mode. I'm willing to bet that if you stock up on food before changing into the Night Creature, the mental strain won't be as severe."

"That makes enough sense," Darcy replied.

Oliver said, "But Varia, you were just fine when you became the Night Creature."

"Yes, but I used magic. When undergoing transformations this way, the magic serves as a substitute for the energy burning. Essentially, it makes it so I can use a transformation spell as often as I need to without side effects. Although once in a large body, I'd still need to care for it and any extra calorie needs it would have."

Darcy said, "I guess Oliver and I's special power doesn't do that."

"Yes, but you *are* immune to dispels, so there are obvious pros and cons here. Now, let's see if you can use two masks at once."

"Oh, good idea."

It took more effort than usual for Darcy to stand up, like trying to get up while wearing a fully-loaded backpack. They picked up the wind mask with a yawn.

"Are you okay?" Asked Oliver.

"Yeh, just..." Their eyes drooped. "Might take a nap after this..."

Darcy tried to put on the wind mask, but it simply wouldn't take. Darcy tried the platinum mask as well, but nothing happened.

Varia said, "I suppose a mask can't wear a mask."

"Or I can only have one of these powers active at a time." Darcy suggested.

Oliver said, "But that doesn't make any sense. After all, you can use your basic powers on top of these extra ones, right?"

"Suppose... suppose so..."

"I wish we still had that hat or coat. Maybe we can combine different articles of clothing."

"Maybe..." Darcy sat down in a corner. "Sorry, can we just... I'll just shut my eyes... just a few minutes..."

# Chapter 20

Darcy woke up so fantastically refreshed that they wondered if they had ever rested before today. Their head felt clear, their muscles were strong, and although they were hungry again, that was easily solved with their food box nearby.

*Wow! I finally know what the phrase "bright-eyed and bushy-tailed" feels like!*

Darcy sat on the floor and ate an entire pound of cooked ham. It was so smooth and satisfying to bite into that Darcy was almost disappointed when they finished eating it.

*Can't just eat the day away, though. I'll need to train for the entire day if I wanna impress the council tomorrow.*

Darcy jumped up and bonked their head against the ceiling. They fell back down with their hands on their head.

"Ow, ow, ow! Darcy, you're tall now. No jumping..."

Oliver and Varia entered the lab. Oliver beamed upon seeing Darcy.

"You're finally awake!"

He and Darcy hugged. Darcy chuckled.

"Feels weird to hug someone smaller than me." They blinked. "Uh... what do you mean by 'finally'?"

Oliver and Varia looked at each other in concern.

Oliver said, "Darcy, you must have been more tired than we thought, because you, um... well, you were just so comfortable that nothing would wake you. And believe me, we tried! But, um... nothing worked."

Darcy slowly stood up. "Oliver, you're freaking me out. How long was I asleep?"

Varia answered, "For and entire night and an entire day. Today is the dragon warrior ceremony."

"Today?" Darcy put their hands against their head. "It's today?! Shit! I'm not even close to prepared!"

Darcy paced back and forth and rambled.

"Maybe... maybe having wind power will be enough. Haha, yeah, being a glorified housefan. Oh, that'll totally work. I got metal, too. If anyone needs their silverware to be moved across the table, I got 'em."

Darcy devolved into a series of nervous giggles. "Oh, man. They're never gonna trust me again. Ahahaha, oh this is great!"

Varia said, "Darcy, it'll be alright-"

"**Don't say that it'll be alright!**" Darcy smashed a fist against the wall. The entire room shook. Darcy's vision clouded, with Varia being the only figure in focus.

Oliver stepped between the two. "Darcy, don't!"

Darcy's vision became clear once more, but their fists clenched.

"What am I supposed to do?" Darcy asked.

Olive spoke clearly and calmly. "We just need to show them what you can do, right? Like an exhibition. It doesn't need to be perfect, just a proof of concept. Your mask abilities may not be the best right now, but the fact that you can control them means that they're useful to the clan. That's what we need right now."

"But-but I can't be the Night Creature and use the other masks at the same time. But if I take this mask off and then transform later, I might not be able to control myself during my job. What am I supposed to do?"

Oliver thought for a moment. "Lend me the Night Creature mask."

"Are you sure?"

"I have more experience with that body than you do right now. I'll wear it during the exhibition, and then after the ceremony, I'll teach you what I know."

Darcy gently held one of Oliver's hands in their own.

"Thank you," They said.

He smiled. "What are partners for?"

*Partners!*

Darcy smiled and focused on their pizzazz. "Okay. Hang on."

The process of taking off the mask was the same as the other transformation mask. Darcy placed their claws around the invisible borders of the mask and removed it.

Their face slowly disconnected from the rest of their body. A warm, gooey substance clung to the inside of the mask, keeping it connected to their head. Darcy kept pulling the mask away until the substance stretched and broke. Darcy tried to breathe to stay calm, but in that brief moment, they had no mouth and no eyes.

Thankfully, one moment later, Darcy's body shifted and became smaller. Their face reformed and they could open their eyes again. They held the wooden mask in their claws. They looked down at themself and found that they had returned to their original arachnomorph body. They breathed a sigh of relief.

"Phew... that was something else."

"Are you okay?" Oliver asked.

"Yeah. I'm sorry for yelling at you guys before. It was uncalled for."

Varia replied, "You're forgiven. But in the future, don't bite the hand that's helping you."

"I'll keep that in mind, definitely."

The moment Darcy gave the mask to Oliver, Rivio entered the room.

"It's time. Come to the council room."

Darcy gulped. "Okay. Be right with you."

Varia said, "Oh, have you noticed the Guard Barracks yet, Rivio?"

"Yes, they smell terrible. But, I must admit, the smoke had cleared out rather well. Now come along."

"Yes, Rivi-"

"Not you, Varia."

"Eh? But why not?"

"We only need to see what the guard can do, not you. Stay here."

Varia frowned, but did not argue. "Yes, Rivio."

Oliver said, "Um, Rivio, permission to join the exhibition along with Darcy?"

"You haven't lost our confidence, but if you truly feel the need to prove yourself, we won't stop you from joining."

"Thank you. It's really appreciated."

Darcy picked up the masks for wind and metal and followed Rivio. Oliver followed along as well with food box and Night Creature mask in hand.

The rest of the council was already in the room, waiting. Terio wore a brown robe with gray accents and intricate red symbols along the cuffs and edges. Grisio sat to their left and Aggis sat to their right.

Grisio said, "Let's get this over with. Darcy, show us what you have learned over the past few days."

Darcy gulped. "Uh, yeah. Well, I think you will all be happy to hear that none of it involves fire."

A collective sigh of relief came from the council.

Darcy said, "But basically, I stored some of my power into these masks and I managed to get that power to mimic Salavite spells. For example, this one has a wind spell inside of it. When I put it on, it gives me air... aero..."

Oliver whispered to Darcy, "Aerokinesis."

"Aerokinesis! So I will show that one first."

Darcy put on the wind mask and shot a gust towards the council. It ruffled Terio's robe slightly, but the robe soon fell back in place. The council's expressions remained neutral.

Terio asked, "Can you create anything stronger?"

Darcy kept up a showman's smile. "Uh, here, let me show you what it looks like from the side."

They blew some wind at a wall and looked back at the council. They all stared at Darcy in silence. A dust bunny rolled across the floor like a tumbleweed.

*Keep smiling, Darcy, keep smiling!*

They took off the mask. "Okay, next is metal. This second mask is actually based on the transformation spell for, um, Platinum Clan! So not only do I gain metal powers, but I also change colors, too. So that's, um... pretty cool."

Terio asked, "Does the change in appearance alter your effectiveness?"

"Not really. I think it's just cosmetic. Still looks cool, though. Watch."

Darcy put on the mask for metal and shifted into a white-and-red color scheme. Aggis's ears shot straight up.

"Oh, you look wonderful!"

"Thank you."

Rivio asked, "If you gained Platinum Clan powers, then that means you currently have ferrokinesis. Did you bring any metal with you for this demonstration?"

Grisio asked, "Also, why did your mask disappear this time? Is that supposed to occur?"

"Uh, for the second question, transformation masks seem to vanish when worn. They're still here, I just need to activate my special power before I can take them off. As for the metal, uh... I, uh..."

Oliver stood next to Darcy and slipped them a spoon.

"Behold!" Darcy held up the spoon. "I shall pull this metal towards me from the other end of the room!"

Darcy set the spoon down next to the council, then ran to the other side as Oliver stepped out of the way. Terio rubbed their chin.

"Ah, I see. Darcy's going to make the spoon fly towards them with so much force that it will become a weapon."

*I can do this,* Darcy thought. *Just bring the metal towards me.*

The spoon slowly dragged across the floor, scraping along loose dirt. Once it reached Darcy's foot, it then lifted up into their outstretched hand.

"Uh... see? So by wearing different masks, I can do different things."

Upon seeing no change in the council's expressions, Darcy made a performer's pose and did jazz hands.

"Ta-daaaaaaa."

Rivio tilted their head to the side. "...Is that it?"

"Um, currently. But, uh, I can get better! After some time and practice and, um..."

Oliver added, "Like all skills, Darcy isn't a master right away, but what they *can* do, they can pull off consistently."

Terio said, "Yes, but it will take a stronger wind force to do anything in battle, and moving metal at your current speed will not be too useful, either. How long will it take before Darcy is be competent with these skills?"

"Well, uh... how long did it take for you?"

Aggis said, "He has a point. Even Salavites need to train for years before their abilities are battle-worthy. It would be unfair of us to expect a newcomer to gain the same results in even less time."

Terio nodded. "Hm. That is true. And having consistent control over what Darcy *can* do means that there is less chance of accidents occurring."

"Yes, exactly," Said Darcy. "And there is one more mask we'd like to exhibit, and this one *can* be used in battle."

Terio's ears pointed upward. "Then let's see it."

Oliver said, "We both have experience with this particular form, so I will be exhibiting it today."

He took off his hoodie so that he only wore the purple bodysuit. He took a deep breath, exhaled, and put on the Night Creature mask.

Oliver's transformation was much like Darcy's, with the new form exploding out of his body, but the bodysuit remained undamaged just as Revi intended.

Every pair of ears on the council pointed skyward. Their eyes widened and one of them even gasped.

"Astounding!"

"Incredible!"

"It looks as strong as Scorpio!"

Darcy put a hand on one of Oliver's elbows. He slightly turned his head towards them and gave a subtle nod.

*Good,* Darcy thought. *He's in control.*

Darcy said, "We call this form the Night Creature. As you can tell, it's super strong, stronger than I could ever be on my own."

"I certainly believe it," Said Terio. "Does it have any other abilities that we should be aware of?"

"Um..." *I swear I felt the urge to use venom earlier, but I never actually tried it. Would it be lying if I said it was possible?*

"Well, spiders have access to silk and venom, which are great for neutralizing their enemies."

*Technically not a lie.*

Oliver stepped forward. He spoke slowly and carefully.

"What's important is that all of the abilities shown don't depend on magic. If the Macbeths visit again, their dispels won't affect us."

Terio nodded. "And with a body like that, even fighting Scorpio would be no problem."

"Indeed," Said Rivio. "I wonder if the silk can be used as a bandage? Or if the venom can be extracted for medicinal purposes?"

Grisio said, "I am particularly interested in the bristles around the neck. Could those be used as tools or weapons?"

Rivio added, "Imagine if we showed this form to the Trio Clan. This, along with possibly freeing Salanon..."

"Ah, yes! That would convince them, I'm sure of it!"

Aggis smiled. "Well, then. I suppose that makes our opinion of the matter unanimous. Guards, we would like to see more of this Night Creature form in the future. It could mean great things for everyone."

"Thank you," Darcy replied. "That means a lot to us."

The council then scattered to prepare for the ceremony. Darcy helped Oliver write down something for the food box.

"I don't understand how you can write with spider claws," He said.

"You just need to get a feel for how they work," They replied.

Oliver graciously ate a bowl full of scrambled eggs when Terio approached the duo.

"Well, color me impressed," They said to Darcy. "You pulled it off."

"Ah, thanks. I wouldn't be able to do it without Oliver, though."

"Yes, you both made a good impression today. I would like to personally apologize for my attitude towards you as of late. I had doubted your abilities, but it was wrong of me to be so presumptuous."

Darcy waved a hand back and forth. "No, no, it's okay. With how impulsive I can be, I totally understand. Plus, I'm still new and we're still getting to know each other, so y'know..."

"Indeed. Still, I see your potential now. If I may make a request, can you be in the Night Creature form during the ceremony?"

"Ah... are you sure? If I were a regular person, I don't know if I would gain much confidence from having a giant spider monster standing around."

"Yes, but the dragon warrior ceremony is a time of transformations. If you reveal your form during the ceremony, everybody will understand its implications and accept it in stride. Then, we can display it with more grace when the Trio Clan arrives."

Darcy glanced at Oliver.

Oliver said, "Sir, what if I watched over the ceremony instead? After all, I'm already the Night Creature."

"Are you comfortable with changing into that form more times in the future?"

"Well... not as much as Darcy would be..."

"Then it would be most efficient for Darcy to be the Night Creature."

"Yes, sir."

Oliver took off the mask and gave it to Darcy.

Darcy said to Terio, "I'll, uh, be right with you guys. I just need a minute."

Terio nodded. "Meet me at the entrance to the underground lake. We'll enter it together."

After they left, Oliver said to Darcy, "You can do this."

"Thanks. How did you feel?"

"In control, thankfully. I feel really full now, though." He put a hand on his stomach. "I think I ate too quickly."

"Haha, yeah, that's easy to do when you're super hungry. Will you be alright being your own?"

"I'll be okay, don't worry. Thanks for looking out for me, though."

"No problem."

The two smiled at each other. Darcy inhaled, then exhaled.

"Okay. I can do this. Tonight is gonna be awesome."

"I believe in you!"

"Yeah! Oliver believes in me!"

This time, Darcy ate before starting the transformation. Just as Varia suspected, their head remained clear, but Darcy kept the food box with them just in case. But once again Oliver looked so small now.

"You sure you'll be alright in the guard barracks?" They asked.

Oliver nodded. "I know how to fight. I'll be fine."

"Okay, but don't underestimate the power of biting people, okay? If all else fails, bite them."

He laughed. "Okay, Darcy."

The two hugged, then went their different ways.

— — —

Darcy caught up to Terio in the hallway.

"Are you ready?" Terio asked.

"Are you?"

Terio grinned. "Fair enough. I suppose we'll be as ready as we'll ever be."

The underground lake reverberated with dozens of voices. Everybody sat on the shoreline and conversed with each other. Aggis sat in a shallow portion of the lake with a pile of newstone next to them. Upon seeing Terio, Aggis made their announcement.

"Everybody! It has been a long time since we have had more than one dragon warrior in the clan. The past years have been filled with uncertainty. But thanks to our new guards, we have gained enough newstone to finally add a new warrior to our ranks, and with the newstone they shall make, we will enter a new era of prosperity."

This was met with many voices of approval. All eyes then turned to Terio. Terio stepped into the lake, next to Aggis, and made their speech.

"I spent much of my early years training to become a dragon warrior, but when the Macbeths took our lives and strained our resources, I gave up on that dream. To finally achieve this dream is not only a gift but also an honor. In the coming years, I vow to serve this clan in every way possible."

The crowd cheered. Terio then swept an arm to gesture towards Darcy, who stood on the shoreline.

"Our guards have also achieved a powerful transformation. With the Night Creature form, Darcy has the strength to match even

Scorpio. Without them and Oliver, we would not be having this ceremony today, and with their new power, we shall be safer than ever before."

This was met with many nods and mentions of agreement.

Aggis then stood up on all fours. "Now, Terio shall consume the newstone and begin the metamorphosis. As they do so, let us meditate on the events that led to this point."

Darcy watched the crowd as Terio did their part. Some Salavites watched while others shut their eyes. Everyone was silent. Everyone was still.

*So far, so good.*

Something pinched Darcy's abdomen. They held back a snarl and twisted their body to look. Kifo nibbled on the side of the abdomen.

"Kifo," Darcy whispered. "What are you doing?"

"I'm bored," Kifo replied. "When will this be over?"

Darcy used one of their lower arms to pick up Kifo.

"Hey, this is important. You're going to have another dragon warrior."

"But why can't *I* become a dragon warrior?"

"I think you're too young. Now let's watch, okay?"

Once Terio had finished the pile, they glowed with a bronze light.

Aggis announced, "This earth shall now test Terio's worthiness."

Terio's entire body became encased in newstone. Their body grew in size until it matched Aggis's. After a long, tense moment, the newstone changed back into flesh and blood.

Terio's gray, metallic scales had become more reflective now. Their rust-red limbs gained new musculature befitting of a dragon. Although Terio stood still and composed, their swishing tail betrayed their excitement. Their orange eyes were full of life.

"The wings," Someone said. "Show us the wings!"

Terio got on all fours and arched their back. The slits on their back opened up and sprouted two pairs of wings: a large primary set and a small secondary set. The wings had metallic, semi-transparent membranes with a rust-red tint. Terio looked at the wings and folded them up like paper fans.

"Now for the moment of truth," They said.

Aggis gathered a clump of earth and handed it to Terio. Terio pressed it between their palms. Light shone from it. Terio hesitantly opened their hands. A small clump of newstone sat in their claws.

Terio held up the newstone for everyone to see. They sat with the posture of a cat with their head held high. They spoke professionally, but everyone could hear the glee in their voice.

"I, Terio Anuren, am a dragon warrior."

Everybody cheered and surrounded Terio. The sudden excitement actually startled Darcy. Their heart jumped and they felt the urge to hiss at them. They locked their jaw shut.

*Stay in control. Everything's fine.*

Kifo squirmed in Darcy's hands. "I wanna see!"

"Oh. Sorry." Darcy let them go.

Someone yelled, "Make more newstone!"

Terio couldn't stop smiling. "If you insist."

Aggis and Terio entered the tunnel. This was the same tunnel that Darcy had first seen Aggis in. The crowd followed them.

"Now, now," Said Aggis. "Let us have some privacy."

Terio flicked their head towards Darcy.

*That must be my cue.*

Darcy stepped in front of the tunnel entrance. "Yeah. Let's, uh... give them the space they need."

Someone argued, "But I want to see the process."

"I'm sure you can see it another time. But let's not drown them, okay? Respect their request."

This was met with faces of disappointment, but nobody else argued.

Terio and Aggis soon returned to the entrance with a hefty sum of earth. Aggis placed their hands over Terio's to guide them.

"Try to position them like this. It will help you put more muscle into the compression."

"Ah, thank you."

With that, Terio held more newstone in their hands. In everyone's excitement, they charged forward to get a closer look. Multiple people bumped into Darcy, and while it wasn't enough to knock them over, the stress was not making a good headspace.

"Hey! Let's calm down now. One... one person at a time. Don't step on each other."

"Darcy is right," Said Terio. "You can follow me into the tunnel now, but there's no need to rush. Walk, don't run."

The crowd listened to Terio's orders. They followed Terio into the tunnel as the latter made more newstone. Aggis stayed at the entrance next to Darcy. Darcy sighed with relief.

*I made it.*

"I am glad the process was successful," Aggis commented.

"Same," Darcy replied. "So do all dragon warriors have wings like that?"

"It depends on the element. Iron Clan and Platinum Clan are both of the metals element, so our wings are the same style."

Aggis protracted their wings. They were indeed in the same style as Terio's, but with white limbs and red membranes. These wings, however, had multiple cracks in them and the edges had become dull. Aggis retracted the wings.

"I am afraid that they aren't flight-worthy anymore."

"Still, they look amazing." *Even if I never want to fly.*

After Terio had made a good number of newstone, they and surrounding Salavites took the stones to the lake to wash them. They sang as they went.

Haul the earth and press it down
Fill it up with magic.
Wash the extra dirt away
The stone's been filled with magic.
Carve them into spheres and orbs
It's the best shape for magic.
Then share them around for everyone
Everyone is magic.

People told jokes and stores to each other as they sorted through the fresh newstone. At the end of it all, Terio had to lie down to rest.

"Do not push yourself too far," Said Aggis. "You did well for your first set of transmutations."

"Thank you," Terio replied. "I never realized how exhausting it is. I am sorry for the hardship I and the council have given you."

Aggis looked at them in surprise, then smiled. "You are forgiven. All I desire is to be happy with my people." Aggis then announced, "Everyone, let us now move to the food halls for the feast! Step carefully now, no need to push each other."

Everyone cheered and went into the hallways. Aggis followed shortly behind them with a new spring in their step.

Terio gestured for Darcy to come close. Darcy knelt down beside them.

"Everything alright?" They asked.

"I'm fine. I wanted to say that you did well. Thank you."

"I'm just glad everything went according to plan."

Darcy's gaze shifted towards the hallways.

Terio said, "You're worried about your friend?"

"I'd like to check on him, if that's alright."

"Permission granted. Aggis can handle everything from here."

"Thank you. I'll join everyone soon, I promise."

Darcy made their way to the guard barracks. They entered the room, only to find pieces of newstone armor scattered across the floor. A large, muscular man held Oliver up with a single hand. Blood painted the back of Oliver's skull and his left leg had been bent in a way it shouldn't. Varia's unconscious body lay in a corner.

A primal growl left Darcy's throat. They could only utter one word before rage overtook them.

"**Scorpio**."

# Chapter 21

Oliver had patiently waited in the guard barracks. He didn't mind being alone—in fact, the quiet felt quite nice. He wished he could grab a book to read. And to his pleasant surprise, Varia soon joined him.

"You're not going to the ceremony?" He asked.

They shook their head. "Crowded events are too loud for me. I likely won't be joining the meeting with Trio Clan, either."

"But you've helped us so much. We wouldn't have made this much progress without you."

"I appreciate it, but I don't need the credit. What I actually need is... far less tangible."

Varia held their hand to their heart. Oliver watched in silence, then looked away.

"I need something as well," He said, "But I think I'm too afraid to ask for it."

"Hm."

After more silence, he said,

"I want to thank you. Even if you don't want credit, I'm so grateful for everything you've done for us. Without you, I would still be turning into the Night Creature against my will. It feels like so much has changed since then. I really feel like myself now."

Varia smiled. "I'm glad to hear it. And I'd like to thank you for putting so much trust in me. We've learned... so much together."

"Yeah."

In the ensuing moments, Varia watched Oliver as if about to say something. They clutched their hand against their chest and made a heavy exhale.

"Oliver... there's something you need to know."

Just then, the entry tunnel's alert system went off. Oliver put a hand against the floor and felt for vibrations.

"Someone's coming. Someone big."

"What?!"

Oliver and Varia ran to the entry tunnel. A man in full armor stood in the center of the hallway. Long blades jutted out from the forearms and pointed forward with a slight curve. A similar blade ran down the middle of the helmet. This black armor reflected the hallway lights, illuminating its white speckles.

Oliver cleared his throat. "Um, good afternoon, sir."

The man lifted his head. He called out,

"Hello, over there! I take it that you're the new guard!"

His friendly tone took Oliver off-guard. Given the rumors, he had expected Scorpio to sound monstrous, but he almost sounded inviting. This sent a shiver down Oliver's spine.

*He sounds like...*

"I-I am the new guard," Oliver replied. "I please request that you leave in the direction that you came."

Varia added, "The Macbeths have no business here!"

"Oh, we have plenty business with your lot. You took my sister's wand *and* you've been messing with Old Newstone. Which one of you took those dispels?"

Oliver argued, "I... I thought you made a deal were you wouldn't bother this clan anymore."

"*Libra* made that deal. I had nothing to do with it."

Scorpio stepped closer. He was only a couple dozen feet away now.

Varia trembled. They had to lean on Oliver for support.

"The dispels on his armor," They whispered.

"Go to the barracks," He whispered back. "I can handle this."

"Are you sure?"

He nodded. "Stay safe."

"You as well."

Varia stumbled back to the guard barracks.

Scorpio said, "You should follow your friend if you know what's good for you."

"I'm sorry, but I can't let you into this clan. Please turn around!"

Scorpio stopped just ten feet away from Oliver. He put one hand on his hip and gestured with his other one.

"Alright, so here's what you're going to do. You're going to give me all of your clan's newstone and give me a headcount of your dragon warriors. Then I will go back home and we will decide whether or not you're playing nice. Or... you could fight back. Then I kill you. I kill your friend. And I kill every filthy lizard that gets in my way."

Oliver got into a fighting stance.

"So you think you can beat me?" Scorpio's voice betrayed his fiendish smile. "I have snapped a dragon warrior's neck with one hand. I've walked through fire without flinching. My armor is so heavy that it crushes the bones of regular people. I've built up a resistance to every type of poison. What makes you think you're special?"

Oliver took a calming breath and exhaled. *Don't respond to him. He's just another supervillain. Figure out his weaknesses and exploit them.*

Upon Oliver's lack of reply, Scorpio rushed to close the gap between them. Oliver was already a step ahead—he jumped onto Scorpio's shoulders. In a single motion, he tore off Scorpio's helmet, turned off its dispel, and threw it down the hall. Oliver then struck Scorpio's temples.

Scorpio reeled back. Oliver leapt away. Scorpio ran his fingers through his platinum-blonde hair and glared at Oliver with charcoal eyes.

"You're fast."

"Thank you. Please leave."

"No."

"I guess we're doing this, then."

Oliver zoomed at Scorpio and leapt on his shoulder. He stuck his hands to a pauldron. Still sticking, he put all his strength into his jump. The pauldron tore away from the rest of the armor. Oliver landed on a wall with ease. Removing the pauldron revealed that Scorpio wore a leather covering just under the newstone armor.

Scorpio looked at his shoulder, then at Oliver. He said in bafflement,

"How did you...?"

"Sorry, it's a secret."

Scorpio swiped at Oliver, but the latter had already jumped out of the way. Oliver landed on Scorpio's other shoulder and removed that pauldron as well. Once he got out of range, he turned off both spells and tossed the pauldrons aside.

Oliver continued with this tactic: stick to a piece of armor, turn off its dispel, and remove it. Now all that was left were the arm-guards, but those had blades attached, and Oliver was running low on steam. He had been putting all of his energy into this fight- ensuring that every attack was perfect- but this also meant that his endurance wouldn't hold out for much longer. Yet every time he tried to remove the arm-guards, Scorpio would swipe at him with his free hand.

Scorpio yelled, "Are you going to keep running? Come down here and fight like a man!"

Oliver wished he was clever enough to say something sassy, but alas:

"Sorry, mister. I don't want to die."

The corner of Scorpio's mouth raised upward. "Fair enough. But if you keep jumping around like this, I'll just have to go and kill your friend." He gestured with his arm blades. "Who knows, maybe I'll cut their eyes out."

Oliver's years of training told him not to give in to the taunt.

*Stay focused on the current tactic. It's worked so far.*

But the thought of someone being hurt made his blood boil.

*If he puts a hand on them...!*

Oliver wished that there was a way to tear off Scorpio's leather armor. It was much thinner than the newstone armor, but still an inch thick—Oliver wouldn't be able to strike any pressure points while it was still on.

*And without the newstone armor, he's probably lighter and faster now...*

Oliver had spent too much time thinking—Scorpio rushed down the hallway, towards the barracks.

Oliver jumped down. "Wait! We're not done fighting!"

Scorpio waved him off. "I'm bored with you. You're not dead yet."

That gave Oliver an idea. He shouted,

"So you only enjoy beating people when you have a clear advantage over them? How pathetic."

Scorpio stopped. He turned his head, but only slightly.

Oliver continued, "This armor looks like it was specially carved to fit *your* body. You probably wear this every time you attack Salavites. Am I wrong?"

"...You're not."

"So the dispels in the armor keep anyone around you from using magic. It weakens Salavites to the point where they can't even move. Then you just execute them, right?"

Scorpio turned to face Oliver. "That's the consequence of being dependent on magic."

"But they don't have a choice. Magic is a part of their biology. They evolved to be like that. And you use that against them. You make it so they can't fight back and then you kill them. That isn't a consequence, it's just slaughter! And you do it because the thought of not being overwhelmingly powerful is too scary for you to handle." Oliver pointed at him. "You're a coward, Scorpio!"

Anger flashed in Scorpio's eyes. He marched towards Oliver.

"You know, Mother wanted me to bring you and the spider creature back alive, but technically, I only need one of you."

He sprinted at Oliver and brought down one of his arm blades. Unfortunately for Scorpio, his anger made this action painfully telegraphed; Oliver could see it coming seconds in advance. He leapt above Scorpio and kicked him in the back of the head, using Scorpio's forward momentum to send him to the floor.

Oliver crouched next to Scorpio and put a hand against the center of Scorpio's back. He pushed downward, pinning him.

"Please leave this place."

"Or what?" Scorpio retorted. "You'll kill me?"

"N-no."

"Then you'll never win. You won't even win this match." He smirked. "Because in wrestling, the bigger opponent always wins."

Scorpio swiped Oliver's legs and knocked him off-balance. The moment Scorpio got to his feet, he grabbed Oliver by the face and slammed the latter's head against his knee. He then held Oliver's left leg in both hands and bent it until he heard a snap. Oliver screamed in pain. Scorpio then dropped him, letting him crumple to the floor.

Scorpio stood over him, smiling with all of his teeth.

"Not so agile now, are you?"

He grabbed Oliver's wrist and dragged him into the guard's barracks.

In the barracks, Varia gasped upon seeing Scorpio with Oliver.

"Oliver!"

"So Oliver is his name." Scorpio raised an eyebrow. "Oliver Vermilio? Mike Harrell's pet?"

Varia growled. "Let go of him."

"Hard pass. Mother will *definitely* want to see him now." He stepped towards Varia. "But I can still kill you to send a message."

The dispel that made up his arm guards caused Varia to collapse, so all that Scorpio had to do was step closer. With Varia now immobile, he readied an arm blade over their neck.

"Goodbye, lizard."

Something bit his other hand, causing him to reel back. Oliver dug his teeth into Scorpio's hand, giving enough pressure to break bones and draw blood. Scorpio dropped Oliver and reeled back.

"You fucking freak!"

Scorpio used his uninjured hand to grab Oliver and tear him away. He lifted him up by the head.

"Maybe I should just bring your corpse!"

Before he did anything, however, a new voice came from the other side of the room.

"**Scorpio**."

A monstrous white spider stood in the doorway. Their dark brown eyes soon went blank with hatred. Azure fangs had protracted from their chelicerae. The spider hissed at Scorpio.

Scorpio could only stare. "What the hell?"

The spider ran at Scorpio. He dropped Oliver and swiped at the spider with an arm blade. The blade struck them, but didn't break through their chitin—it didn't even leave a scratch.

Scorpio stepped back. "What are you made of?"

Now it was the spider's turn. With one hand, they grabbed Scorpio's arm, then they used another hand to tear off the blade.

Scorpio punched at them with his free arm, but the spider blocked it with their extra hands. They tore off that blade as well.

Now that the spider had him in their clutches, they dragged him to the wall, then climbed to the ceiling. They dangled Scorpio below them.

"What are you doing?!" Scorpio yelled. "You freak!"

The spider either didn't understand his words or didn't care. They readied their spinnerets and twisted Scorpio in place. The silk from the spinnerets wrapped Scorpio until he was covered head-to-toe in webbing. The spider then dropped him to the floor.

Scorpio wriggled and fought against the silk. The spider tackled the webbed-up body like a cat with a mouse. Scorpio made mumbling sounds, but the spider didn't care. They placed their fangs where the neck would be and readied to take a bite.

"No!"

Oliver placed their hand on the spider's leg. He stood up, placing all of his weight onto his right leg, but wobbled in place. The spider turned their attention away from him and back to their prey.

Oliver pulled at them. "We don't kill."

The spider pushed him back to the floor. Oliver got up with a whimper and put himself between the spider and their prey.

"Please, Darcy," He said. "Don't do this."

The spider tilted their head to the side.

Oliver said, "Your name is Darcy Aran. Remember? My name is Oliver Vermilio. You know us."

Recognition flashed in their eyes, but it apparently wasn't enough. The spider pushed him again. This time, Oliver used his left leg to steady himself, only for pain to shoot through the entire limb. Oliver clenched his teeth and grabbed a nearby wall to keep steady.

"Wait, Darcy! Wait just... hang on!"

Moving was agony and the blow to his head made the world spin, but Oliver knew that if he didn't stop Darcy now, they would do something that they would regret.

"We showed him that we can beat him. We don't need further violence. So please, Darcy, come back to me."

He curled his fingers around one of Darcy's claws. He said gently, "I need my partner back."

Darcy squinted at him. They blinked and said,

"Oliver?"

Oliver nearly cried from relief. "Yes! Yes, that's right!"

Darcy shut their eyes and rubbed their head. "I... I almost... oh, god."

"It's okay. It's over now."

Darcy glared at the webbed-up Scorpio. "Not just yet."

Darcy placed their claws against his head. "You think you can hurt my partner and get away with it?!"

Scorpio gave out a muffled response. Darcy didn't care to decipher it. They said,

"How 'bout I break *your* leg, huh? How would you like that?!"

Oliver said, "Darcy-"

"I'm sending a message." Darcy snarled at Scorpio. "That's what you Macbeths do, right? Cruelty for cruelty's sake?"

"Darcy, don't," Oliver begged. "Just let him go. We don't need to become him."

Darcy emitted a low, constant growl. Oliver held one of their hands.

He said again, "Let him go."

Darcy ceased their growling. They opened up the silk around Scorpio's head. Scorpio gasped for breath.

"I relent," He said. "I'll retreat! Just don't eat me! Please!"

"Fine," Darcy replied. "But if *anyone* sees you within the Refugee Clan's borders again, I will not hesitate to **tear you apart**. And I'll do it so you're alive as long as possible, so you can watch me consume your body **bit by bit**. Understand?"

Scorpio nodded. "You won't see me here again."

Darcy cut open the silk with their claws. Scorpio ran off as soon as his legs were free and vanished into the hallway.

Oliver felt for the vibrations in the hallway. Once he was certain Scorpio was gone, he fell to his hands and knees.

"We're alive."

"Yeah. And... thank you for stopping me. You can rest now."

"Will you be okay on your own?"

"I will, don't worry. I'll gather up this newstone and talk to the council. You need medical help."

"Okay. Help Varia, too."

"I will."

Darcy carried Oliver and Varia on their back as they went along. Oliver tried to stay awake to explain things, but his injuries and exhaustion from the fight caused him to slip in and out of consciousness. In his last waking moment, he recalled being placed onto a cot somewhere. Darcy sat by his side. They stroked his hair.

"It's going to be okay, Oliver."

# Chapter 22

In the infirmary, Darcy watched Oliver rest. Rivio had set his bones back into place and stitched up the left side of his skull. The hard-light threads glowed under his red hair.

Rivio said, "I put him under for the operation, so he won't wake up for a few more hours."

Darcy asked, "Is it okay if I stay with him?"

"Just as long as you don't move him."

Darcy tried not to let themself slip into fearful thoughts, but the anxiety couldn't help but build up inside them. They considered taking off their mask and giving it to Oliver, but with him being unconscious, it wouldn't result in anything good.

After an hour or so, Rivio returned to check on Oliver.

Darcy asked them, "What if he doesn't make it?"

"If he has strength similar to Akio, then he will make a full recovery."

"But I've never seen him so injured. If I lost him... god, I don't know what I'd do."

"He won't die. I have years' worth of medical training, both for Salavites *and* humans. I know what I'm talking about."

"Sorry. I'm just scared."

Rivio put a hand on one of Darcy's arms. "Empathy is valuable, but don't let its fears consume you. If there is anything I've learned from recent events, it's that you and Oliver are capable of miracles."

Rivio then spoke quietly, as if they themself could not believe the next words to leave their mouth.

"You, Oliver, and Varia are the first people ever to survive an attack from Scorpio."

"But he'll be ready next time. He said he'd stay away, but..."

"Does he have anything that could stop the Night Creature?"

"I don't know."

"Hm. We will have to plan our next move. But for now, you need rest. Like the saying goes, you can't cast spells from an empty stone."

"...Okay."

Darcy returned to the barracks. The beds were too small for a Night Creature, so they simply sat down with their shoulder against a wall. They watched the entrance just in case anything else happened.

Just in case.

— — —

Darcy awoke to find that someone had draped a blanket over their shoulders. Aggis sat a few feet away with a watchful eye.

Darcy rubbed their eyes. "How long was I out?"

"About twelve hours. How do you feel?"

"Exhausted. Worried. Guilty."

"Guilty? What source of guilt could you have?"

"I gave myself this body so I could fight against Scorpio, but when I got mad, I couldn't control it. If Oliver wasn't there..."

"But he *was* there, was he not?"

"Yeah, but still, when I think about Oliver's injuries, I just... it doesn't seem fair."

Aggis replied, "Darcy, it is not fair to blame yourself for circumstances outside of your control. I understand being lost in the past, but it is important to remember that what happened *has happened*. All we can do now is to try to learn from history."

"How do I do that?"

"Well, you are trying to master your new form, yes? So, the next thing to focus on would be exactly that."

"Right... you're right. I have to keep moving." Darcy worked up a small smile. "And maybe I can have this body with different articles of clothing."

"What would that do?"

"Well, theoretically, I'd be the Night Creature on top of having other powers. Like wind or water or fire." They gave a weak chuckle. "Although maybe not fire."

"Yes, preferably not."

The two laughed together.

Varia entered the room. "Oh, fantastic! Darcy's awake!"

Darcy gave them a nod. "Hey, Varia. How's Oliver?"

"He's been awake for a couple hours now. He keeps asking for you, so I promised him to let you know the moment you woke up."

"Tell him I'll be right there."

Darcy made a beeline to Oliver's room in the infirmary. Oliver's left leg had been placed in a cast and kept raised. His bandaged head rested against the softest pillow Darcy had ever seen. Oliver saw Darcy and immediately smiled.

"Hi."

Darcy sat next to him. "Hi. How are you feeling?"

"Rivio has me on pain medicine, but I'm mostly coherent. You?"

"I'm doing much better now. I should probably eat soon, though."

Varia stepped in. "Um, if it's alright, I would also like a word with Oliver. He isn't in trouble, I simply... well, there are certain things that need to be said."

Darcy asked, "Want me to leave?"

"No, no. You can stay."

Varia knelt down on Oliver's other side. They gazed longingly at him.

"I wish I could have protected you."

"It's okay," He replied. "He was literally covered in dispels."

"Still..." Varia made a long pause. "...A mother should protect her child."

Oliver's eyes widened. He was silent as the information clicked.

"Doctor Vermilio?"

Varia nodded. "I'm sorry I didn't tell you. I was scared. In a perfect world, we would have never separated."

Instead of regret and frustration, Oliver's eyes filled with joy and relief.

"You're here. There's so much we can do together now. We can get to know each other as a family."

Varia nodded. They had begun tearing up as well.

"I promise to be a good mother for you."

"And I promise to be a good son." He sniffed. "Wow. This is amazing. I have a mom."

"I would hug you, but I'm worried about aggravating your injuries."

"Haha. That's okay. When I recover, we'll catch up on twenty-five years of hugs."

Darcy stood up with a smile. "Well, I need to go eat. I'll check in on ya in a couple hours."

Oliver said, "Oh, can you can me some food, too? I'm really hungry."

"Of course, bud. I'll bring the food box here so you can eat as much as you want."

"Thank you, Darcy."

# Epilogue

Darcy sat at the bar with Dusk and Sky.

"...So Akio finally returned today. Apparently the Trio Clan wanted to wait ten or so days to make sure Scorpio wouldn't come back."

Sky asked, <And he hasn't appeared since your battle?>

Darcy shook their head. "The council is convinced that I scared him bad. I'm just relieved that everything worked out. I think I officially have their trust now."

<They *should* trust you,> Said Dusk with a grumble. <You found a way to translate spells into pizzazz; what could be more impressive than that?>

"It isn't what's impressive, but what's dependable. And since it was the Night Creature form that defeated Scorpio, the council expects me to keep training that ability." They sighed. "I think they've lost all interest in my other ventures. Everyone but Aggis."

<Have you told Revi about what you've learned?> Asked Sky.

Darcy shrugged. "Don't really see the point, to be honest. I'm not qualified as a power tester. And I just... my brain just isn't built for all those videos and quizzes."

<Yes, but you could share your findings with a warlock who *is* qualified, right?>

"Maybe. Akio about how they've already asked the other warlocks. Nobody else wants to help the Salavites."

Dusk said, <But that was before you defeated Scorpio. Now you have a victory under your belt. *And* you can use your pizzazz findings as leverage. Trade knowledge for power.>

"Huh." Darcy scratched their head. "You're right! I'll try that!" They checked the time on their phone. "...Just as soon as I have more free time."

Darcy returned to the guard barracks. Oliver was still in the infirmary, so Darcy arrived alone. Or, they thought they were alone.

"Darcy?!"

A familiar Salavite from the Ruby Clan jumped up. Darcy threw up a smile.

"Oh! Hey, Pyrus. Didn't see you there."

"And I literally did not see you. How did you appear out of nowhere like that?!" Pyrus looked up and down at them. "Have you always been so tall ?"

"Uh, being a spider creature has given me many abilities. So what about you? How have you been doing?"

"Well enough, considering the tongue-lashing I got from my council. Oh, and here. I've been looking for you to give you these."

Pyrus handed Darcy a bundle of ruby-red flowers. Darcy forced themself to keep smiling.

"Oh... they're so pretty."

Pyrus's tail swayed from side to side. "Yes, and since it seems like our clans will be conversing for quite some time, we'll have many opportunities to be together."

"That... that is true."

Pyrus played with one of their ears as they spoke. "And, well... I was wondering if you wanted to have lunch together sometime."

Darcy considered saying yes, if it would only make Pyrus happy.

*But would I really want to draw out a relationship like this? The longer it goes on, the more it will hurt Pyrus when the truth comes out.*

They sighed. "Pyrus, I'm sorry, but I just don't see our relationship that way."

Pyrus's ears dropped. "What?"

"I'm aromantic. I don't feel romantic attraction to people, no matter how close I am to them."

"Oh." Pyrus laughed and put a hand against their forehead. "I feel so silly now! I had a crush and everything. I'm sorry!"

Darcy shrugged. "I mean, as long as you're understanding about it."

"Of course, I just..." They laughed sheepishly. "I suppose the sensation of being held in a hero's arms swept me off my feet."

"I'm honored to be that hero." Darcy offered Pyrus half of the set of flowers. "Friends?"

Pyrus smiled. "No. Bros."

Darcy exploded into giggles. "Bros! I forgot about that!"

After having a good wheeze, Darcy and Pyrus made their way to the meeting hall. On the way there, Pyrus asked,

"So I heard about Scorpio!"

"Yeah. The victory still doesn't feel real." They clasped their hands together. "Oh! And I set myself on fire the other day!"

"Awesome!"

"Yeah, but now I'm soft-banned from doing anything fire-related."

"Sorry to here that, bro. I'll start some fires in your name."

"Aww, thanks."

Refugee Clan now had visitors of Ruby, Sapphire, and Emerald: the Trio Clan. Their scales shined like gemstones and had large, wavy lines around their eyes. Their dragon warriors had insect-like wings: the ruby ones with damselfly wings, sapphire with beetle wings, and emerald with dragonfly wings. They had six dragon warriors in total, two of each type.

Pyrus mingled with other clan members while Darcy lingered at the edge of the room, not wanting to draw too much attention to themself.

Akio approached Darcy and asked, "What's the news from the other side?"

"There's a chance that we might be able to get more of our kind to help out. We'll just need to play smart with our resources and promises."

"I'll help with that however I can. The more spiders we have protecting the clans, the safer we'll be. By the way, did you get qualified?"

"Ah, no. I didn't have the time for those things."

"Damn."

"Sorry."

Darcy shook their head. "Not your fault. Let's do more planning later."

"Definitely."

Terio then went up to Darcy. "Here is your assignment for this event: first, the respective councils will speak with each other on introductory matters. During this time, you'll be stationed at the southern doorway with a guard from Trio Clan. Afterwards, I'll summon you to the center of the room to display your abilities."

"Alright, understood. Is there anything in particular I should focus on?"

"Act as though you're a full-fledged member of Refugee Clan. Loyalty will inspire confidence and we'll have better chances for the desired outcome. Also, don't answer any questions that you don't know the answer to. Simply say that it's for your council to know."

"Okay. Thank you for trusting me again."

Terio smiled. "Oh, you're certainly earned it."

Everybody ate together as the Trio Clan leaders introduced themselves. There was Iiris of Sapphire Clan, Silki of Ruby Clan, and Miym of Emerald Clan. To Darcy's surprise, none of them were dragon warriors, although each did have a special pattern on their scales to indicate their political power.

Darcy stood at one of the room's exits along with a dragon warrior from the Emerald Clan. Two other dragon warriors stood guard at the other exit, at the opposite side of the room.

The emerald dragon warrior said to Darcy, "So you're one of the guards that we've been hearing about."

"Uh, yeah. You a guard, too?"

They nodded. "In Trio Clan, you're required to be a dragon warrior before you can qualify as a guard."

"Oh, wow. I heard that becoming a warrior takes a lot of work."

"It does, but the stronger a person is, the better they can protect their clan. Although I suppose for someone who's immune to dispels, you have less to fear. Is it true that you defeated Scorpio?"

*Would taking all the credit make the Trio Clan want to join even more? But I don't want to leave Oliver out of it... I should be honest.*

"Well..." They replied in a whisper, "Just between you and me, the other guard did most of the work. I just scared him off."

The warrior's goldenrod eyes beamed with fascination. "You frightened Scorpio? You made him *run away*?"

Darcy nodded. "We'd be dead right now if we didn't."

"Wow. That is... *amazing*. How in the world did you pull it off? Ah, or is it a clan secret?"

"I'm afraid that a lot will have to be kept secret. Sorry."

The dragon warrior looked at the combined councils at the center of the room. "Well, either way, I can't help but feel that these factors will give you an edge in diplomacy. Once word gets out that Refugee Clan can defeat the Macbeths, Salavites from all over will come flocking." They looked towards Darcy. "I hope there are more of you."

Worry crossed Darcy's face. They responded quietly,

"I hope so, too."

— — —

Libra paced in the Macbeth mansion's drawing room. She paid no heed to the opulent chalcedony walls or golden chairs. She eyed the mahogany grandfather clock in the corner.

Scorpio trudged into the room and sat on one of the chairs.

"What is it?"

"You're late again."

"Just tell me what you want to talk about."

"We need to formulate a new plan for dealing with the lizardfolk. If we keep putting it off, they will gain confidence. They may even try to take back their city."

Scorpio leaned forward in his seat. "Look, I'd love to bash some skulls in, but those guards were something else."

"We'll just have to use regular spells against them."

"And then we'll have to face an entire clan of angry magic reptiles." He added sarcastically, "Good idea!"

Libra snapped, "Well, we can't have regular spells *and* dispels active at the same time!"

"What about Mother? Can she deal with this?"

"She's still bedridden. She's too ill to even sign documents these days."

She looked at the bandages on Scorpio's hand. She sighed, regaining her composure.

"Are you certain that these guards were spider creatures?"

"I'm sure of it. Even the human." He raised an eyebrow. "He belonged to Mike Harrell."

Libra put a hand to her chin. "Harrell... every single one of his ambassadors had spider powers."

"Maybe we should forge an alliance. He would know their strengths and weaknesses."

"True, but this is Mike Harrell we're talking about. If we get any help from him, he'll lord it over us until the end of our days."

The siblings rolled their eyes in unison. "Pass!"

Libra thought for a moment. "Although... if the white spider has the same powers as Red Arachnid, then if we find a weakness for one, then we can weaken the other as well. If we could just gain Harrell's data without him knowing..."

"Company sabotage?"

"No. Something more low-key, like corporate espionage."

"That dragon warrior from the Pearl Clan works for Harrell now. Think we can get her under our thumb?"

"Even if we did, I don't know if she would have the clearance to access ambassador information." She snapped her fingers. "Mother has a list of contacts in her personal study. I recall reading it while I was... checking on her health. I know someone who can provide us with a spy. But with my responsibilities with the museum and running the estate in Mother's place, I won't have the time to visit this person myself."

"Tell me where it is and I'm there."

"Have you ever been to Utah?"

Scorpio furrowed his brow. "Not lately. Who the hell is in Utah?"

Libra made a fiendish grin. "Her name is Doctor Phoenix."

## Don't miss out!

Visit the website below and you can sign up to receive emails whenever Sol Quasar publishes a new book. There's no charge and no obligation.

https://books2read.com/r/B-A-MBMIC-YQJCF

# Also by Sol Quasar

**Banana Split Timeline**

BST Book Zero

Death Timeline

Life Timeline

Revival Timeline

## About the Author

Sol Quasar chose their name to represent outer space, something that they have always loved. The wonder of the stars remains constant in their life. Along with writing books, Sol enjoys petting cats, taking photos of spiders, and drawing art. They hope that their stories can help other people someday.

Sol currently lives in Wisconsin, but prefers to keep specific information obscured.